For Stacy Schiff
And once again for
Stephen Reibel

To hate except in the abstract is more
difficult than it might seem.

Flora Groult, *Diary in Duo:*
Paris, 1940–45

Do not judge your fellow human being
until you have stood in her place.

Hillel the Elder

The Tattooist of Auschwitz

'This is an exquisite novel – one that gives us what we're hungry for: an intelligent, complex female character who challenges our ideas of right and wrong, morality and immorality. We're reminded, too, of the dangers of drawing easy, swift conclusions. Feldman achieves all of this with wholly admirable precision and wit; she takes aim and does not miss.' **Elizabeth J. Church, author of** *The Atomic Weight of Love*

'Feldman's characters – in the Paris bookstore that harbors many secrets or the Manhattan publishing house with its marvellous cast of misfits – are both terrifying and utterly engaging. With more twists and turns than the back streets of Paris, the story is as propulsively readable as a spy novel, and as rich and psychologically rewarding as only the finest literature can be.' **Liza Gyllenhaal, author of** *Local Knowledge*

'Completely compelling. I tore through it. This novel pivots on how we manage to survive surviving . . . Charlotte's visceral story will stay with me.' **Naomi Wood, author of** *Mrs. Hemingway*

'Feldman's powerful exploration of some of the most profound questions about love and loyalty resonates strongly today: What would you do to save your child? What is morality in wartime? How do we make peace with the past?' **Christina Lynch, author of** *The Italian Party*

'Fans of Anthony Doerr's *All the Light We Cannot See* and Kristin Hannah's *The Nightingale* may want to pick this up.' ***Booklist***

'A memorable, thought-provoking moral conflict, and dialogue [that] crackles like a duel . . . *A Bookshop in Paris* succeeds as a meaty moral tale.'
Historical Novel Society

'The best works of historical fiction have a way of illuminating the present, allowing readers to better understand themselves through well-defined characters reflected in the prism of time . . . Feldman does this beautifully in a multi-layered, tender story that explores the emotionally charged, often parallel terrains of truth, deception, love and heartbreak.' **Shelf Awareness**

'Nothing is quite what it seems . . . Wartime Paris is described in vivid, sometimes harrowing, detail . . . [An] engrossing page-turner.' *Kirkus*

'A nuanced WWII story of love and survival in Occupied Paris . . . With its appealing heroine and historically detailed settings . . . a dangerous secret gives Feldman's story a gasp-worthy spin.'
Publishers Weekly

A Bookshop in Paris

Ellen Feldman

SIMON &
SCHUSTER

London · New York · Sydney · Toronto · New Delhi

First published in the United States by St. Martin's Griffin, an imprint of
St. Martin's Publishing Group, 2020
First published in Great Britain by Simon & Schuster UK Ltd, 2020

Published in the United States and Australia as *Paris Never Leaves You*

3 5 7 9 10 8 6 4

Simon & Schuster UK Ltd
1st Floor
222 Gray's Inn Road
London WC1X 8HB

Simon & Schuster Australia, Sydney
Simon & Schuster India, New Delhi

www.simonandschuster.co.uk
www.simonandschuster.com.au
www.simonandschuster.co.in

A CIP catalogue record for this book
is available from the British Library

Paperback ISBN: 978-1-4711-9781-9
eBook ISBN: 978-1-4711-9780-2

Printed and bound in Great Britain by CPI Group (UK) Ltd, Croydon, CR0 4YY

A Bookshop in Paris

Prologue

Paris, 1944

They were ripping off the stars. Filthy fingers with broken dirt-encrusted nails were yanking and peeling and prying. Who would have thought they still had the strength? One woman was biting the threads that held hers tight to her torn jacket. She must have been a good seamstress in her day. Those who had managed to tear off their stars were throwing them to the ground. A man was spitting on his. Who would have thought he had the saliva as well as the strength? Charlotte's mouth felt dry and foul from dehydration. Men and women and children were stomping the worn scraps of fabric into the mud, spreading a carpet of tarnished yellow misery over the fenced-in plot of French soil.

Charlotte crouched beside Vivi and began pulling out the stitches that held her daughter's star to her soiled pink blouse. The law had stipulated that only children six or older had to wear the star, and Vivi was four, but the blouse had been left behind when another child had been abruptly added, in a moment of bureaucratic desperation, to a transport that had come up one short of the required one thousand bodies. Charlotte had taken the blouse before anyone else could—they were permitted possessions in the camp, if they still had any—but she hadn't removed the star. Wearing a blouse with a dark six-pointed shadow where a star used to be, denying, even if you were only four, was asking for trouble. Now Charlotte could remove it. Only when she had did she straighten and start pulling off her own.

For the rest of her life, every time she sat on an airplane and listened to a smiling stewardess warn that in case of trouble she was to put on her own oxygen mask before taking care of the child traveling with her, she would remember this morning and think the airlines had logic on their side but no heart.

ೀ

She'd come across the scene in a square in Drancy, the suburb ten kilometers northeast of the city, not the camp for the detention and deportation of Jews, communists, socialists, and other enemies of the Reich. If she hadn't already known staying in the area was safer than returning to her old haunts, the incidents that day would have persuaded her. She hadn't wanted to watch, but neither had she been able to tear herself away. She'd stood riveted to the spot, mesmerized by the hatred, immobilized by the fear.

They had stripped the woman down to her brassiere and underpants, threadbare graying scraps of dignity or modesty or some barely remembered decency from better times. The brassiere was torn at the nipple, whether from current violence or past passion was impossible to tell. An old man with a tobacco-stained beard reached out a filthy hand and pinched the pink flesh. The crowd roared its delight. A young man brandishing a rifle used it to prod the woman first one way, then another, until she was stumbling on the high heels she was still wearing. The shoes made her nakedness more obscene. As she lurched, the crowd caught sight of a brown stain on the seat of her torn underpants. Again it was impossible to tell whether it was the sign of current terror or past slovenliness, but the jeering grew louder. It drowned out the sound of the church bell that had begun to toll and continued after the bell went silent. It was only two o'clock.

Collabo, a woman in the crowd howled, *collabo horizontale,* another screamed, and the women in the mob took up the cries and passed them around as they would, under other circumstances, have handed a baby from one to the other. Both instincts were primitive and protective, though in this case of self. Only the hardest or most forgetful among them, those who had never given a civil nod to a billeted soldier or uttered a *merci* for a door held, could fail to see themselves in the place of that woman huddled in shame as her hair fell to the ground in greasy clumps. Her days of black market meat and eggs and shampoo were long gone.

Charlotte thought of the patches of hair missing from her own scalp as a result of the malnutrition. She'd been able to live with that, but when the tufts of Vivi's fine baby hair had begun to come away in her hands, she'd stopped brushing it, as if that could do any good.

The women in the pack howled their rage, but the men, especially the silent men, were more dangerous, and not only because they brandished the rifles and wielded the shears and razors. The men reeked of sexual malice. Some of them clutched their crotches as they heckled and punched and kicked the woman. Others sweated and smirked and wiped the spittle from their mouths with the backs of their hands, then ran their tongues over their lips as if they could taste the thrill. Their country had been defeated. They had been humiliated. But this wreaking of vengeance, this rendering of justice, this half-naked woman, stained with blood and tears and feces, made them men again.

Two boys—they couldn't have been older than sixteen or seventeen—began pushing the woman, her bald head glistening in the afternoon sunlight that slanted past the church steeple, toward a truck parked in a corner of the square. The three women, one almost naked, two half dressed, who were sprawled in the flatbed didn't look up when the boys shoved the newcomer among them.

Now the crowd was tightening the circle around another woman. This one was holding a baby. Her soiled cotton dress hung beltless, one sleeve torn away, but she was still wearing it. Perhaps the presence of the baby shamed the men, or perhaps it only tamped down the sexual voltage. She wasn't cradling the baby against her, the way a woman usually holds an infant, but carrying the child under one arm like a package. Its legs hung limp; its head, unsupported, drooped to one side on its fragile neck. Its eyes were closed, and its small face was screwed tight against the world.

Charlotte picked up Vivi, who'd been clinging to her skirt, and hid her daughter's face in her neck. This was nothing a child should see. This was nothing anyone should witness.

One of the men who seemed to be in charge, if anyone could be said to be in charge, grabbed the woman by the hair and yanked her head back. The sound she let out was more a bleat than a cry. Charlotte waited for the baby to begin to wail. It merely screwed its face tighter.

The hair began to fall to the ground. It was longer than the short bob of the woman they'd stripped to her underwear and took more time. Perhaps that was what made the man in the crowd do it. He was getting bored. While the *tondeur* was still shearing the woman, the man darted forward and inked a swastika on her forehead. The crowd roared its glee.

Still whimpering, still clutching the silent baby, the woman was shoved toward the truck, and another was hauled into the center of the square. Holding Vivi tighter, Charlotte began pushing her way through the mob. Drunk now on justice and the wine an enterprising woman and her young son had begun selling, but not yet satiated, the crowd pushed back against her, urging her to stay, sneering at her for her tenderheartedness, taunting her for her lack of patriotism. She put her hand on the back of Vivi's head to shield her and kept going.

At the edge of the crowd, Berthe Bernheim, the woman from the camp whose stitches had been so expert she'd had to bite off her star, stopped her.

"You can't leave," she said, and pointed to a group of

women and one man in a corner of the square waiting their turn with the *tondeur*. "It's not over."

Charlotte shook her head. "As long as this goes on, it never will be," she said, and kept going.

Berthe Bernheim stood looking after her. "Holier than thou, that one," she observed to no one in particular.

One

New York, 1954

Charlotte spotted the letter as soon as she stepped into her office. There was no reason it should have caught her eye. The desk was littered with papers and envelopes. Stacks of manuscripts and books filled the shelves of the small cubicle and spilled over onto the two chairs. Certainly the airmail envelope didn't make it stand out. Most of the books she published were American editions of European works, and a good deal of her mail arrived in those tissue-thin blue envelopes. The only explanation for its attracting her attention was that she'd already gone through her morning mail and the afternoon delivery hadn't yet arrived. Perhaps the letter had gone to another editor by mistake, and he or she had left it on Charlotte's desk while she was upstairs in the art department. Or perhaps the mailroom had overlooked it in the morning sorting.

Gibbon & Field was a prestigious publishing house, but a certain loucheness lurked behind the scenes. That was the fault of Horace Field, the publisher. He was too forgiving, or perhaps only cannily manipulative. She'd had her earliest inkling of the trait the first Christmas after she'd come to work at the house. Leaving the office one evening at the same time, she and Horace had entered the elevator together to find a young man from the production department struggling to balance two or three oversize art books and several of a more conventional trim size. When he saw Horace, he colored an unhappy Christmas red.

"I see you've taken our ads to heart, Seth," Horace said. "'There's a book for everyone on your Christmas list.'"

The young man turned a deeper red and shot out of the elevator as soon as the doors opened. That was unusual. The staff usually deferred to Horace getting on and off elevators, and everywhere else.

"Are you going to take the books out of his salary?" she'd asked as they'd followed him across the lobby.

"Not on your life."

"It would teach him a lesson."

"The only lesson I want to teach him, Charlie, is to work his tail off for the greater glory of G&F."

"And you think encouraging him to walk out the door with an armful of purloined books will do that?"

"I think the next time he asks for a raise and doesn't get it, he'll remember all the books he's filched and feel guilty, or at least compensated. Same with the expense accounts the editors and travelers turn in. They think they're stealing me blind, but a guilty conscience breeds contrition. Maybe even loyalty. They feel they owe the house something in return. That's why I worry about you. Those expense accounts you file are a travesty. If the other editors get wind of them, they'll never forgive you for spoiling the game."

Horace's philosophy permeated the entire publishing house from the grand larceny of the production department, run by a man rumored to have ties to the Mafia, to the petty pilfering and general slacking off of the mailroom. That must be why the letter had been delivered late. And the timing was the only reason she noticed it. It had nothing to do with a sixth sense, in which she definitely did not believe.

She sat behind the desk and picked up the envelope. Her name and the G&F address were written, not typed. The handwriting wasn't familiar. There was no return address on the upper left-hand corner. She turned it over. As soon as she saw the name, she realized why she hadn't recognized the handwriting. When had they put anything in writing? No, that wasn't true. He'd written her once, a year or so after the end of the war. The letter had taken months to wind its way through the Drancy records and the various agencies to reach her in New York. She'd taken solace in that. He didn't know where she was, and he was still in Germany. She'd never answered that letter. The return address on this one was Bogotá, Colombia. So he'd got out after all. She was glad. She was also relieved. South America was still a long distance away.

What troubled her was not where he was but that now he knew where she was. She'd thought she'd been so careful. Neither her address nor her telephone number was listed in the book. The people who had tried to help her settle into her new life—social workers and do-gooders from various refugee organizations; her colleagues here and at other publishing houses; Horace Field's wife, Hannah—had found the omission foolish and antisocial. "How do you expect to make a life for yourself in a new country," Hannah had asked, "if no one can find you?" Charlotte hadn't argued with her. She'd merely gone on paying the small fee to be unlisted. Gradually Hannah and everyone else had stopped asking and chalked it up to what she'd been through. No one, including Hannah, knew what that was, but that didn't stop them from speculating.

She wasn't much easier to find in the office, though

apparently he'd managed. Her name didn't appear in the list of editors that ran down the left-hand side of the company stationery. Most publishing houses didn't list editors on the stationery but that was another of Horace Field's peculiar indulgences. A year after she'd come to work at G&F, he'd asked if she wanted to be included.

"Think of it as a sop," he'd said.

"A sop?" She spoke four languages, could read two others, and had taken her degree at the Sorbonne in English literature, but in those days she was still having trouble with some American slang.

"Compensation for the slave wages we pay you."

"At least you didn't suggest I make up the difference by stealing books," she'd said, and added that she didn't want her name on the stationery but thanked him all the same.

Nonetheless, despite her absence in the phone book and on the company stationery, her name did occasionally turn up in acknowledgments in the books she worked on. *And my gratitude to Charlotte Foret for steering my vessel safely through the turbulent waters of American publishing. My thanks to Charlotte Foret, who first saw that a book about the Dutch Golden Age written by a Dutchman would appeal to American audiences.* The question was how he'd managed to get his hands on a US edition in Europe, or now South America. The various consulates had libraries to spread the American gospel among the local populations, but the books she published rarely spread the American gospel. Nonetheless, he must have found one. Or else he'd tracked her down through a refugee agency. Once in America, she'd distanced herself from the émigré or immigrant or refugee—choose your term—groups, but she'd had to file the usual papers and obtain the necessary documents to get here. She was traceable.

She sat looking at the envelope. It wasn't registered. There was no proof that she'd received it. Even if there had been, no law said she had to answer every letter she got. She did try to respond to the ones accompanying manuscripts from would-be authors, but she had boiler-plate for that. *While your thesis is cogent, I'm afraid the subject matter doesn't quite fit our list. While the book is beautifully written, I fear the characters are not fully re-alized / the plot strains credulity / there isn't an American audience for this sort of story.* But she had no form letter to cover this situation, whatever this situation was. Remi-niscences? He wouldn't want to remember those days any more than she did. Love? Even then she'd told herself not to be ridiculous. Money? As of last year's naturalization ceremony, she was an American, and everyone who wasn't an American knew that everyone who was, was rich, but of all the indictments she'd brought against him, that one was the least likely.

She heard the sound of voices in the hall and inhaled

the aroma of pipe tobacco floating over the frosted glass
partition of her cubicle. The pipe would belong to Carl
Covington, a faintly foppish man with a mane of white
hair that he wore just a little too long. Carl aspired to
be a grand old man of publishing, but it was difficult
to be a grand old man of publishing when the house you
worked for was owned by an only slightly aging wunderkind of publishing. The voices belonged to Faith Silver,
whose claim to fame was a brief friendship with Dorothy
Parker in their heyday, and Bill Quarrels, a swaggering
overgrown boy with a big brutal body and an adolescent
mind. According to one of the secretaries who commuted
from the same Westchester town as Bill, every morning
as he stepped off the train in Grand Central Terminal, he
put his hand in his pocket and slipped off his wedding
ring, and every evening as he boarded the train home, he
slipped it on again. The three of them were on their way
to the Wednesday editorial meeting.

Faith stuck her head with its dark, dated Dorothy
Parker bob around the partition of the cubicle. "Time to
gird the loins for combat," she said.

Charlotte looked up from the pale blue envelope. As
if it had a will of its own, it fell into the wastebasket. She
stood. "I'll be along in a minute."

The voices moved on down the hall.

She began gathering papers, then thought better of

it, opened the bottom drawer of the desk, lifted out her handbag, and took out her compact and lipstick. She believed in going into these meetings with all flags flying.

As she lifted the powder puff and began to dab, she brought the compact closer to examine her skin. The fine porcelain grain that had made her vain as a girl was coarser now, but at least the sickly yellow cast of those years was gone. She smoothed the streak of white that ran through her dark hair. Occasionally she thought of dyeing it, but somehow she'd never got around to doing so. She wasn't hanging on to it as a reminder. She just liked the dramatic effect. Her fingertips smoothed the web of fine lines beside her eyes, as if she could massage them out of existence, though she knew that was impossible. Perhaps it wasn't even desirable. A few weeks earlier, an enterprising saleswoman in the cosmetics department of Saks Fifth Avenue had tried to sell her a cream to get rid of them. "It will erase your past," she'd said.

The promise had been so terrifying in its appeal that she'd put down the tube of Helena Rubinstein lipstick she'd been about to buy, turned, and walked out of the store. No one but a fool would try to erase the past. The only hope was to stand guard against it.

Even now, in her dreams, she heard Vivi crying, not the childish whimpers and sobs of temporary discomfort but a shrieking rage born of an empty belly, and chilled-through bones, and the agony of rashes and bites and festering sores. Sometimes the crying in the dream was so loud that it wrenched her awake, and she sprang out of bed before she realized the sound was only in her head. Then, still sweating, she took the few steps down the short hall from her room to her daughter's and stood beside the bed, listening to Vivi's breath coming soft and safe in the miraculous New York night that was broken not by boots on the stairs or banging on the door but only by the occasional siren screaming that help rather than trouble was on the way.

Waking hours brought different nightmares about her daughter. Every cough was the first sign of tuberculosis, every stomach upset the harbinger of a bug that had been lying dormant, every rash the return of disease, and the knowledge that these days there was penicillin to treat it didn't mitigate the terror. Vivi could not possibly have escaped without consequences. Her slight fourteen-year-old body had to be pregnant with dormant disaster.

Sitting in the audience at school performances, she measured Vivi against the other girls. Was she the runt of the litter? Were her bones permanently deformed by malnutrition? Had her mother's fear and remorse scarred her psyche? But standing beside her classmates in her starched white blouse and blue jumper, Vivi bore no evidence of earlier hardships. Her hair gleamed dark and glossy in the glare from the overhead lights. Her legs stretched long and coltish in the navy-blue knee socks. Her wide smile revealed a sunny streak and improbably white teeth. All the hours Charlotte had spent queueing for food, every mouthful she hadn't eaten so Vivi could, every chance she'd taken, even the compromises she'd made had been worth it. Vivi looked just like her classmates, only better.

Nonetheless, some differences did set her apart. She was one of twelve students, a single representative in each class, on scholarship. The other girls inhabited sprawling apartments, duplexes, and penthouses on Park and Fifth Avenues filled with parents and siblings, dogs and domestic help. Vivi lived with her mother in four small rooms on the top floor of an old—in America, a seventy-year-old building was considered old—brownstone on East Ninety-First Street. At Christmas, other girls headed to grandparents who inhabited Currier and Ives landscapes, or north or west to ski, or south to the sun. Vivi and her mother carried a small tree home from a stand on Ninety-Sixth Street, put it up in a corner of the living room, and decorated it with ornaments bought at B. Altman the first year they were here, and added to annually. The ornaments were new, but the tree, Charlotte insisted, was a tradition. Her family had always celebrated Christmas. It had taken Hitler, she liked to say, to make her a Jew. That was the other thing that set Vivi apart. There were fewer Jewish girls in the school than scholarship students. Neither condition was ever mentioned, at least in polite company, as the phrase went.

The point was, despite those deprivations and disadvantages, Vivi was flourishing. Only the other night, sitting in the living room, Charlotte had looked up from the manuscript she was reading and seen Vivi at the dining table doing her homework. There was a desk in her room, but she liked being near her mother. The experts whom Charlotte read said that would soon stop, but she didn't believe them. Experts dealt in generalizations. She and Vivi were singular. Vivi had been sitting with one foot in her regulation brown oxford tucked under her, a silky curtain of dark hair falling forward as she bent over her book, her mouth pursed in concentration. Looking across the room at her, Charlotte had barely been able to keep from shouting with joy at the sheer miracle of it.

She put her handbag back in the drawer, left the cubicle, and started down the hall to the conference room.

Horace Field was already in his place at the head of the long table. He was always the first to arrive at meetings. That was partly the result of his impatience, but only partly. He sat, leaning back in his chair, but the relaxed pose and the loose Harris tweed jacket couldn't hide the dormant power of his muscled shoulders and arms. Sometimes Charlotte wondered if, in his mind's eye, he was still the lean loping young man, the former college tennis player, she'd seen in a photograph in an old issue of *Publishers Weekly* from before the war. In the picture, he sported a trim mustache, and as she'd sat at her desk studying it, she'd been sure he'd grown it to look older. She'd met him once briefly at the time, but she had been too young herself to realize how young he was. He really had been a boy wonder. The mustache was gone now, and his hairline was beginning to recede. She'd noticed that when Carl Covington looked at him, he couldn't help stroking his own white mane. Horace must have noticed it, too, because once he'd barked at Carl to stop petting himself like a goddamn dog. Horace's face, beneath the receding hairline, was still boyish, except occasionally, when he didn't know he was being watched. Then frown lines, no, fury lines settled between his eyes, which were icy blue and watchful. No one was going to blindside him.

"Nice of you to join us, General," he said using the French pronunciation of the title as she took a chair. In private, she was Charlie; before others she was Charles or General, both pronounced with French accents. She wished she weren't. The nicknames, even the formal nicknames, implied an intimacy that didn't exist. He'd been kind to her, and she was grateful, but generosity and gratitude were not intimacy. As far as she was concerned, they necessitated the opposite relationship. Especially with him. The youthful man in that old photograph had been reputed to be, if not a wolf, then a dangerous heart-breaker, though she was pretty sure those days were behind him.

The other editors were already seated around the table, restive as racehorses at the starting gate, mentally snorting and pawing the ground in their eagerness to break away from the pack with a surefire bestseller, or at least an enviable quip in their own presentation or a droll jibe at a colleague's. They got started.

Carl Covington had a biography of Lincoln by a leading scholar.

"Not another one," Bill Quarrels said.

"One-decade rule," Carl answered. "If there hasn't been a biography in ten years, it's time for a new one. And books about Lincoln sell."

Walter Price, the sales manager, nodded. "Books about Lincoln sell. So do books about doctors and books about dogs. So what I don't understand is why none of you geniuses has managed to find a book about Lincoln's doctor's dog that I can sell."

The discussion turned to the author's previous sales figures, the likely sum for paperback rights (a new phenomenon since the war), and how little the agent would take. Horace didn't say much, but his nod at the end of the discussion was eloquent. Carl said he'd make an offer.

Bill Quarrels had a novel by a marine who'd fought his way through the Pacific.

"Wait, let me guess," Carl said. "The author's name is James Jones."

"The market for war books has peaked," Walter warned.

He and Carl had been too old for the war, Bill too young. None of them looked at Horace as they spoke.

They moved on to Faith. She had a first novel about life in a small New England town. It was quiet, she admitted, but beautifully written, and didn't they publish moneymaking potboilers precisely so they could afford to publish small literary gems like this? No one bothered to answer that particular question, though Charlotte, who'd read the manuscript, seconded Faith's literary opinion. Horace gave a nod of approval. No one mentioned money. No one had to. Faith had been in the business long enough to know that an appropriate advance for a book like this would be a few hundred dollars.

Charlotte presented a book about the interaction of politics, diplomacy, and art in Renaissance Italy. That met with silence, too. She had what amounted to her own little fiefdom at G&F. Only Horace cared about the books she brought in, unless they were foreign novels that might be banned. Then suddenly everyone wanted to take a look.

But this one squeaked through with a nod of approval. Again a paltry advance was taken for granted.

They went on that way for the better part of two hours. Editors presented books, formed alliances, switched sides. The process reminded Charlotte of the papal conclaves she'd read about. Only the white smoke at the end of the meeting was missing.

She had gathered her papers and was starting for the door when Bill Quarrels caught up with her.

"Did you have a chance to look at that novel? The one about the American spy dropped behind the lines in France before the Invasion?"

"Didn't you get my memo?"

"All you said was that it was incredibly steamy."

"I said it was steamily incredible. Any spy who spent that much time between the sheets would have been dead twenty-four hours after parachuting in. Forty-eight at the outside."

He leaned his big body toward her. "Are you speaking from experience?"

She was debating whether to bother answering when it happened. Standing in the doorway with their backs to the conference room, neither of them saw it coming. Horace Field, his massive arms propelling the wheels of his chair, came barreling between them. He missed her by a hair's breadth but managed to career over Bill Quarrels's cordovan-clad right foot. Horace arrived early at meetings because he didn't like people watching him maneuver his wheelchair, but that didn't mean he wasn't skillful at it.

"Ouch," Bill shouted, and jumped out of the way, too late.

"Sorry, Bill," Horace called back as he sped down the hallway.

❦

She hadn't forgotten the letter she'd tossed in the wastebasket. Now and then during the editorial meeting, she'd found herself thinking about it. She didn't want to read it, but she knew she would. She wasn't sure why. She couldn't erase the past, despite what the woman in the Saks makeup department had promised, but she had no intention of wallowing in it. Still, it didn't seem right not to read it. She'd resolved to fish it out of the wastebasket as soon as she got back to her office, but she hadn't counted on finding Vincent Aiello, the head of production, waiting in her cubicle.

"You know that mystery of yours set in Morocco?"

For a moment she thought he might actually have read one of the books he steered through production and wanted to tell her he liked it.

"We got bound books," he said.

"They're early. That's good."

"Not so good. They're missing the last page."

"This is a joke, right?"

He shrugged.

"It's a mystery, Vincent. Not that it wouldn't be a disaster if it weren't. But readers do tend to want to find out who did it."

"Look on the bright side. Now it's a do-it-yourself whodunit. We could be starting a whole new trend."

"The entire print run?"

"Every last copy."

"This is coming out of your budget, not mine."

"To hell with budgets. I'm taking out a contract to have the binders' kneecaps broken." He smirked, as if daring her to believe the rumors about him.

❦

She was standing on Madison Avenue, waiting for the bus and brooding about the entire print run of the unsolved mystery, when she remembered the letter. For a moment, she thought of going back, then looked at her watch and decided against it. She didn't mind leaving Vivi alone for a few hours after school, especially if Hannah Field had finished seeing patients for the day and lured Vivi in for her homemade cakes and cookies, but she did like to get home in time to make dinner and sit down to it properly.

She'd fetch the letter out first thing in the morning. And if this was one of the nights the cleaning crew came through and emptied the baskets, so much the worse. It wasn't as if she had any intention of answering it. In fact, so much the better. The matter would be taken out of her hands.

Two

She stepped down from the bus and started along Ninety-First Street, careful of her footing in the gathering dusk. The rain had stopped, but a carpet of wet leaves made the sidewalk slippery. Light spilled out of the wide bay windows and intricately worked fanlights of the brownstones and lay shimmering in the puddles. Occasionally she stopped on the street and stood looking into those brilliantly lit rooms. The life going on within them intrigued her. The aura of safety mesmerized her, though she knew that was a mirage. As she stood there now, the faint aroma of a wood fire made her nostalgic, though she couldn't have said for what. Certainly not for the acrid stench of burning papers. Then it came to her. The scent reminded her of a fire burning in the hearth on a damp night at Grandmère's house in Concarneau. She and her mother had always wanted to go south for the summer holidays—one of the few issues on which she and her mother were arrayed against her father—but her father had been adamant about visiting his own mother. The older Charlotte had got, the more bored and sullen she'd grown during those weeks in Brittany, but what wouldn't she give for them now, for herself, and for Vivi. She imagined the two of them walking down the long poplar-lined road and saw Vivi break into a run at her first glimpse of the sea. She straightened her shoulders against the image and started walking again.

Halfway down the block, she opened the wrought-iron gate and descended three steps. A short cement ramp ran alongside them. Some people said sheer perversity made Horace Field go on living in a brownstone. If he and Hannah had moved to an apartment building, he could have whizzed from street to lobby to elevator with ease. Others insisted his remaining in the house he'd grown up in proved he wasn't the cynic he pretended to be. Charlotte had a third explanation, though she'd never mentioned it to anyone, not even Horace, especially not Horace. The doorman and elevator operators in those apartment buildings would have fallen over themselves trying to assist a man in a wheelchair, and not merely for Christmas bonuses. They were, by and large, a respectful lot, at least on the surface, and many of them had been in the war. Horace could not have tolerated that. The solicitude would have embarrassed him. The condescension would have infuriated him. So he'd built the ramp for the steps outside the brownstone and installed an elevator inside.

She closed the gate behind her, crossed the flagstone enclosure blooming with planters of orange and yellow mums that glowed in darkening evening, and pulled open the wrought-iron and glass door to the foyer.

Later, when she thought about the incident, she'd blame it on the letter she'd thrown in the wastebasket. She wasn't thinking of it at that moment, but it must have been lurking in her unconscious. There was no other explanation for her hallucination.

A woman was standing with her hand to her head, her fingers pointing to her temple as if they were the barrel of a gun. Suddenly Charlotte is back in the cold dank hall of the house on the rue Vavin. The concierge's eyes, hard and black as lumps of coal, follow her and Vivi across the shadowy space. Just as they reach the stairs, the concierge in that old apartment house where her memory has transported her moves her finger at her temple as if she is pulling a trigger. "*Après les boches,*" she hisses, and the words scald like steam.

Then another night, and this is shortly before the

Liberation, when Charlotte is carrying Vivi in her arms,
the concierge steps out from the loge to block her path.
Standing only inches away, she raises her cocked-pistol
hand not to her own temple but to Vivi's forehead. "*Après
les boches,*" she croons, as if she is singing a lullaby, and
pulls the imaginary trigger.

Charlotte grabbed hold of the doorknob and closed
her eyes. When she opened them, she was back in the
elegant little foyer with the black-and-white-tiled floor,
watching a woman who was not her former concierge but
must be one of Hannah Field's patients tugging her hat
into place in front of the gilt-framed mirror. The woman
turned from her reflection, nodded to Charlotte, pulled
open the heavy outside door, and disappeared into the
night.

Charlotte went on standing in the foyer, suddenly
sweating in her trench coat, though she hadn't bothered
to button in the lining that morning. She hated herself
for the fear, but she hated the woman, too, for bringing
it back. *Après les boches.* The phrase was always lying there
in the murky polluted depths of her unconscious, just
waiting to rise to the surface. That and the other expression that was even more chilling, but she wasn't going to
think of that.

She started up the stairs. She rarely used the elevator
in the house. It always seemed like an invasion of Horace

and Hannah's privacy. Besides, the American habit of descending on anything other than one's own legs struck her as self-indulgent. And she liked the exercise. She was glad the gauntness was gone. She'd read somewhere that the average Parisian had lost forty pounds during the Occupation. But she didn't want to put on too much weight.

When she reached the first landing, it seemed gloomy. She looked up. One of the bulbs in the overhead fixture was out. That was uncharacteristic. Hannah ran a tight ship. She glanced back down at the entrance hall. It was cast in shadows. And the woman had been standing half turned away as she adjusted her hat. Anyone could have mistaken the woman for someone else.

❦

They sat basking in the glow of the white-sprigged yellow wallpaper that Hannah had chosen for them before they'd moved in. Most landlords, Charlotte had since learned, would have slapped a coat of paint on an apartment in preparation for a new tenant and let it go at that, but as Hannah had often said since she'd met Charlotte and Vivi at the ship that morning almost nine years ago, they were more than tenants. Horace had known Charlotte's father before the war, and Hannah was looking forward to having a child in the house. So she'd wallpapered as well as painted, taken Vivi shopping for curtains and a rug, and even replaced the old dying refrigerator with a new model. Charlotte hadn't realized it at the time because all she'd seen at first was America's abundance, but she knew now that Hannah's managing to get her hands on a new appliance so soon after the war was a testament to her resourcefulness.

The wallpaper pattern Charlotte and Vivi sat basking in was called Innocence. Where but in America, Charlotte thought, would people believe they could shroud a room in naïveté? Nonetheless, she admired Hannah's taste.

The mirror over the mantel was tilted so she could see the reflection of the two of them sitting at the small table angled between the fireplace and the swinging door to the kitchen, her in the shirt and trousers she'd changed into to cook dinner, Vivi still in her school uniform. The wallpaper was so sunny, the light from the wall sconces and lamps so soft, they really did seem to be basking in radiance. Then Vivi spoke.

"How come you never talk about my father?"

"Why don't you ever talk about my father?" Charlotte corrected her. She wasn't stalling for time. At least that wasn't her only motive.

"Why don't you ever talk about my father?" Vivi asked.

The question wasn't new. Vivi occasionally asked about the father she'd never known. But this was the first time she'd framed it as an accusation. Or did Charlotte hear it that way only because of the imaginary encounter with the concierge in the foyer?

"I talk about him. I talk about him all the time. What do you want to know?"

She shrugged. "What was he like?"

Charlotte thought about that for a moment. Now she wasn't stalling. She was trying to remember. But it was like trying to capture the feeling of a fever dream after your temperature is back to normal. After the whole world's temperature is back to normal. Sometimes she wondered if they would have married if the war hadn't come, if he hadn't been called up, if they hadn't felt time bearing down on them, if they hadn't seen themselves as actors in a tragic play or movie. Would her skin have gone so hot at his touch in less heated times? Would they have been able to hold each other with tenderness rather than desperation? She didn't regret any of it. She was grateful for what they'd had. And without Laurent, she would not have Vivi. But the haunted intensity was not something you could tell a child.

"He had an original mind," she said finally.

"What does that mean?"

"It means I was never bored with him. More than that,

I was dazzled by him. He saw things other people didn't, made connections others didn't." This was better. She was getting the hang of it.

"What else?"

"He had a finely calibrated moral compass."

"A what?"

"A well-developed sense of right and wrong."

"Oh."

This clearly was not what Vivi was looking for.

"He would have been proud of you." Charlotte tried again.

"How do you know?"

"Because you're smart. He cared a lot about that. And pretty." Vivi made a self-deprecating face. "He cared a lot about that, too, at least in women. And you have a moral compass, too."

"I do?"

"You care about other people. You try to do the right thing."

Vivi considered that for a moment. "Sometimes I'm not sure what the right thing is."

"You're in good company there."

"Even when you're a grown-up?"

"Especially when you're a grown-up."

"But you said my father knew."

Charlotte thought about that. Laurent had had principles and scruples, but he hadn't faced many choices. One of the advantages, perhaps the only advantage, of dying young. She wasn't about to tell Vivi that. "He did his best," she said.

Vivi took a bite of her omelet, finally. "Tell me more about him."

Charlotte sat thinking. She was an editor. She dealt with words and images and stories all day. Surely she could create a father to capture Vivi's imagination.

"He was over the moon when you were born."

"I thought he wasn't there when I was born."

She is alone in the bare white room, more alone than she has ever been in her easy cossetted life. The nuns come and go at intervals, but the nuns are no help. At least, they are no comfort. She is on her own. We are born alone and we die alone, Laurent used to say. We also give birth alone, she wants to tell someone, but there is no one to tell. Laurent is off at the front, though in this rout no one knows where the front is. The nuns and other patients sob as the radio, taken over by the Germans, blares that the French army is nothing more than a rabble with no idea in which direction to flee. Her mother died three years ago. Charlotte still hasn't got over the unfairness of the timing. She'd been a rebellious child, closer to her iconoclastic father than her more conventional mother, but just as she'd begun to know the vulnerable woman behind the exquisitely dressed, irreproachably behaved public persona, her mother had succumbed to a rapid and virulent cancer. Her father, a leftist publisher who was a friend of the Jewish socialist prime minister Léon Blum, barely got out before the Germans marched in. He hadn't had to be told that his name was on their list. Laurent's elderly parents are safe, she hopes, in the South of France. They'd wanted her to go with them, but she was afraid of delivering the baby on the road. Besides, what if Laurent somehow finds his way home? She has to be there for him. She'd refused to go with Simone for the same reason. "In that case, I'll stay with you," Simone said, but Charlotte was adamant, and in the end Simone didn't put up much of a fight. They'd been friends, almost like sisters, they always said since neither of them had one, from the days when they'd played together as little girls in the Luxembourg Gardens, but now Simone had her own child to worry about. She'd taken three-year-old Sophie and left, too. Even the local tradesmen had fled. She'd seen them as she'd made her way on foot to the hospital, people hijacking taxis, tying their possessions to automobiles, piling wagons with beds and pots and pans, portraits of ancestors and cages full of canaries and parrots. She doesn't understand that. Dogs and cats, yes, but birds, when the city is hemorrhaging, when the world is coming to an end? Ashes rain down from the sky. Smoke stings her eyes and sears her nose and throat. The government offices and foreign consulates and embassies are burning their records.

Then, she doesn't know how much later, Paris goes silent. She hears the hush in the intervals when she stops screaming. The lack of sound is thunderous. The city cannot be this still. No automobiles, no horns, no cacophony of human voices. She lies there, thinking she is dreaming. That is the only explanation for the silence. Then she hears the birds. She's not dreaming. She's dead. Why else is a nun hovering, her wrinkled gray face smashed out of shape by the tight wimple, telling her it's all over. So Laurent and she were both wrong. There is an afterlife, and it's silent, antiseptic smelling, staffed by nuns who appear harried but not unkind.

Only later when they put Vivi in her arms does she realize that she's not dead, and the city is silent because it's empty, and she has a daughter. The terror closes in. Before this, she had only her own survival to worry about. Now she looks down at this small purple-faced package and knows the meaning of responsibility. Suddenly she understands her mother's caution. Her childhood had been lived in a less dangerous time, but there is no such thing as safety. The dread grows worse as the newspapers begin to publish again, and she reads the ads. Mothers looking for babies who have gone missing in the stampede. People searching for someone, anyone, to claim lost infants whose only answer to questions of who they are and where they come from is a single bleating plea. *Maman.*

She stays in the hospital for how long, a week, ten days? Long enough for the city to start to stir again, but the noises are new and unrecognizable. The first uproar sounds like an avalanche or hurricane, nature wreaking its vengeance. She asks the young nun, the one whose face swims pale and thin inside her wimple, what she is hearing. "Boots," the nun says. "Every day they stage a parade down the Champs Élysées. Complete with a military band." Sure enough, Charlotte recognizes the strains of music beneath the roar of the unnatural disaster. "You can hear it everywhere. In case we don't remember they're here," the nun adds.

It's not only the parade. The boots are all over the city, pounding sidewalks, punishing cobblestones, kicking in doors, stomping through buildings, even here in the hospital. They go from ward to ward, room to room. When they come to the mothers and babies, they are polite, even avuncular. One stands beside her bed. He asks for her papers. She hands them over. His glance is cursory. He hands them back. Then, just as she is about to exhale in relief, he leans over and cups Vivi's head in his big hand. It's lucky she's frozen with terror. Otherwise she would slap his hand away.

Gradually people begin to return. Simone comes back with Sophie in tow. Many other friends do as well, but some cannot or do not. Josephine, who was in Portugal visiting a man she'd fallen in love with when the border was closed, is trapped in safety; Bette is teaching in Grenoble; Laurent's parents remain in Avignon; her own father keeps moving; or so she has heard about all of them. There is little or no postal service to or from the unoccupied zone.

"How do you know he was over the moon," Vivi insisted, "if he'd already left for the war?"

Caught in the lie. "Letters, of course. He was the one who named you." That at least was true. "I wanted to call you Gabrielle, but he wrote saying you had to be Vivienne." If you were a girl, she didn't add. "You had to be life."

Vivi sat with her fork in midair, staring at her mother. "You mean he knew he was going to die?"

"He was in the army. He knew it was a possibility. That's why you were so important to him. To both of us."

Vivi didn't say anything to that, and Charlotte didn't tell her the rest of the story. It was true that Laurent would have been thrilled and proud and hopeful, but he hadn't had the opportunity. By the time Vivi was born, he was dead, though she didn't know it until later. The army, which, like the country, was in disarray and disgrace, had taken almost two months to notify her. These were not details she wanted to pass on to Vivi. The hole left by Laurent's absence yawned wide enough. The chasm left by his never knowing of her existence would be unbridgeable.

"Do you mind if I ask what brought this on?"

Vivi shrugged. "I was just thinking."

Charlotte didn't believe that for a minute. She took a sip of wine and waited.

"We had to go around the class today," Vivi said finally, "saying what our fathers did."

Charlotte could kill them, she really could. The insensitivity. The stupidity.

"Barbara Sinclair's father is something at the UN. Kitty Foster's is a doctor who invented an operation. I forget what kind. Camilla Brower's father owns a magazine."

"Your grandfather owned a publishing house."

"They didn't ask about grandfathers."

"They should have."

"It's okay, Mom. I wasn't the only one who couldn't answer." The solicitude in her voice was like a nail going down the blackboard of Charlotte's heart. She was supposed to take care of her daughter, not the other way around. "Pru McCabe's father died in the war, too. Only . . ." Her voice drifted off.

"Only what?"

"She has a picture of him in his uniform on her dresser."

"You'd have one of your father, too, if both of your grandfathers' apartments hadn't been appropriated by the Germans, and ours hadn't been looted by the French when we were taken away. We never went back after the camp. There was no point. It wasn't as if we had good memories to return to."

"I know. I didn't mean it was your fault I don't have one. What did he look like?"

Charlotte poured more wine into her glass. Surely she could remember what the man she'd fallen in love with looked like, but no matter how hard she tried, no face came into focus, only fragments. A tanned throat disappearing into the open neck of a shirt as she lay with her head in his lap, looking up at him, on the beach where they'd gone for two days after the wedding. Eyes narrowed against the smoke as he lit a cigarette. A way of holding his head to make him look taller. He was sensitive about his height. Long fingers, moving incessantly, practicing surgical knots when he had thread, imaginary knots when he didn't, a doctor's trick. No, those weren't his hands.

"He was dark. Dark hair. Dark eyes."

"Do I look like him?"

"You have his eyes. Not just the color, but the shape," she said, though she couldn't remember that either. She was ashamed of herself. This really was willful amnesia. "And his long lashes and brows. He had beautifully shaped eyebrows. I used to joke that the lashes and brows were unfair on a man."

"I wish I had a picture."

Charlotte sat looking at her daughter. "So do I, sweetheart, so do I."

She did, she really did. She'd even thought of trying to get her hands on one. How hard would it be? A few letters, some anodyne requests. Not everyone's apartment had been appropriated or looted. Surely some friend or relative had a photograph of Laurent. All she had to do was write. Sometimes she thought it was the least she could do for Vivi. Sometimes she thought it was the most foolish thing she could do for her.

❦

It was after ten when Charlotte looked up from the manuscript she'd propped against her knees and found Vivi standing in the doorway to the bedroom, her pink pajamas a pale glow against the background of the shadowy hallway.

"I thought you were asleep."

Vivi took the few steps into the room and sat on the side of the bed. Charlotte moved over to make room for her. She slept in a single bed. The room wasn't large, and there was no need for anything more accommodating.

"You know what you said before, about doing the right thing?" Vivi asked.

Charlotte waited.

"And how sometimes it's hard to know what the right thing is?"

"I have a feeling we're not talking about hypothetical situations anymore. I have a feeling we're talking about you."

Vivi nodded.

"Do you want to tell me about it?"

"I'd be tattling."

"My lips are sealed."

"What if you have to choose between what the rules say and something your best friend did?"

Charlotte decided this was not the time to quote E. M. Forster about having the courage to betray his country rather than his friend. "You mean Alice?"

Vivi nodded.

"Which rules did she break?"

"The school honor code."

"Alice cheated?"

"On a Latin test."

"Are you sure?"

"She had some declensions written on the inside of her blouse cuffs. She showed them to me before the test."

"What did you say?"

"I didn't have a chance to say anything. The teacher was handing out the questions."

"Did you say anything to her after class?"

She shook her head. "I can't tell on her. She's my best friend. But when you were talking about my dad"—she almost never used the word, and now she pronounced it hesitantly, as if she weren't quite entitled to it—"being moral, I started thinking maybe I had to do something. I just don't know what."

Charlotte put the manuscript aside and reached for her daughter's hand. It was soft and damp from the cream she'd begun slathering on at night. "It's a moral conundrum, all right."

"That makes it sound even worse."

"Okay, let's look at the alternatives. You can turn her in."

"She'll never speak to me again. No one in the whole class will."

"Or you can say nothing and just try to forget about it."

"But what if she does it again? I mean, if she got away with it this time and thinks it's okay, won't she do it again?"

"I think you just found your solution."

"I did?"

"What if you tell her you're not going to say anything this time, but it's not right, and if she does it again, you'll have to report her."

Vivi thought about that for a moment. "I don't know. That feels as if I'm trying to get away with something myself. I'm not really following the honor code, but I'm not being such a good friend either."

"I think you're being a very good friend. You're trying to save her from a life of crime. And what you're getting away with is a compromise. That's what most of life is, unfortunately. Or perhaps fortunately. The world isn't black and white. It's a gray and shadowy landscape out there."

"I guess," Vivi said, but she didn't look persuaded. She stood and started for the door. When she reached it, she turned back. "Technicolor."

"What?"

"If the world's not black and white, can't it at least be Technicolor?"

Charlotte grinned. "I love you, Vivienne Gabrielle Foret, I really do."

Three

"Please, Mom." Vivi turned from her image, from the replicas of her image that went on and on into infinity in the three-way mirror of the fitting room, to her mother. "I'll never ask for anything ever again. I promise."

"You wouldn't care to put that in writing, would you?"

"In blood if you want."

"Let's not get carried away."

"Oh, come on, let's get carried away." Vivi twirled around the small fitting room, the burgundy velvet skirt swirling about her long legs, until she came to a dizzying stop against a wall. "Pretty please with whipped cream."

Charlotte reached out, lifted the price tag that swung from the sleeve of the dress, and read the number again, as if the figure might have changed since the first time

she'd looked at it. Forty-nine ninety-five was an unconscionable sum to pay for a dress for a girl Vivi's age. Even
if they had the money, she'd be reluctant. The debate had
been raging in her head for some time now. Where did
compensating for the hardship and deprivation of Vivi's
early years stop and spoiling her rotten begin? True, the
dress was for a special occasion, but Charlotte was ambiv-
alent about that, too.

The grandmother of a girl in Vivi's class had become
obsessed with her mortality. The woman, who was living
out her days in a great heap of limestone on Seventy-
Ninth Street, was certain that not only wouldn't she live
to witness her only granddaughter's wedding, or even her
coming-out party, but that it would not be held in the
family mansion, which, in view of property and inheritance taxes and the cost of help, would by that time have
been sold to a foreign country to serve as a consulate or
embassy or turned into the wing of a museum. With those
bleak prospects in mind, she'd decided that rather than
wait, she'd give her granddaughter a dance while she was
still alive and kicking and the impressive building with
its soaring ballroom still in the family clutches. Charlotte
wasn't sure she approved of dances for fourteen-year-old
girls. The idea carried more than a whiff of the unsavory
side of Colette. But she wasn't foolish or cruel enough to

try to keep Vivi from going to one when the rest of her class was.

Vivi watched her mother studying the price tag.

"If it's too much money, I bet Aunt Hannah would give it to me for Christmas. She's been asking what I want."

Charlotte dropped the price tag. "It's not too much money. And we are not a charity case. You're right, let's get carried away."

The smile that cracked open Vivi's face easy as an egg went on and on in the line of mirror-reflected girls. Later, when Charlotte returned the dress, she'd remember that bevy of euphoric Vivis stretching into eternity.

᭟

Charlotte never would have been blindsided if she hadn't still been smarting from that absurd encounter with Hannah's patient in front of the gilt-framed mirror in the foyer. She should have forgotten the incident by now, but it kept sneaking up on her at odd unexpected moments, like some vulgar practical joker with a bag of nasty tricks up his sleeve. That was the only explanation for what happened in the museum that afternoon, not that anything did happen in the museum that afternoon.

In earlier days, when Vivi was small and they were

new to New York, they'd spent weekends wandering the zoo or the Museum of Natural History hand in hand, wondering at the outrageously expensive and opulent toys at F. A. O. Schwarz, and ending up at Rumpelmayer's, where Vivi sat with a hot chocolate mustache on her small face and one of the resident teddy bears tucked beside her. But Vivi had outgrown those childish pleasures as well as weekend afternoons with her mother, unless they were shopping for a dress for a dance or some other momentous event. These days she heard the siren call of her peers. The attraction was normal. Vivi's guilt was not.

"What are you going to do this afternoon?" she'd ask Charlotte as she put on her coat. Occasionally the question was even more deadly. "Do you want me to hang around and we can do something together?" Even when Charlotte outlined her plans in careful detail—lunch with a colleague from another publishing house, a visit to the Frick to see her old friends the Rembrandts and the Turners—Vivi had a way of hesitating on her way out the door and turning back to look at her mother. Once she'd asked if Charlotte would be okay. That was when Charlotte began leaving the apartment when her daughter did. Striding away from Vivi on the street was easier on Vivi.

That afternoon, they walked down Park Avenue to the building on the corner of Eighty-Eighth Street where Alice and her family lived. The compromise solution to

the cheating incident had worked: Alice had been de-
terred from a life of crime, and she and Vivi were still
best friends. Standing on the street under the dark green
awning, Charlotte kissed her daughter quickly, told her
to have a good time at the movies, and started off. Then
she turned back.

"I forgot to ask what you're going to see."

"*The Last Time I Saw Paris*."

"Have fun," Charlotte said again, and this time she
kept going.

She told herself not to be ridiculous. It was only the
title of a movie. Not even the real title. The F. Scott Fitzgerald story the film was based on was called "Babylon
Revisited." Nonetheless, Vivi's words followed her down
Park Avenue and over to Fifth and all through MoMA
until finally she gave up trying to see the art and sat on
a bench in one of the galleries. The paintings and sculptures and other museumgoers fell away as everything had
in the foyer that day, and she was back there.

❦

The bell above the door to the shop jingles, and she looks
up, but she can see nothing. The awning over the window
is useless at this time of year. It's the end of June, and the
sun refuses to set. It slants into the shop, blinding her and
turning him into a silhouette. She cannot see his face or

what he is wearing. He is merely a black outline carved from the brilliance of the evening. But the two young students who are browsing must be able to make him out against the glare, because they move toward the door, each slinking around either side of him, and slip out of the shop into the dazzling setting sun.

Bon soir. The words are almost out of her mouth when he takes another step toward her, and she recognizes the uniform. For more than a year now, they have been marching around the city, swaggering up and down boulevards, scattering people in their wake, shouldering their way into restaurants and cinemas and shops, buying up everything in sight. She cannot keep him out. But she does not have to welcome him. She does not have to speak to him at all. She swallows the greeting and goes back to the book she is reading, though she knows she will not be able to concentrate, not with him in the shop. In the storeroom in back, Vivi whimpers in uneasy sleep.

He asks in fluent but accented French if she minds if he browses. She keeps her head down, her eyes focused on the unintelligible words, and nods her head in a noncommittal way. He begins wandering around the store, taking books off the tables and down from the shelves, leafing through them, putting them back. She keeps track of him out of the corner of her eye. He is returning the books where they belong. He is one of the correct ones.

He keeps browsing. She keeps pretending to read. Her silence apparently doesn't bother him. Why should it? He's the conqueror, the occupier, the one who has nothing to fear. But she feels the quiet as a palpable presence, almost as loud as the fretting that is mounting in the back room. She stands and starts toward the sound. She doesn't have to worry about keeping an eye on him. Conquerors don't steal, they appropriate. Apartments, factories, haute couture salons, publishing houses. No, they didn't have to appropriate the publishing houses. Most of the publishers were eager to cooperate. How else could they get their hands on the necessary paper and turn a profit? And they are turning a profit. Book publishing came to a halt during the first months of the Occupation, then roared back to life, albeit an insipid spineless version of it. Henri Filipacchi at Hachette drew up a list of books to be banned. Many of his colleagues contributed to it. Bernard Grasset of Editions Grasset sent out a letter to his fellow publishers advising them to censor themselves, thereby sparing the German Propaganda Office the trouble. Most of them went along with the unholy suggestion, though some have begun to play a dangerous double game. Gaston Gallimard dines with Propaganda Office officials— the shortage of paper again—while turning a blind eye to the communists who put out their underground publication from his firm's offices. It's lucky her father has fled.

ELLEN FELDMAN

He would not countenance a double game. He would
go before a firing squad, or under the guillotine, which
the Germans are using again in public executions at La
Santé Prison on the rue de la Santé in Montparnasse, before he'd sell his beloved Éditions Aumont, which was his
soul, to the devil. Instead, he'd closed it down. That was
how Charlotte, who'd begun working there after university, had ended up running the bookstore on rue Toullier,
that and the fact that her father's old friend Étienne de
la Bruyère, the owner of Librairie la Bruyère, had been
called up by the military, captured by the Germans, and
sent into forced labor. As a child, she'd spent blissful hours
in the shop, curled up in one of the vaulted corner alcoves
with all the books she could ever want while her father
and Monsieur de la Bruyère discussed what her father
was publishing, and Monsieur de la Bruyère was selling,
and people were buying. The shop, like all of Paris, has
lost some of its luster since the Germans marched in. The
beautiful herringbone patterned floor is scuffed. There is
no floor polish available in Occupied Paris. At least, none
is available to anyone except the Occupiers and their col-
laborators. The old India rugs are showing wear. But the
carved art deco mahogany panels still frame the sections
of shelves, and she still has, if not all the books she could
ever want, thanks to Nazi censorship, then more than she

will ever be able to read. The point is, the browsing officer can take anything he wants, and he knows it.

She steps into the back room, lifts Vivi out of the crate she has lined with a quilt, and begins to jiggle her against her shoulder, trying to fool her out of her hunger pains. Simone has been gone for more than an hour. The queues often go on for longer. She and Simone take turns, one queueing for whatever is meagerly available that day, the other minding the store. Simone's daughter has a J1 card that entitles children between the ages of three and six to extra rations. Charlotte has a card that permits nursing mothers, or those who claim to be still nursing—even the most efficient German does not try to determine if a woman's milk has dried up—to go to the head of the queue. Her card is more valuable than Simone's. Extra allocations mean nothing, when there is nothing left to allocate. A week earlier, two thousand people queued for three hundred portions of rabbit, or so the word that went down the line said. The queues are rumor mills. It's hard to believe what people say, impossible not to.

She returns to the front of the store, still jiggling a crying Vivi against her shoulder. He is standing, with a book in one hand, beside the mahogany counter where the cash register sits. As she goes behind the register, she keeps her head down, refusing to look at him. His free hand

comes into her line of vision. His fingers are long and
slender. She wonders, irrelevantly, if he plays the piano.
Germany wasn't always like this. It was the land of Bach
and Beethoven and Wagner, people told one another in
an attempt to console themselves when the troops first
marched in. But Wagner played at full volume, it turns
out, is good for drowning out the cries of the tortured,
or so rumors go. These days the city runs on rumors, as it
used to on petrol when there were still automobiles. The
hand seems to be moving toward Vivi, as if to soothe her.
Charlotte stops herself from taking a step back, but she
cannot help stiffening. The hand withdraws. Perhaps he
is not insensitive. Perhaps he has intuited how repugnant
she would find his laying an Aryan finger, even a long
graceful Aryan finger, on her child. The hand returns into
her line of vision. Now it is holding francs. Still refusing
to look at him, she takes the bills, puts them in the cash
register, counts out change, starts to hand it to him. Only
then does she notice the title and author above the price
on the volume he is holding. She had been too scared to
before. It is Stefan Zweig's book with a section on Freud.
It is on the so-called Otto list of banned books. Works by
or about Jews are forbidden, and this is both. They were
supposed to turn it in to be sent to the vast warehouse
where outlawed books are pulped or left to molder, but
Simone took the copies they had in stock and hid them in

the storeroom. Many booksellers are selling banned books under the counter, partly in defiance, partly for profit. Only this purchase is not under the counter. Simone either missed the book or left it on the shelf intentionally, another of her futile dangerous gestures. Charlotte loves Simone, like a sister they always say, but sometimes she could kill her. She supposes that's sisterly, too.

Her hand is still hovering near his with the change. Does she hand it over and let him walk out of the store with the book? She could be arrested for less. Does she tell him it's a mistake, that they have turned in the other copies, that they must have missed this one in their eagerness to comply? She cannot sell it to him, to anyone, she will insist. It is against the law. The explanation sickens her, but she knows she will make it to save her skin, hers and Vivi's.

She looks up and, frightened as she is, she almost has to laugh. The joke about Hitler, the epitome of blond, blue-eyed, strong-jawed Aryanism, is standing in front of her in the flesh. This Wehrmacht officer has dark hair, black eyes set deep behind rimless glasses, and the long ascetic face of a saint. While she is staring at him, he takes the change from her hand, executes a slight bow, and starts toward the door with the contraband book. As she watches him go, she notices that he slips the volume into his tunic before he steps into the street. So he knows it's banned.

A moment later, the two students who had fled at the sight of him return, and shortly after that the bell jingles again, and Monsieur Grassin, another friend of her father's, comes through the door. Grassin, an ethnographer at the Palais de Chaillot, visits the shop periodically. He has promised her father to look after her as best he can. Unfortunately, he is not up to the task. A member of the Resistance, or so she suspects, he sleeps in a different place every night or two. He is not easy to find, but he has told her that if she ever needs his help, she is to put his book, *Seeing and Writing Culture,* in the window as a sign. "But be careful of the stampede," he'd joked at the time. "You know how popular the subject is."

"I was waiting for the boche to leave," he tells her now, then asks after her and Vivi. He doesn't stay long, but she knows that, despite the nonfunctioning postal system, he will get word to her father that she and Vivi are, if not safe, then surviving.

৵

She loses sleep over the Zweig book with the section on Freud. She and Simone both do. But no military car pulls up in front of the store, no Germans come thundering in, not even a gendarme appears. The officer, however, returns. She is in the store alone again. He asks if he may browse again. She remains silent again. Why doesn't he frequent the stalls along the Seine? The quays are crowded with Germans trying, unsuccessfully, to saunter like Parisians, hoping to blunt their barbarism with an infusion of purloined French culture and style. Why doesn't he take his business to the Rive-Gauche, a big slick bookstore run by a collaborationist, backed by the Occupation authorities, and stocked with German propaganda and approved French trash? But he has developed a liking for the shop. He comes in the following week and the one after that. Sometimes she is sitting behind the cash register, sometimes Simone is, sometimes they're both there. Books and money pass between one or the other of them and the officer, but few words. Occasionally he will inquire about a book. One day he asks for *Moby-Dick*. Charlotte stiffens. Melville is on the Otto list. Is he trying to trap her? She explains she is forbidden to stock the book. The next time he asks for a volume of short stories by Thomas Mann, who has also been banned. When she tells him that, too, is forbidden, he buys a volume of Proust, who, strangely enough in view of his Jewish ancestry, is not. The week after that he purchases a copy of *Being and Time* by Heidegger. Perhaps he is not a spy, merely a man with eclectic interests.

"The boche has good taste," Simone says after another of his visits. "That's one more thing I hate about him and all the rest of them with literary pretensions."

Charlotte knows she is thinking of the high-ranking official who threatened to close down Shakespeare & Company and confiscate all its stock after Sylvia Beach refused to sell him her last copy, or so she said, of *Finnegans Wake*. As soon as he left the shop, Sylvia sent out the call to friends and colleagues. Within two hours, they had emptied the store of all the books and even the shelves and electrical fixtures. By the time the official arrived with his men to carry out his threat, Shakespeare & Company had ceased to exist, thanks to a house painter who had obliterated the name on the front of 12 rue de l'Odéon. They never did find the shop, though they arrested Sylvia and put her in an internment camp. She was released after six months, and gossip has it that she's in hiding here in Paris. Charlotte could swear she saw her one evening just before curfew standing in the shadows on the rue de l'Odéon, staring at number 12. She didn't approach her.

Sylvia should have gone into hiding in the south after the incident, as Gertrude Stein and Alice Toklas did, not that they're actually in hiding. From what Charlotte has heard, they're living safely and well at their house in the Bugey under the protection of Gertrude's old friend Bernard Faÿ, a notorious anti-Semite who was appointed director of the Bibliotheque Nationale after a Jew was fired from the position. Stein, a Jew, is another example of literary figures playing both sides of the game. Before

the war she told an American newspaper that Hitler deserved the Nobel Peace Prize, but her admiration didn't
stop the censors from putting her books on the Otto list.
Charlotte's father had broken with Stein over the Hitler
remark, as well as her support for Franco, though the
latter hadn't seemed to bother Stein's friend Picasso, who
plays perhaps the most dangerous double game of all. He
gives money to the Resistance and has been known to
harbor fugitives (or so people say; no one knows for sure,
and most people don't want to; the less you know, the
safer you are), but he entertains German visitors in his
studio, while instructing Françoise Gilot to follow them
around to make sure they don't plant anything. Nonetheless, artists have an easier time under the Nazi boot than
writers, whose messages are more explicit.

This German officer, however, seems less dangerous.
He is unfailingly polite. He tries to fit in, as much as a man
in that hated gray-green uniform can fit in. He is almost
successful. The other customers begin to grow accustomed to him. They no longer put down the books they're
looking at and drift out of the store when he arrives. Even
the elderly teacher who has been dismissed from the
Lycée Condorcet for being Jewish and frequently comes
to the shop to sit in the worn leather chair in a nook and
read the volumes he can no longer afford to buy ignores
him, but then these days the professor seems to notice

less and less. He lives in a world created by the words on the page.

One day when she is at the cash register she steals a glance at the officer, who is standing with a book in one hand, the fingers of his other hand doing some kind of intricate exercise as, she has noticed, they frequently do, but he is not looking at the book. He is staring at the clock on the back wall. It is set to French time. The Germans have decreed that all of Occupied France must now run on German time. Charlotte keeps setting it to German time. Simone keeps moving it back an hour. Damn Simone and her meaningless bravado. They need no excuse to arrest and appropriate, but still, why give them one to hide behind?

The officer looks from the clock to his watch, then back up at the clock. She drops her eyes and waits for him to speak. Except for the labored breathing of the old professor, who is not well—how could he be under the circumstances?—the shop remains silent. The officer walks to another shelf and takes down a book. She almost wishes he had said something about the clock. It is harder to hate the polite ones, the ones who seem reasonable, who let you keep time by the sun rather than by force. She does not want to begin to see this officer, any officer, any German as human. It is too dangerous.

The next time he comes, a week or ten days later—

she refuses to keep track of his visits—she is alone in the shop. Simone is queueing for their rations, and there are no other customers. That is unusual these days. Despite the shortage of paper, the Occupation is turning out to be a boon for both publishers and bookshops. Between the curfew and shortages, there is little to do at night other than read or make love, and there isn't much opportunity for the latter. Too many of the men have disappeared into POW or labor camps, fled to England or North Africa, or been killed in the fighting. She is sitting in the torn leather chair in the corner with Vivi on her lap, paging through a picture book.

"*Bonjour,*" he says.

She doesn't answer.

He begins to browse. She drops her voice to a whisper as she reads the nonsensical rhymes to her daughter. When she looks up after a while, she sees he is watching them.

"How old is she?" he asks in his correct but accented French.

Charlotte does not mean to answer, but how can she resist talking about Vivi? "Eighteen months."

The look of surprise that crosses his face is the confirmation of her worst nightmares. The lack of food is taking its toll. Vivi will be sick and stunted for life.

The next day, he returns with his wiliest ploy or most

generous gesture. Who can tell? He is carrying an orange. "For the child," he says, and puts it on the counter.

She stands looking at it. How can she look anywhere else? She doesn't remember the last time she saw an orange. It glows as if lit from within.

"Vitamin C," he adds.

She goes on looking at it.

"I am a physician," he says, as if you had to have a medical degree to know a growing child needs vitamin C.

Still she goes on looking at it but doesn't reach for it.

He turns away, takes a book off a table, glances at it, returns it, says *au revoir,* and leaves the shop. He is making it easy for her.

❧

"How was the movie?" Charlotte asked when Vivi got home that evening.

"Sad. Elizabeth Taylor dies because Van Johnson gets drunk and locks her out in a snowstorm. Then Elizabeth's sister, Donna Reed, won't let him have custody of their daughter. She says it's because he's a bad father, but really it's because Donna Reed was in love with him, but he chose Elizabeth Taylor instead." She stood looking thoughtful for a moment. "But the girl goes to live with her father in the end, so it all works out."

Charlotte started to say that in the Fitzgerald story the

protagonist doesn't get custody, then changed her mind. It was like the yellow wallpaper. She wanted to preserve the illusion for Vivi as long as possible.

⚘

Charlotte was at the stove sautéing mushrooms when Vivi got home several evenings later. She stood in the doorway to the kitchen, leaning against the jamb, still wearing her camel's hair coat, hugging her books to her as if they were armor.

"You can return the dress."

"What?" Charlotte turned off the burner under the skillet and faced her daughter. She really did think she hadn't heard her correctly above the faint flickering of the gas.

"I said you can return the dress. It's too expensive anyway."

"It's not too expensive. It's fine."

"I don't need it. I'm not going to the dance."

"Of course you're going to the dance."

"I'm not invited."

"What do you mean you're not invited? The invitation is on your dresser."

"It's been rescinded. That was the word Eleanor used." Eleanor Hathaway was the classmate whose grandmother was facing her mortality. "She says it's not her fault."

"What's not her fault?"

"That she can't invite me. She says her grandmother won't let her."

Impossible as it would seem to Charlotte later, she still didn't understand. She racked her brain trying to remember if she'd offended the old woman or Eleanor's mother in some way. Vivi's classmates' mothers were polite, but Charlotte didn't fool herself into thinking that she was one of them or even that they liked her. They pitied her—poor Charlotte Foret had to go out to work—but mostly they disapproved of her. She managed to dress with twice the style, they told one another, on a quarter of what they spent on clothes. The observation, which Vivi had passed on, was not meant as a compliment, at least not entirely. There was also some speculation about her accent, which seemed to wane and wax. She had to admit they had a point there. In the years she'd been living in America, she'd found that a rolled *r* or elongated *e* occasionally came in handy. And once, from the stall in a school ladies' room on some parents' night, she'd overheard one mother telling another that Charlotte Foret had a way of lighting a cigarette and throwing away the match that told you to mind your own damn business. It was lucky she wasn't much of a smoker.

"Her grandmother doesn't even know you."

"She knows I'm Jewish. I know what you always say.

You weren't a Jew until Hitler made you one. But that's not the way other people see it."

"Even here?"

Vivi lifted her thin shoulders in another shrug. The gesture was meant to be insouciant. It came out as defeated. "I hope the dance is a flop. I hope Eleanor comes down with a bad case of pimples the night before."

"And I hope her grandmother rots in that special circle of hell reserved for bigots," Charlotte said.

So this was the way they got to you in America. No roundups, no camps, merely insidious cruelty to your children.

⚜

Vivi came back to the subject over dinner.

"What about my father?"

"What about your father?"

"Did he need Hitler to make him a Jew?"

"He wasn't any more of a believer than I am."

Vivi didn't say anything to that, but her expression gave her away. She was skeptical. She was also desperate to have something to hang on to. That was all right. Charlotte wanted her to have something to hang on to. But not this.

Four

Carl Covington, the would-be grand old man of publishing, prided himself on his publication parties. The guest list was select. No junior editors or advertising assistants getting drunk and making a dinner out of pigs-in-blankets and angels-on-horseback. The setting was dazzling. He and his wife lived in a penthouse on Central Park West with a view of the shimmering reservoir and a book-lined living room that rose two stories. His own little Morgan Library, he liked to say. His toasts to the author of the evening and his or her new book were effusive. The parties were great successes. Some people were said to enjoy them.

The celebration that night was in honor of a writer who every twelve months turned out a thriller that could be relied on to nibble at the lower reaches of the *Times* bestseller list. Charlotte had congratulated the author, paid her respects to a few reviewers, chatted with a foreign agent, compared notes with an editor from another house, thanked Carl's wife for a delightful evening, and started down the hall in search of her coat, which a hired man had taken when she'd arrived. As she passed the first door, open to a dimly lit study, she noticed Horace sitting in a circle of light from a floor lamp. He must have sensed her in the doorway, because he looked up from the book he was reading.

"Anything good?" she asked as she stepped into the room.

"Doesn't get much better." He held up the book with the spine turned toward her. *The Portable F. Scott Fitzgerald* was imprinted in black on the burgundy binding. "Why didn't we think of reissuing *Gatsby*? Viking was damn smart. Have a seat. Unless you're eager to get back to that." He gestured toward the living room.

"About as eager as you appear to be."

She took the chair on the other side of the reading lamp. He squinted at her through the glare, then reached up to pull the chain of one of the bulbs. "The mornin' light does not become me." He closed the book and gestured to her empty glass. "You want to freshen that? I'd offer, but it's easier for you."

She was surprised. He never referred to his incapacity. At least she'd never heard him do so.

"I'm fine. In fact, I was about to leave." She leaned forward and put the empty glass on the table just as Bill Quarrels stuck his head in the doorway.

"Am I interrupting something?"

"Yes," Horace barked.

Bill reared back as if he'd been punched. "Sorree." He drew out the word as he left.

"You have to watch that surfeit of charm," she said.

"And you have to watch him."

"He's harmless."

"If you say so." He sat studying her for a moment. "How are things on the fourth floor?"

"Fine. Whatever the problem with the water pressure was, Igor fixed it."

"My wife and the handyman are a formidable team, but I wasn't inquiring about the physical plant. I meant on-site morale. How's Vivi?"

"Fine," she said again.

"That's not what I hear in my part of the house."

"What do you mean?"

"When I got home last evening, I went into the kitchen to get some ice. Vivi was there with Hannah. Your daughter looked as if she was the one who needed a drink."

"I'm sorry. If she gets underfoot, just send her home."

He shook his head. "Come on, Charlie, we both know the one thing Vivi is not in our household is underfoot. Hannah would move her in if you'd let her."

"I know, and I'm grateful."

He raised one eyebrow. The problem with Horace was that he observed people too closely.

"Hannah said it had something to do with a party at school."

"It's a dance, not a party. And it isn't at school." She told him about the grandmother facing her mortality and the rescinded invitation.

"You sound surprised."

"Shouldn't I be?" Her voice was incredulous.

"Does the name Dreyfus ring any bells? Not to mention more recent events, of which I believe you've had some firsthand experience."

"That was France. Europe. The Old World."

"Oh, I forgot. Human nature changes when it crosses an ocean."

"I just didn't think it would be as virulent here. And I didn't think they'd visit it on a fourteen-year-old girl."

"That's your problem. You don't think."

"Thanks."

"I'm sorry. What I meant was your lack of antennae."

"Now you're saying I'm insensitive?"

"Not in the way you mean it."

"Then how?"

"Most Jews, even Jews like me—"

"You're Jewish?"

He sat staring at her for a moment, then threw back his head and started to laugh. "That's what I mean. You have no antennae."

She felt her face getting hot. "I assumed Hannah was. Because of her practice. But I didn't think you were. You don't act it. You don't seem it."

"Now you sound like that anti-Semitic latter-day Miss Havisham sitting in her beaux arts mansion, spewing venom. What does a Jew act or seem like, Charlie?"

He'd caught her out, all right. "All I meant was that you never said anything. You never do anything religious."

"As opposed to you, you mean?"

"I wasn't brought up as a Jew. I don't call myself one."

"No, you leave that to others. What I'm trying to say is you're the only Jew I've ever known who isn't aware of it. No, I take that back. Your father wasn't either, but then all he and I ever talked about was books. He was a helluva publisher. But most Jews, including the ones in publishing that I met abroad, are obsessed with the subject. Even the Jews who are trying to pass, especially the Jews who are trying to pass, which incidentally I'm not accusing you or your father of doing, are always thinking about it. Who is and who isn't. Who hates us and who pretends not to. Who tries to ignore it, who goes around with a sandwich board advertising it, and who's looking for a fight about it. It's a survival tactic. And it's universal. At least I thought it was until I met you. You're the only Jew I ever met who's tone-deaf."

"You make paranoia sound like a virtue."

"It's not paranoia when there's a real threat. I take it you've heard of quotas. I came up against them when I was at Harvard. They still exist. Are you familiar with the word 'restricted'? I have a picture of a hotel in Maine. 'No dogs or Jews,' the sign outside says. That was before the war. These days it's a little more subtle. If you don't believe me, try renting an apartment in certain buildings in Manhattan or buying a house in parts of Connecticut, not to mention various other states in this great union of ours. I had a friend who pulled it off, but he had to have his lawyer front for him. Still, look on the bright side. That anti-Semitic old bitch is preparing Vivi for the world."

"Which you're suggesting I'm not?"

His only answer was that cold blue stare.

❦

She hadn't even had a chance to take off her coat when Horace wheeled into her office the next morning.

"I've come to apologize. Something, incidentally,

Hannah says I'm incapable of doing." He'd dropped his voice for the second sentence, and she wasn't sure she'd heard him correctly.

"For what?" She hung her coat on the standing rack in the corner and walked around him to sit behind the desk.

"That lecture last night. I don't know where I got off, pontificating to you about being a Jew. It's as if you decided to enlighten me about the proper way to go through life as a cripple, if you'll excuse the expression. Don't look so surprised, Charlie. Did you think I didn't know I was in a wheelchair?"

"I just never heard you talk about it."

"Any more than you talk about what happened to you in Paris. You and I are two of a kind. The walking wounded. Or in my case, the wheeling wounded. Which also makes us the two great mysteries of this place. Subjects of infinite curiosity and speculation. 'Is it true he was wounded on some heroic mission?'" He shook his head. "It wasn't a mission, only a battle, and there was nothing heroic about it, but a heroic mission makes for a better story, and we're in the business of selling stories. 'Is it true she was tortured in a Gestapo prison? Or managed to sneak herself and her baby off the last transport that left Drancy for Auschwitz?'" He held up his hand. "I'm not asking. I'm just telling you the kind of gossip that flies around here precisely because we don't say anything.

I'm not suggesting we start undressing in public." He was silent for a moment, and she wondered if he was thinking of the most intense speculation about him. "But," he went on, "we don't have to be quite so squeamish with each other. So I'm apologizing for that ridiculous lecture last night."

"It wasn't actually a lecture."

"Whatever it was, I was out of line, and I'm sorry."

He navigated his chair around, started to wheel out of the cubicle, then stopped at the entrance but didn't turn back to face her, merely sat staring out into the open area of secretaries' desks. "And while I'm throwing around apologies, I might as well toss one in for that crack about Hannah saying I'm incapable of them. The line smacks of my-wife-doesn't-understand-me." He gripped the wheels of the chair with his big hands and gave them a fierce turn to propel himself out of the cubicle. "Hannah does," he said as he rolled away. At least, that was what it sounded like.

☙

Charlotte sat thinking about the sentence Horace might or might not have spoken. From the moment she'd met Hannah Field in the noisy sprawl of the vast metal customs shed her first morning in America, Hannah had made it clear that she was going to take both Charlotte and Vivi under her wing. Most new arrivals would have been grateful, and Charlotte had been. But she'd also been on her guard. She was reserved by nature. The last few years in Paris had made her more so. And then there was the warning, though that came a year or two later.

Ruth Miller was an editor at another house with whom Charlotte struck up a friendship. She was also a friend of Hannah's from college.

"Be careful of her," Ruth said one day when she and Charlotte were having a non-expense-account lunch at Mary Elizabeth's, a tearoom serving crustless sandwiches and mysterious meat and fish swimming in equally mysterious white or brown sauce. The place depressed their spirits and offended their palates, but it was convenient, inexpensive, and a step up from Schrafft's.

"She's been extremely generous," Charlotte said, her voice even.

"Hannah's nothing if not generous. You know that character in *The Forsyte Saga*, the one who takes up lame ducks? That's Hannah. But just let the duck get back on its little webbed feet, and out it goes."

"I'm not sure I know what you mean," Charlotte said, though she had a feeling she did.

"After the war, I got mixed up with a bad egg. He drank, chased women, and was always in need of money, which I, of course, handed over. What're a few dollars where love's concerned? I'm not a very good judge of character. At least I wasn't in those days. Hannah could not have been more sympathetic. She listened to my laments, did her best to find some redeeming traits in him, and never once urged me to throw the bum out. But when I did throw the bum out, when I got back on my little webbed feet and took up with Nick, she dropped me like the proverbial hot potato. I think Nick's admirable qualities are what did it. She stopped calling, stopped returning my calls. Once I swear she even crossed the street to avoid me. The funny thing is, if she were a man, I would have caught on immediately. But she was another woman and so sympathetic. It took me longer to realize the friendship with Hannah was over than it did to throw out the bum."

Charlotte sat in her office remembering the story and thinking about Horace's comment. Even in a wheelchair, he wasn't a lame enough duck.

༈

"I've been thinking." Vivi straightened from her prone position on the living room floor and sat up to face Charlotte, who was on the sofa. They'd been handing sections of the Sunday *Times,* fat with ads for gloves and ties and other Christmas gifts, back and forth between them. Thin winter sunshine trickled through the two south-facing windows overlooking the street that dozed in Sunday morning tranquility, interrupted only by the occasional pedestrian walking a dog or taxi cruising for a fare.

"Always a good endeavor. About anything in particular?"

"The dance."

Charlotte put the section she'd been reading down. "The fact that you weren't invited has nothing to do with you personally," she said again. "Only with that bigoted old woman."

"I know that. But it made me think about something else."

Charlotte waited.

"If I'm Jewish, I ought to be Jewish."

"Apparently you are," Charlotte said after a moment.

Vivi thought about that. "I wish I remembered more about being in the camp."

"I'm glad you don't."

"I can't even picture it."

"You were too young. And we were only there for a short time before it was liberated."

"How did we manage before that? I mean, if they were rounding up Jews, how did they miss us all that time?"

"We had forged papers. Sometimes we hid out. The Germans weren't always as efficient as they thought. And let's not talk about the French gendarmes. In other words, we were lucky."

"That's what Aunt Hannah says her patients who are survivors tell her. They also say they never knew who to trust. An old friend could turn you in or a complete stranger could risk his life to save you."

"I suppose that's true," Charlotte said.

"The people who helped us—"

"Vivi! It's the past. It's over." Charlotte held out the theatrical section she'd been paging through. "I know you think *Peter Pan* is infantile—"

"I'm too old to sit in the audience screaming 'I believe' so some silly light onstage doesn't go out."

"Note taken. But is there anything else you'd like to see over the holidays? *Fanny* might be fun. We could go to a Saturday matinee or even in the evening during school break. Anything you want to see, within reason."

"A Jewish church."

"What?"

"I want to go to a Jewish church. Synagogue," she corrected herself. "See what I mean. If I'm Jewish, I ought to know something about it. Couldn't we go just once to see what it's like?"

"I know what it's like."

"I thought you didn't know. I thought it took Hitler to make you a Jew."

"That's my point. I think religion is dangerous."

"But that's *my* point. If people are going to treat me a certain way because I'm Jewish, I ought to know why."

"There's no logic to intolerance. Any more than there is to the rites and rituals of religion. Any religion. You think if you were Catholic, saying a dozen Hail Marys would cleanse your soul?"

"You always do that."

"Do what?"

"I ask about being Jewish and you tell me some story about going to confession with your friend Bette or how all the other girls you played with got new white dresses for their first communion."

"I grew up in a Catholic country. Most of my friends were Catholic, except for one Jewish girl. All I'm trying to say is I don't trust any religion. Your father agreed with me. We were both atheists. I don't think we ever talked about religion, except to agree on how much harm it did. He wouldn't be any happier than I am with this religious awakening you seem to be having."

She knew she was playing dirty, but it was necessary under the circumstances. And the ploy worked. Vivi took the theater section and began paging through it.

Five

Charlotte wasn't sure how it had happened. Surely a letter she hadn't even read couldn't upend her life so completely. Still, something had breached the barrier she'd erected between then and now.

When she had first arrived in America, she'd found life less the challenge she'd braced herself for but more of a shock to her sensibilities. She couldn't get used to people hurrying along the sidewalks with long confident strides or sauntering as if they hadn't a care in the world instead of skulking with shoulders hunched and eyes averted, crossing streets and cowering in doorways to avoid anyone in uniform, and flinching with fear when a soldier stopped to ask directions because he might just as easily be bent on harassment, or worse. She was amazed at the

absence of signs forbidding her to cross this thorough-
fare or enter that area, and the press of traffic swarming
the avenues and jockeying on the cross streets, and the
lights that turned night into day. Paris had been so dark
for so long. But the greatest surprise was the abundance.
She had sailed away from a world still stalked by hunger, stunted by shortages, mired in misery. She'd landed
in a country booming with optimism and hell-bent on
making up for lost time. People were gorging on steaks
and whiskey, butter and sugar. They were building houses,
and buying cars and appliances and clothes, and going
on holidays. Gradually, as she grew accustomed to this
overstocked new world, the astonishment had worn off.
Some mornings she'd opened her eyes and felt as if she
were waking to a sunny day after a long sheet-twisting
nightmare. Now the nightmare was beginning to shadow
not her nights but her days again. Now the nightmare
was becoming more immediate than her real world.

One day, standing in front of the display case in the
butcher shop, she'd grown lightheaded at the profusion
of steaks and roasts and chops and offal and ordered a
dozen lamb chops. "Having a dinner party, Mrs. Foret?"
the butcher asked as he wrapped them in the heavy waxed
paper. Too embarrassed to say she'd lost track of where
she was, she'd spent a quarter of an hour rearranging the
refrigerator's freezer to fit them in. As she was coming out

of the subway on Eighty-Sixth Street, just on the edge of Yorkville, the sound of a German conversation stopped her dead on the steps so a logjam piled up behind her. An anodyne piece in the newspaper about the Coney Island Polar Bear Club that swam every Sunday from November to April yanked her down the rabbit hole.

✿

At first she and Simone and all the Parisians laugh at them. They need something to laugh at as they pedal their bicycles beneath the huge Nazi banners that snap and shout in the wind, and the signs that tell them they have the English and the Jews to thank for their defeat, and the darkness that hangs over the city on even the sunniest days. Who can help but laugh at these overgrown boys in shorts and underwear, marching in lockstep to pools and playing fields, roughhousing in the open air, splashing and shouting and showing off their raw high spirits and robust health. Their bare chests glisten with sweat in the summer and as fall comes shine hard and white as marble in the cooling air. The muscles in their arms and legs ripple as they move. At rest after their exertions, lounging on lawns and benches and, worst of all, national monuments under the French gaze, they parade their erections with childish pride. Look at us, they seem to say, look at our disciplined, beautiful, brimming-with-life bodies and what they're capable of. Not like you broken defeated French. And gradually the populace begins to look. Some of the women stare, and others try to turn their eyes away in anger, and in fear, not of those bodies but of themselves. The men watch, too, some in rage, some in envy, and some surreptitiously, longingly, hungrily. And gradually the joke becomes a dread. Even those who are risking their lives to sabotage them aren't free of the lure of sex and danger and death all mixed up in a murderous erotic cocktail. Once, acting as a courier for an organization she has joined, Simone finds herself in a railroad compartment full of German officers. Instead of changing compartments, she spends the trip flirting with them. That is before the decree about the stars comes down. Wasn't that clever of me, she asks Charlotte when she returns, hiding in plain sight that way. Clever yes, though something else, too, Charlotte thinks but does not say. She is too busy fighting the fascination herself.

Spring comes again after another unbearably frigid winter without heat. Spring is nature's thumb in the eye of the German Occupation, now about to begin its third year. In the absence of exhaust fumes, the city reeks of lilacs. In the absence of engines and horns, there is a symphony of birdsong.

One Sunday she puts Vivi in the basket of her bicycle and pedals to the Luxembourg Gardens. She is not worried that the Germans have taken over the Luxembourg Palace and are entrenched around the park. Or rather, the Germans have taken over Paris. She is worried no matter where she goes. But the sun has come out after several days of rain, and the feel of the warmth, spring thin but still tender on her skin, makes her brave, or at least restless.

She leans her bicycle against a tree, and she and Vivi settle on a patch of greening grass. She will not take one of the benches where signs warn Jews it is forbidden to sit. She could get away with it, but the ban is morally repugnant. Though she's not as brave as Simone, she has her scruples. And she and Vivi are happy on the grass. She is so happy that at first she doesn't notice them. But little by little, the thump of the ball and the shouts and laughter intrude. She glances up, then away, then at them again. Some are playing in shorts, some in boxy under-wear, some in thin briefs that cover little. The Third Reich worships the cult of the body. Nakedness is a sacrament.

The noise and exuberance catch Vivi's attention, too. She has stopped playing with the handful of blocks Char-lotte has brought and stands, her small hand resting on her mother's shoulder, her eyes wide. She has never seen such uninhibited joy. She is accustomed to whispers and wariness and fear.

Charlotte turns away from the sight, picks up a block,

holds it out to her daughter, but Vivi is not interested. Charlotte gives up and leans back on her elbows, lifting her face to the sun. One of the men kicks the ball. It lands a few feet away and rolls over to where they sit. Another player comes running after it and skids to a stop in front of them. His sweat-slicked chest is brown. How did it get so brown so early in the season? The muscles in his thighs strain against the skin. He stands looking down at them. A white smile slices his broad easy face in two. For a moment she wonders if the rumor that Goebbels, the propaganda genius, sent the Wehrmacht's handsomest soldiers to occupy Paris is true. He bows. "*Verzeihung,*" he says, and as he reaches for the ball, Vivi reaches for him. Charlotte pulls her back, but Vivi tries to squirm out of her arms. The German laughs, leans toward them, and ruffles Vivi's thin cap of dark hair. He smells of sweat, not the stale sour stench of the Parisians, of Charlotte herself, who lack adequate water and have no soap, but the smell of recent exertions in the open air. And sitting there, watching him trot back to the game, she feels her own perspiration between her breasts and beneath her arms and in the small of her back, and is ashamed.

She begins gathering Vivi's blocks, her book, and their hats and sweaters. That is when she hears the familiar voice behind her. She turns and looks up, but the sun is behind him and in her eyes, as it was the first time he walked into the shop.

"Let me help you," he says, and reaches for her things. She swats his hand away, stands, scoops up Vivi, and, pushing the bicycle with her other hand, walks away from him without a word. Only when she's at a distance does she stop, strap Vivi into the basket of the bicycle, and climb onto the seat.

As she pedals out of the gardens and through the streets, she tries to avert her eyes, but everywhere she looks, she sees the same sight. It enrages her. Lovers lie entangled on the grass. They embrace on benches. They walk in step, hips grazing, arms entwined, bodies melded. When had so many men returned? She veers toward the Seine and passes the spot where later the dead body, the first dead body, will turn up, but the bodies she is thinking of now are fiercely, offensively to her, alive. The faster her long legs pedal, the angrier she gets. Not at Laurent. How could she be angry at Laurent?

Six

Vivi hadn't meant to buy it. Actually, she hadn't bought it, merely taken it, not swiped it as some of the girls did candy bars and packages of gum just to prove they could, but accepted it as a gift.

Her mother had sent her to Goodman's, the hardware store around the corner on Madison Avenue, to get replacement bulbs for their Christmas lights. They hadn't even got the lights and ornaments out yet, but her mother liked to be prepared. She was always afraid that stores would run out of things.

Vivi was wandering the aisles, carrying the bulbs, looking at the candles and ornaments and gag gifts. Her favorite, because it was so stupid, was a John Wayne piggy bank that drew a gun from his holster every time you put in a coin. Then she spotted it, a kind of candelabra with eight arms and one taller arm in the middle. She was surprised it caught her attention. It wasn't silly like the John Wayne piggy bank or shiny or glittering like the Christmas decorations. It had a dull bronze glow. Later, she'd say something about it had called out to her, and her mother would tell her not to be ridiculous. The only thing that had called out to her was Mr. Rosenblum. Her mother didn't like Mr. Rosenblum. She said he was too friendly. When Vivi asked how anyone could be too friendly, her mother said she meant too familiar. It wasn't until later that Vivi understood what her mother meant by that.

Mr. Rosenblum was wearing his usual shabby brown sweater with the familiar brown checked shirt and brown woolen tie. The sleeves of the sweater were pulled all the way down. That was usual, too. When the weather got hot and even the fans couldn't cool the store, he took off the sweater but kept the sleeves of his shirt buttoned around his wrists.

He approached her now as she stood holding the Christmas bulbs in one hand and the candelabra, which was heavier than she'd expected, in the other. He had a long hangdog face, but his smile, when he chose to show it, was big and wide and white. It was so big and wide and white that it didn't seem to belong to him. It looked like one of those masks held in place by an elastic behind the head.

"So which is it going to be, Miss Vivienne Foret"—he must have known her last name because of the charge account, but she didn't know how he knew her first name—"the Christmas lights or the Chanukah menorah?"

That was what it was. She must have sensed it. She put it back on the counter. "I was just looking at it," she said guiltily. "My mother sent me for the lights."

"So maybe this year a surprise you should give your mother."

She shook her head. "My mother doesn't believe in religion."

He looked at the lights she was holding. "So what's that you got in your hand?"

"She says Christmas is different. It doesn't have to be religious."

"But Chanukah does? This is America. The land of the free. The home of the brave. Go ahead, have both. No one's going to charge extra."

"Are you Jewish?" she asked.

"Does a bird fly?"

"I am too."

"News this isn't."

"My mother says she didn't know she was a Jew until Hitler made her one."

He shrugged. "Some of us knew. Some of us weren't so smart. In the end a difference it didn't make." He went on looking at her. "But a smart girl like you, you're curious, right?"

"Well . . ." She hesitated. "I figure if other people know I'm Jewish—"

"That you can count on."

"Then I ought to know something about being Jewish."

"Like I said, a smart girl. I tell you what." He picked up the candelabra. "The menorah you take."

"I couldn't. My mother sent me for the lights."

"So the lights you buy. The menorah you take. A present from me to you." He smiled that borrowed white smile again. "It's okay. For working here I get a discount. I'll even throw in the candles. So now you don't have to wait for another Hitler to let you in on the secret."

It had seemed like a good idea when he'd said it, but now, standing in the black-and-white foyer of her own house, holding the bag with the Christmas lights and the candelabra, she wasn't so sure. No, she was sure. It was a terrible idea. Her mother would be furious. She could take it back to Mr. Rosenblum, but she didn't want to hurt his feelings. She could ask Aunt Hannah to keep it for her. Aunt Hannah liked Mr. Rosenblum. She was the one who'd told Vivi his teeth were so big and white because they were false. He'd lost all of his in a camp, and the dentists at Montefiore Hospital, where they treated refugees for free, had made him a whole new set. But though Aunt Hannah let her get away with a lot, she wouldn't help her keep a secret from her mother. And if Uncle Horace got wind of it, neither would he.

The only solution was to hide it. She'd put it in the back of her closet or in the bookcase behind the books she'd outgrown but didn't want to give away. It wasn't as if she was going to light the candles he'd given her or anything like that. She just wanted to have it.

❦

Her mother always apologized for all the Christmas parties she had to go to for work, but Vivi didn't mind. Sometimes when her mom and Uncle Horace were both at a party, she and Aunt Hannah had dinner at the big farmhouse table in the kitchen with the stone floor and the old dumbwaiter that still worked, though no one ever used it. At Aunt Hannah's she had the kind of dinners she had at her friends' houses. A lamb chop or hamburger, green beans, and a baked potato. She liked her mother's cooking, but she knew her friends thought having an omelet for dinner was weird, and more than once when they'd come for supper she'd seen them trying to hide uneaten mushrooms on their plates. Sometimes she just liked being alone in the apartment. At least, she didn't mind being alone. It made her feel less guilty for the times she went out and left her mother alone. And tonight she had a reason for being glad she was on her own.

She took the menorah from behind the set of Betsy-Tacy books, put it on the radiator cover in front of the window, and stood looking at it. That was when she got the idea. She hadn't planned to light the candles Mr. Rosenblum had given her, but what harm could there be if she did it and then blew them out right away? It wasn't as if she were playing with fire. She was just lighting a couple of candles. She was seeing what it was like to be Jewish.

She went back to the bookcase, took out the candles, and carried them to the menorah. Mr. Rosenblum said she was supposed to light the top candle first, then use it to light the others going from right to left. Backwards from the way you read, she'd said. Not in Hebrew, he'd answered. You were supposed to light one candle on the first night, then add one each night until the holiday was over. She had no idea when the first night was, but who knew if her mother would be out then? Besides, she wasn't celebrating the holiday. She was just seeing what it would be like if she did.

She put a candle in the top and another in the first holder on the right, then struck a match, lit one candle, and used it to light the second. The flames shimmered. Their reflection danced against the darkened window.

She crossed the room to the switch beside the door and turned out the overhead light. That was even better. That was beautiful. She didn't care what her mother said. She bet if her father were alive, they'd celebrate Chanukah. If her father were alive, she'd be like everyone else, almost.

☙

Horace opened the back door and wheeled out into the small garden that was clipped and pruned and shrouded for the winter. Hannah was indefatigable. He wasn't being ironic, even in the privacy of his own mind. She took care of the house and the garden and a full load of patients. She would have taken care of him, too, if he'd let her. That was why he was out in the garden on an icy December night. No, that wasn't true. This had nothing to do with Hannah. This was all his.

He grasped the wheels in both hands and propelled himself forward, seventeen feet away from the house, nineteen and a half across the bottom of the garden, seventeen feet back. A handkerchief-sized yard is no place to work off anything, but he had no choice. In the beginning, when he'd gone careening up and down streets, or tried to, someone had always stopped him. Can I get you a cab, sir? You all right, mister? Hey, buddy, need some help? Hannah left him alone. At least she did now. She hadn't the first few times. She'd come crunching down the gravel path in her high heels—her legs were her best feature, next to her mind she liked to say, and she enjoyed showing them off—and stood in front of him blocking his path. Even in the darkness, her eyes blazed with her determination to help, and her hair, which had a tendency to escape its French twist, made a pale halo against the sky.

"What are you doing out here alone in the middle of the night?" she'd ask.

"It's not the middle of the night."

"What are you doing out here alone in the dark?"

"What does it look like I'm doing?"

"I don't know, that's why I'm asking."

"I'm going for a walk, my version of it. And alone is the point, Hannah."

He knew that was cruel, but he couldn't help himself.

"It would be better if you'd talk."

"So says the William Alanson White Institute."

That was another low blow. She was proud of her professional affiliation. She could never have been a physician, she admitted. She was too squeamish. But accreditation by the institute let her treat people's minds without having to deal with their bodies. Still, his making fun of the place made her the grown-up and him the child taunting her.

At least those arguments in the yard had stopped before Charlie moved in. He would have hated to subject her to them. No, he wasn't worried about subjecting her; he was concerned about exposing himself. Not that he and Hannah had to go outside to argue. Charlotte had probably overheard her share of indoor disagreements. She never said anything. Unlike Hannah, she did not believe in the healing power of the spoken word. He and Charlie were two of a kind, all right, wary, secretive, shamed, though he'd be damned if he knew what she had to be ashamed of. No, that wasn't true either. Survival never comes with a clear conscience.

He reached the end of the path, swung the chair around, spun along the bottom of the garden, and turned right again. That was when he saw it. He grabbed the wheels to stop the movement and sat looking up at the window on the top floor. Flames. There were goddamn flames in the window. They leapt and flickered and burned holes in the night.

His hands spun the wheels forward. The chair shot up the path, through the back door, and down the hall to the elevator. His fist hit the button. The cage began to lumber down the shaft. It shook. It growled like a menacing animal. It took forever.

When it finally arrived, he yanked the outer door and pushed the cage door open. The metal screamed in protest. He wheeled in with such force that his withered knees hit the back of the cage. His fist jabbed the button that said four. The inner door slid closed. As the elevator began to inch upward, he rotated the chair to face the door. The climb was a nightmare in slow motion. One slid by, then two, then three, finally four appeared. He wrenched the cage opening halfway across and began pushing on the outer door, but he'd been too impatient. The grating had frozen halfway. The door was locked in place. He pushed against it, though he knew force wouldn't work. His sweat-slick palms slid down the door. His breathing rasped in the silent cage. He closed his eyes for a moment and tried to regulate his breathing. He opened them and managed to force the cage door closed, then pushed the four button again. The cab lurched into place. He slid the grating across, pushed open the outer door, and spun himself out into the hall.

The door to the apartment was closed. He rang the bell and hit the knocker against the plate and banged with both fists.

"Charlie," he howled. "Vivi!"

He waited. There was no answer. He rang and knocked and banged and shouted again. Later, he'd realize she had taken so long because she was trying to hide the evidence, but that would be later. Now all he knew was that someone was in there playing with fire.

The door opened. Vivi's eyes were terrified saucers in her white face.

"The candles," he shouted. "Put out those goddamn candles!"

"What candles?" she asked.

"Don't 'what candles' me. The goddamn candles you're burning in the window. Put them out!"

She went on staring at him.

"I said put them out!"

"They're out."

He closed his eyes for a moment, opened them, sat up in his chair, and tried to hide his humiliation, but it was no good. He was sweating the way he used to after a couple of hours on the tennis court in the midday heat. He could feel the veins in his temple pulsing.

"Your mother isn't home, is she?" At least his voice wasn't shaking.

She shook her head.

"Didn't she tell you? In this house we do not play with fire."

She stood looking at him for a moment. "I wasn't . . . ," she began, then stopped. "I'm sorry. I forgot."

❦

Hannah was waiting for him in the hall when the elevator door opened. He wheeled past her into the parlor. She closed the door behind them and stood watching as he made his way across the room to the marble-topped

Victorian sideboard that served as a bar. It seemed impossible to her now that she'd once taken such pride in this room, in the whole house. She'd had the moldings restored and the marble mantels over the fireplaces rebuilt, the hardwood floors refinished and the generations of paint and wallpaper scraped and stripped. Beautiful, friends had said. So authentic, they'd added. But it wasn't authentic. It was a stage set, and she was stuck in it for the run of the play.

She stood in the middle of the room, watching him as he poured a drink. His hands were shaking so badly that the bottle clinked against the glass. His back was to her, but his face, reflected in the mirror over the mantel, was distorted with rage, and something else. Shame. The shame should have stopped her from speaking, but it didn't.

"Don't you think you were a little rough on her?"

Holding the glass in one hand, he maneuvered the chair around with short angry jerks until he was facing her again.

"I just reminded her that in this house we do not play with fire."

"Just reminded her? I was in the bedroom, you were on the fourth floor, and I could hear you."

"Maybe now she'll remember."

"Oh, she'll remember, all right."

He wheeled away from her toward one of the tall front windows, then pivoted again to face her.

"Okay, I was a little rough on her. I'll apologize tomorrow. To her. And to Charlotte."

"You didn't shout at Charlotte."

He took another swallow of his drink.

"I'm not stupid, Horace."

"I never thought you were."

"I see what's going on."

"Nothing is going on."

"I'm not talking about sex. I wouldn't mind that. Not anymore."

"Not anymore? You wouldn't have minded it the day I came home from the hospital. Hell, you would have been grateful if I'd taken my so-called affections elsewhere. You may not be stupid, but you're lousy at hiding disgust."

"I was trying to help."

"You were trying to manage. Do this, don't do this. It's supposed to be sex, not physical therapy."

"Actually, it's supposed to be making love."

He sat staring at her for what felt to both of them like a long moment. "Let's not ask for the impossible."

"That's not fair."

"Fair! You've walked this earth for thirty-eight years, you're married to a cripple, and you still think life is fair?"

"What I think is that there's such a thing as emotional infidelity."

"If only that were grounds for divorce in New York

State. But even then you couldn't do it, could you? You couldn't bear to look in the mirror and have the kind of woman who leaves a crippled husband look back at you."

She started to say that wasn't fair, then caught herself. Not because he'd come back with the same line about life not being fair, but because he was right. And she hated herself for it.

❦

"You didn't shout at Charlotte."

The sound of her own name on the other side of the wall stopped her on the stairs. She didn't think of herself as an eavesdropper, but even the most scrupulous woman does not keep going when she hears herself being discussed in what people think is private, especially if voices are raised.

She went on standing there. The accusations were mounting, but her name wasn't mentioned again. She took two more stairs.

"I'm not talking about sex. I wouldn't mind that. Not anymore."

She stopped again. She couldn't help herself. She wasn't like everyone else in the office, wondering, speculating, could he, couldn't he. Their interest was prurient. And what, a voice masquerading as her conscience asked, is yours? She had no answer to that, or rather she had an answer, but it was even worse than prurience. It was personal.

🙜

"What I don't understand," Charlotte said, "is what you were doing lighting candles in the first place." She and Vivi were standing in the living room facing each other. Vivi had confessed as soon as her mother walked in the door.

Vivi shrugged.

"That's not an answer."

"I just wanted to see what it looked like."

"What what looked like?"

"The menorah when it was lit."

"The candles you were lighting were in a menorah?"

"I only lit them for a minute. At least that was what I was going to do. I would have blown them out even if he hadn't come up here screaming bloody murder."

"What on earth were you doing with a menorah?"

"Mr. Rosenblum at Goodman's gave it to me."

"That little old man who works in the hardware store gave you a menorah?"

"When I went to buy the lights for the tree. He said America was a free country. I could celebrate as many holidays as I wanted."

"Since when did Mr. Rosenblum become the arbiter of your behavior?"

"I don't see what you're so upset about. It's only a kind of candlestick. Even if it is Jewish."

She hears the explosions going off. Seven of them. Seven synagogues. Does she count them or does she learn the number from the rumor mill? The next morning, people pick their way through the debris. She stumbles over a candelabra melted almost beyond recognition. She closed her eyes for a moment. When she opened them, the image was gone and she was facing Vivi again.

"It has nothing to do with the religious significance," she said.

"Oh, sure."

"It doesn't. But we do not keep secrets in this family."

She could have sworn Vivi smirked at that.

❧

Half an hour later, she was waiting in the hall when Vivi, smelling of soap and peppermint toothpaste, came out of the bathroom. Vivi dropped her eyes and started to slide past. The gesture cut Charlotte. She blocked the way and lifted Vivi's chin so she was forced to face her.

"You don't have to agree with me about religion," she said, "but you do have to promise me you won't play with fire anymore."

Vivi slumped against the wall and dropped her eyes again. "Lighting candles for two minutes isn't playing with fire. I'm not a five-year-old."

"I know that. But it's still dangerous."

"According to Uncle Horace's phobia."

Charlotte felt herself stiffen. "A phobia implies an extreme or irrational fear. I see nothing extreme or irrational in being afraid of fire if you're in a wheelchair. He can't navigate stairs, and elevators are dangerous in a fire, or so say the signs. 'In case of fire, use stairs.'"

Vivi shrugged. "Aunt Hannah was the one who called it a phobia. And she's a psychiatrist."

"She may be a psychiatrist, but she's certainly not a semanticist."

"What's a semanticist?"

"A woman with compassion."

Now Vivi's eyes snapped up to meet her mother's. "I don't believe you said that."

They went on standing face-to-face in the narrow hall.

"I'm sorry. You're right. That wasn't exactly compassionate on my part. A person who studies the meaning of words."

❦

The night after Vivi lit the candles in the menorah and Horace lost his temper at the top of his lungs, he took the elevator to the fourth floor again. This time there was no assaulting of buttons, wrenching open of steel cabs, or pounding on doors, though his manner was still brusque.

He rang the bell and waited. Charlotte opened the door. He was sorry he hadn't come earlier. He would have preferred to do this without her in the apartment.

He wheeled past her into the living room. "Is the kid around?" he asked without meeting her eyes.

"If you mean Vivi, she's in her room doing her homework."

He looked up at her, finally. "I suppose you know why I'm here."

"Do you want me to get her?"

"Do you mind if I go in there?"

"Tread gently."

"I put on my kid gloves before I came up here." He wheeled across the living room and down the short hall.

She didn't follow, but she was listening.

"Hi, kiddo." His voice carried to the living room. It was too hearty.

If Vivi replied, Charlotte couldn't hear it.

"Mind if I come in?"

Again she couldn't make out Vivi's answer, but she heard the rubber wheels roll over the place in the floor that always squeaked.

"About last night," he said, and now his voice grew

so quiet that she couldn't make out his words either, but later Vivi told her about the conversation.

"He said he was sorry he lost his temper, but he hoped I'd understand. He couldn't go up or down stairs, and you're not supposed to use an elevator in a fire. He said he had nightmares about it all the time. He said President Roosevelt used to, too, though no one knew it until after he was dead."

"I told you all that," Charlotte said, "except the part about the late president."

"Yeah, but it was different when he said it. He sounded ashamed. Like a little kid who doesn't want to admit he's afraid of the dark. He wasn't making fun of himself, like he always does, or of other people. He does that a lot, too. He was just . . . I don't know . . . ashamed," she said again. "I felt so sorry for him."

"Just don't let him know it."

"I'm not an idiot, Mom."

"And don't light any more candles."

"I already promised him that."

❦

Vivi saw it standing on the mantel in the living room as soon as she got home from school that evening. It looked a lot like the one Mr. Rosenblum had given her, but instead of space for candles there were small bulbs in the holders. The bulbs weren't lighted, but a cord ran to the electric outlet beside the fireplace.

"What's that?" she asked as Charlotte came out of the kitchen.

"What does it look like?"

"I thought you didn't believe."

"I don't, but I decided if we're going to have a tree, we might as well have a menorah. An ecumenical celebration. Peace on earth. Good will toward man. And God bless us, every one."

She stood watching as Vivi crossed the room to the mantel. "How do you light it?"

"Twist the bulb."

Vivi turned the top bulb. It lit up. She stood staring at it for a moment, then turned to her mother. "Where did you find it?"

"New York City is full of menorahs. But this one came from your friend Mr. Rosenblum."

"Mr. Rosenblum gave you another menorah?"

Charlotte smiled and shook her head. "One free gift to a family. My rule, not his. I bought it."

"You bought a menorah?"

Now she laughed. "I wish you'd stop repeating everything I say as a question. It's not so strange. I may not believe in organized religion, but I'm not exactly Scrooge or whoever the Jewish equivalent is."

Vivi turned back to the menorah and twisted the first bulb on the right. It went on.

"I think it goes in the other direction," Charlotte said.

Vivi shook her head. "That's what I thought, but Mr. Rosenblum says you light it from right to left. The way you read Hebrew."

"I didn't know that."

Vivi turned to her mother. "Like you always say—"

"As you always say."

"As you always say, you could put what you know about being Jewish on the head of a pin and still have room for a couple of million angels."

֍

The laughter stopped Charlotte on the stairs. This time she couldn't justify eavesdropping by hearing the sound of her name. It was pure curiosity. No, pure snooping. She wanted to know what Hannah and Horace were laughing at. No, that wasn't true either. She wanted to think that she was mistaken. How could they be laughing together so easily, so intimately, after the argument she'd heard the other night? But they could be and they were.

Several months earlier, Vivi had returned from a visit downstairs to say Hannah had shown her an album of pictures from their wedding.

"She was really pretty."

"She still is—for somebody even older than your mother."

"And you should have seen her dress. It was long and slinky with a train that went on forever. Like something out of the movies. But it was weird seeing him standing next to her. It made me kind of sad."

"More than kind of."

"There was one picture of them kissing. That was weird, too."

"Married couples have been known to kiss. Especially at the end of the ceremony."

Vivi made a disparaging face. "I know that, but this was so, I don't know, smoochy. I mean, I just don't think of them that way."

"We were all young once."

"Were you and my father smoochy?"

"How do you think you came about?"

"Would you have stayed smoochy, do you think? Or would you have been like Aunt Hannah and Uncle Horace?"

"We would have stayed smoochy," she said, but the question made her wonder, not only about her own brief marriage and what would have happened if Laurent had lived—would they have aged toward each other or away?—but about Horace and Hannah's. Had it begun to go sour before the war, or was it, like Horace's body, one more casualty of the conflict? Or maybe it hadn't gone sour at all. One overheard argument does not drive a marriage onto the rocks. Perhaps her own wariness of Hannah was coloring her view. And what she took as Horace's flirtatiousness might be mere friendliness. She could decipher Frenchmen, but she was still a naïf when it came to Americans. If it was a cliché that no one knew what went on in anyone else's marriage, she knew less than most. She simply didn't have the experience.

Seven

❧

On a wet morning, the first week in January, Horace wheeled into Charlotte's cubicle, managing to avoid the umbrella she'd left open in the corner to dry, and swung the chair around until he was facing her across the desk. Rain streaked down the single window, and the office was gloomy even with the overhead light on.

"I tried to give you a lift this morning, but when I rang your bell from the downstairs hall, no one answered."

"I left early," she lied. "I wanted to talk to one of Vivi's teachers."

She'd heard the bell and stood behind the curtains peering out the living room window until the car that came for him every morning pulled away from the curb. Living on the top floor of his brownstone made her suspect enough among her colleagues. She could imagine what they'd say if she began arriving with him in the morning and leaving with him at night. Nonetheless, she'd had second thoughts as she'd stood in the rain waiting for the bus.

He took a manuscript box from his lap, leaned forward, and dropped it on the desk. She glanced down at the title page. *Under the Yellow Stars.*

"It's not an astronomy book or guide to camping, in case you were wondering," he said.

"I wasn't."

"I don't know why the agent didn't send it to you. It's up your alley, not mine. Anyway, take a look at it and let me know what you think."

"I can tell you what I think now."

"Isn't that a little precipitate?"

"My judgment may be precipitate, but the book is premature. Maybe in another ten years. People might be ready by then. But not now. Not yet." She thought of the afternoon in the square just after the Liberation, the woman in the torn and soiled underwear, the mother holding the baby like an unwanted package, the jeering crowd. "Emotions are still too raw."

"That's what they thought about Anne Frank's diary. It was turned down by five houses in England and nine here. It's too soon after the war, they said. Who's going to fork over three bucks for the musings of an adolescent girl locked in an attic, they asked. But a junior editor by the name of Barbara Zimmerman had another idea. Doubleday printed five thousand copies. The *Times* ran a review on Sunday, and the entire print run sold out on Monday. That was three years ago. Do I have to remind you what's happened since then, other than the fact that Barbara is no longer a junior editor?"

"Barbara also wrote an introduction to it that she got Eleanor Roosevelt to put her name to."

"You have any objection to ghosting introductions?"

"I just don't think lightning is going to strike twice. Not this soon."

He sat looking across the desk at her. She forced herself to hold his gaze. She refused to feel guilty. Strangling a book couldn't hold a candle to the other crimes she'd committed.

"So much for bearing witness," he said, and wheeled out of her office. This time, he resolved as he got back to his own, he was not going to apologize. She had to stop hiding eventually.

She went on staring at the manuscript box he'd left behind. She had no intention of reading it. She'd already given him her opinion. She didn't even want it in her office. She stood, picked it up, walked across the open area, and put it on Horace's secretary's desk. The woman glanced over at it. "*Under the Yellow Stars,*" she read. "Is it a romance?"

Charlotte could have slapped her, but you didn't go around slapping motherly women whose only flaws were a penchant for office gossip and naïveté about the world. She couldn't even blame her for the latter. Half the people who'd been affected had been in the dark, or denial, at least at first.

༘

Surely the decree doesn't apply to French Jews, they insist, only foreigners. Surely it doesn't mean me, a decorated veteran of the last war, the head of an important corporation, the hostess of a salon that half the German generals would give their eyeteeth to be invited to, a nonbeliever. But the proclamation is clear even if people who are still insisting that what is happening isn't refuse to believe it. All Jews over the age of six are required to wear a six-pointed yellow star, as big as the palm of an adult hand, outlined in black, sewn, not pinned, securely to the garment on the left side of the chest and visible at all times, with the word *JUIF* printed on it in black letters. That is where another question, or hope, of exemption comes into it. To French Jews, the word *juif* connotes immigrants from other countries, especially eastern Europe. French citizens of the Jewish persuasion, especially those whose families have been here for generations, refer to themselves, if they refer to their religious affiliation at all, as *Israélites*. The Germans make no such distinction. A Jew is a Jew is a Jew, and as such, must be herded into this psychological ghetto of humiliation and shame, as inescapable in its way as the physical camps created by barbed wire and guards and dogs. No longer will Jews be able to masquerade as ordinary French men, women, and even children. They must be marked. It is for the public good.

At first it seems as if the plan might backfire. Some gentile French citizens begin wearing stars, either blank or with other words such as *GOI* or SWING printed on them. The protest is lighthearted, but the punishment for it is swift and serious, and as the gentiles are arrested and imprisoned, fewer risk it. Until now, Jews have been slipping into first-class Metro cars, which are forbidden to them, unnoticed, despite Nazi assurances that Jews can be spotted by long hooked noses, pendulous lips, and other surefire physical giveaways. When a woman without any of those telltale features but wearing a star boards a prohibited car, an outraged German officer pulls the emergency cord and orders her off. The rest of the car follows, leaving him alone in his pure Aryan solitude. Other Christians express support by smiling, nodding, and offering words of encouragement as they pass on the street. And some Jews, determined not to be cowed, parade the boulevards with their yellow stars, heads high, faces daring others to disapprove or pity. A few even sit beside

Germans in cafés. Simone is one of these. At first she refuses to wear the badge; then she takes it up as a cudgel.

But there are others, and as time passes and the novelty wears off, they become more bold. People stare at the gaudy yellow stain and whisper among themselves that they never would have guessed, he or she had seemed so refined, so intelligent, so French. Thugs, and some who do not think of themselves as thugs, slap, punch, and kick old men, boys, even women wearing the star. In cafés, solid citizens usurp outdoor tables where Jews sit and force them inside. Supposed friends are suddenly busy. Perhaps cruelest of all, children taunt their classmates with ugly words, blows, stones, and exclusion.

Then the other ordinances come down. Jews are forbidden to frequent restaurants, cafés, cinemas, theaters, concerts, music halls, swimming pools, beaches, museums, libraries, expositions, historic monuments, sporting events, racecourses, parks, and even phone booths. Their personal telephones have already been confiscated. The roundups grow more sweeping and violent. And still no one can believe. The French tell one another they're arresting only the communists, the foreigners, the criminals, despite the doctors and lawyers, the writers and respectable businessmen, who are beginning to disappear.

The professor who has been driven out of the Lycée Condorcet is sitting in the leather chair in the corner reading, his yellow star bright against his drab frayed coat. If the two customers who are picking up books and paging through them notice the insignia, they give no sign of it. Neither does the German officer, who is back again. Charlotte has got used to him. So have the regulars. He causes no trouble. He is scrupulous about not getting in anyone's way, stepping aside to let people pass or reach for a book, executing that small stiff bow in greeting, as if he knows how hated his uniform is and wants to prove that not everyone who wears it is the enemy, though of course that is exactly what he is.

The shop is quiet, as is the city outside. There is no warning, no screaming of sirens, only the muffled sound of automobile doors being slammed and feet moving rapidly across the sidewalk. True, the bell above the entrance rings for longer than usual as each of the four officers lets the door go and the next pushes in behind him. Who would think they need that many for the task at hand? They are not, Charlotte notices, Gestapo or even Wehrmacht but French gendarmes. The flames of anti-Semitism, anticommunism, and xenophobia that have always smoldered among the French gendarmerie have been fanned to a bonfire by the occupying forces. Even among those who are not so inclined, fear for their own skin makes them execute the Nazi orders.

Once inside, they stop and look around, not at the

books but from one customer to the next. Charlotte and the others pretend to go on with what they are doing, but each of them is suspended, senses sharpened, muscles tensed, waiting. Out of the corner of her eye, she glances at the German officer. Even he seems suddenly wary. She wonders if he is part of this, an agent masquerading as an observer. Or perhaps he has no more knowledge of what's going on than the rest of them.

Without a word or even a sign to one another, the four policemen move to the alcove and surround the professor. And here is something Charlotte will remember. He does not look up from his book, Montesquieu, she notices, but goes on reading. He is still clutching the volume as two of the officers grab him by the arms, lift him from the chair, and begin hauling him across the shop, his worn trousers and scuffed shoes dragging after him as if he is a rag doll. When they reach the door, one of the other gendarmes knocks the book out of his hands.

Charlotte and the two customers stand watching them push and pummel the professor into the car. Now he is trying to struggle, but he is outnumbered, and they are younger and better fed. She looks from the scene to the German officer. He is pretending—surely it's a pretense—to page through a book.

She thinks of all the books he buys, and his correct manners, and the orange.

"Stop them!" she says before she can stop herself. "He's an old man. He hasn't done anything."

The German officer lifts his gaze from the page. He looks at her, rather than the scuffle going on beyond the shop window, but doesn't speak.

"Please," she says.

He goes on looking at her, but she has the feeling he is not seeing her. His eyes are dead. His face is a mask. "I can do nothing," he says finally.

"Of course you can. They're French gendarmes. You're a German officer. Of the occupying force."

"I am sorry, Madame. I have no authority."

Later, after the war, when she reads about the trials—I was only following orders, the defendants will plead, one after another—she'll remember the German officer's words. But by then she won't be so eager to sit in judgment on anyone.

❦

It's Charlotte's turn to queue for their rations, but she pleads with Simone to go in her place. Vivi's cough has grown worse. The spasms rack her small body. Her forehead is hot, and she probably has a fever, though Charlotte can't be sure. When the Germans appropriated her father-in-law's apartment where she was living, she had to leave behind most of her possessions, including the thermometer. She can't get her hands on aspirin anyway. Medications are in even shorter supply than food.

But Simone is adamant. "Now that I've sent Sophie to my mother we don't have her card, and last time I tried to use yours, it didn't work. Maybe I can fool the boches, but no Frenchman will believe I'm nursing. Not with these." She opens the heavy sweater, which she hasn't taken off since the weather turned cold at the beginning of October, to reveal the flatness of her breasts beneath her dress. Charlotte's breasts are dry of milk but not as flat as Simone's.

"Then I'll take Vivi with me."

"In this rain? Do you want whatever she has to turn into pneumonia? She'll be fine with me."

Charlotte gives in. Later, she'll tell herself that her acquiescence has nothing to do with the fact that it's Saturday, and the German officer frequently shows up on Saturday. She doesn't want to see him. She never wanted to see him, but her aversion has grown since the day he pleaded a lack of authority. She is too angry, or is it conflicted? How can someone who reads philosophy and history and fiction and brings an orange to a child let an old man be dragged off for no reason?

She takes the sheet of ration cards and her string bag and leaves the shop. Her high platforms are hard to walk in. If she has to resort to wooden soles, she should find flat shoes. These are absurd, like the towering turbans some women have begun to wear to hide unwashed, unstyled hair. The presence in the city of more and more of those pathetic gray mice, the stubbornly unstylish German women in their drab uniforms who serve as nurses, secretaries, typists, and telephone and telegraph operators, and venture out only in twos and threes, like nuns, makes the Parisian women only more determined to hold on to some vestige of chic. But she finds nothing chic in those exaggerated hats, though her hair is a ragged mess, thanks to Simone's way with a scissors. The cut accentuates how thin her face has grown and makes her mouth look even wider and more vulnerable. Now, rain drenches her kerchief and turns the shoulders of her gray coat black with moisture, but she still tries to walk like a Frenchwoman, not plod like a German in heavy oxfords.

As she gets nearer, she sees that the line snakes down the street and around the corner. People snarl at her as she makes her way to the front. She waves her special ration card as she goes. Some become apologetic, even wishing her well. A baby is cause for rejoicing in these unrejoiceable times. Others shout that she is an impostor, a cheat, a *collabo* even.

She reaches the front of the line and is allowed to pass into the market. The woman whose turn she has usurped mutters angrily. She ignores her. No, she does not hear her. Vivi's cries echoing in her ears drown out the sniping.

She moves quickly, determined to get what she can while it lasts. She negotiates for a kilo of butter and some black bread. There is no meat or even rabbit. If only she had friends or relatives in the country nearby she could take the train or even bicycle out for food. A few weeks earlier, Simone's mother sent a sausage. By the time it arrived it was purple. They'd tried to cure it with vinegar but finally given up. She turns to the sack of beans. They're not rationed but still scarce. A woman jostles her, making her spill the beans she is trying to scoop. She drops to her knees and begins shoveling them up. She can tell even before she picks over them that they're full of weevils.

She produces her ration card, pays, and leaves. The transaction has taken more than an hour. It would have taken far longer without her special card. There would have been no transaction at all without her special card. The meager supplies are already running out.

As she makes her way back down the line with her purchases in her string bag, she keeps her eyes on the cobblestones. She cannot meet the gazes of the people still waiting, some huddled under torn and broken umbrellas, others resigned to the wet, to one more indignity. Their looks are too full of hatred. Even those who'd murmured about a baby when they'd let her pass before cannot camouflage their envy now. Why should she eat, why should even a child eat, when their bellies are empty?

She hears the howls before she turns the corner onto the rue Toullier. She tells herself it's her imagination, but she knows it isn't. It's Vivi. She breaks into a run. Her wooden platforms clatter over the pavement. She careens through the few pedestrians who are out. Even in good weather people no longer stroll for pleasure. The *flaneur* is dead. A woman tells her to stop. "*Les boches,*" she warns. Sure enough, two soldiers head her off as she nears the bookshop. Standing in front of her, blocking her way, they demand to see her papers.

Don't you have anything better to do than stand in the rain, waiting to ambush innocent people, she wants to shout at them. Instead, clutching the string bag in one hand, she fumbles for her papers with the other. The older of the two takes them from her, moves under an awning, and begins studying them. The younger one, so young that his face is still ravaged with acne, stands guard over her, as if she is a criminal about to bolt. The one with the papers says something in German to his colleague. She cannot make out the words. He speaks a mixture of dialect and slang too quickly. Besides, she can't hear anything above the sound of Vivi's cries. She tries to explain. Her baby. That is her baby crying. The younger soldier grins as if a child in pain is a joke. The older one comes out from under the awning, hands her back her papers, and tells her not to run. She will alarm people. She will cause a disturbance. When they stand aside to let her by, she can barely keep from breaking into a gallop. It is harder as she gets closer to the shop and the sound of Vivi's screams grows louder. Then they stop. The silence settles on her like sunshine breaking through the clouds. Simone has somehow managed to calm her. Or she has finally cried herself into an exhausted sleep. Charlotte feels her shoulders relax. She keeps walking, steadier now on the ridiculous wooden platforms.

She reaches the shop, pulls open the door, and steps inside. The only sound is the bell. Then that goes silent, too. The store is even quieter than the street. Simone is nowhere in sight. There are no customers. The place is empty. But this is odd. There is a metal canteen standing on the counter beside the cash register. She looks around the shop again. In the alcove, sitting in the worn leather chair, still the professor's chair as she thinks of it, is the German officer. He is holding Vivi in his arms, and— Charlotte cannot believe her eyes—giving her a bottle. Vivi's rash-covered cheek rests against the rough cloth of his uniform. Her mouth sucks violently at the rubber nipple.

The officer looks up and smiles. "I found the bottle

in the back of the shop. I was careful to wash it first. I thought the child could use some milk. I brought it from the mess." He points to the canteen on the counter, then drops his eyes for a moment, as if he is embarrassed. How did he know her milk has dried up? "There is other food, too." He indicates the black doctor's bag that sits on the floor beside him.

She opens her mouth to say she can't take it, but she knows she will.

The bottle is almost empty. Vivi's lids are drooping. Slowly, as the level of milk goes down, she stops sucking. Charlotte stands looking at the man who sits gazing down at the child, her child, whom he is cradling. Something in her chest lurches. Who is this man?

She straightens her shoulders and stiffens her back. She will not be taken in.

She crosses the room and takes Vivi from him. He stands.

"I brought the milk and the food because every time I am here the child seems hungry."

"All of Paris is hungry."

He ignores her and goes on. "When I found her unattended, I gave her the bottle."

"She was not unattended," she says indignantly. "I left her in good hands. It was my day to queue for food. The two of us take turns."

"The child was alone when I arrived," he insists. "Your sister must have gone out for a moment."

She starts to say that she and Simone are not really sisters, they simply behave that way, but before she can, the knowledge dawns on her. No, the horror dawns on her. Simone would not have left Vivi alone unless she was forced to. Simone has been arrested.

She sees the shadow pass across his face as he comes to the same realization. Now he is implicated. Now he is the one who can be accused. The Germans, his people, have taken Simone away.

"You've arrested her." She's half shouting, half crying.

"I have arrested no one," he answers quietly.

"Oh, yes, you arrest no one. You can do nothing. You have no authority."

Instead of answering, he lays two fingers on Vivi's forehead. "She has a fever. I took the liberty of giving her half an aspirin." He nods toward the black bag still sitting beside the chair. "I am a physician," he tells her again.

Oh, he's clever, all right. He has no authority to save Simone or the old professor, but he has the ability to heal her child, he is telling her.

She opens her mouth, though she doesn't know if she's going to thank him or spit in his face. She does neither. She just goes on holding Vivi and watching him as he takes the rest of the food from the black doctor's bag, puts it on the counter, turns, and leaves the shop. Vivi doesn't stir at the sound of the bell over the door.

ֆ

When he comes again the next day, he asks about Vivi. She tells him she is napping in the storeroom. "Thanks to you," she adds before she can stop herself. He smiles, and she realizes she has been had, again. He has got her to be civil. More than civil, friendly, grateful, indebted.

He puts the black doctor's bag on the counter, opens it, and begins taking out food. A loaf of bread, a piece of cheese. They haven't had cheese in months. He is still putting out food when the bell over the door jingles. She turns to the sound and recognizes the man immediately. He rarely comes into the shop, but she sees him often on the street, or in other shops, or playing cards with the concierge in her loge. He and the concierge are great friends. Every time Charlotte encounters him, she has to force herself not to look away. The man was wounded in the last war, and like so many other injuries suffered in the trenches because only the head was above ground, it destroyed his face. The plastic surgeons did a good job of giving him a new one. From a distance he looks almost normal. Close up he is terrifying. The replacement face is rigid and waxy. It can express neither joy nor sorrow, rage nor affection. A week or so ago, she saw him on the street berating a young woman who'd said thank you to a German soldier who'd picked up an envelope she'd dropped. His fierce patriotism and violent hatred of the Germans are understandable in view of what they did to him, but something about the contrast between the vehemence of his anger and the impassivity of his expression made him seem like a deadly mechanical doll, capable of destruction but immune to reason.

She turns back to the German officer. The food is no longer on the counter. He is standing in the far corner, an open book in his hands, the black doctor's bag on the floor beside him.

The man wanders around the shop, picking up books but not opening them, returning them to the wrong place, staring from the German officer to her and back again. Finally he leaves.

The officer picks up his bag, crosses the shop, and hands it to her. "Put the food in the back where no one can see it."

When did they become conspirators?

ꝗ

The next time he turns up, several days later, she asks him about Simone. When she sees the expression that crosses his face, she knows he has made inquiries but wasn't going to tell her unless she asked.

"She is in Drancy. Two policemen—gendarmes, not Germans—took her, first to the station on the rue de Greffulhe, then to the German office to be interrogated. Apparently it went well. She would have been released if it were not for her star."

"What about her star?"

"It was attached with press studs rather than sewn."

"She did that so she could wear it on a dress or sweater or coat. She never went out without it."

"The regulations say it must be sewn to the garment."

"And for that they put her in a camp?"

"They are scrupulous about such things."

"They? Aren't you one of them?"

His only answer is the blank stare, the one that says he has no authority.

"Can I visit her?"

"Visitors, even relatives, are not permitted."

"Can I send her something? Some of this food?" She indicates his latest gift. "Warm clothes?" She knows from what remains in the closet in the back that they took Simone away in only the dress and sweater on her back, and another brutal winter is setting in. "Books?"

"It is difficult. Now that the SS have taken over the camp from the French." He hesitates.

"But not impossible?"

"Guards can be bribed," he admits. "If you make a package, I will see that she gets it."

After he leaves and the full horror of the situation sinks in, her first thought, after Simone, is of Simone's daughter and mother. Should she get word to her mother? Which is kinder, information or ignorance? She remembers a day, when they were perhaps thirteen or fourteen, that she and Simone sneaked out of school and spent the afternoon larking in the Bois de Boulogne. When they were found out and given extra essays to write and hours of atonement after school, Charlotte confessed her transgression to her parents, but Simone managed to hide the punishments as well as the crime. Then, Simone was saving her own skin. Now, Charlotte has the feeling, she'd want to save her mother's peace of mind, or the little of it there is these days.

She decides not to contact Simone's mother in the hope she'll be released soon, but she does put together a parcel. He delivers it and returns with word that Simone is still in the camp. At first she is furious. How long can they keep someone for not sewing on her star properly? Then she interprets his words. He means Simone has not been put on a transport. She has heard about the transports, though like almost everything coming out of the rumor mill, the stories are unbelievable. Salt mines in Poland and forced labor camps in Germany make a horrible kind of sense, but can a crippled and bent old woman, a man who has lost his sight, a three-year-old child work?

❦

He continues to turn up in the shop. If he were a normal customer, if these were normal times, she would discuss the books he buys with him or at least comment that he is a voracious reader. She holds her tongue. Except to say thank you. Oh, you're scrupulous, she chides herself silently. You keep him at arm's length, except when you reach out to take the food he brings. But she does not argue with herself too vehemently. Vivi's legs are no longer spindles. She is beginning to have a small belly. She cries, but not incessantly.

Of course, the silence cannot last. He is too wily for that. He asks her name. She doesn't answer. She is fairly sure he already knows her name, but volunteering it in polite conversation feels too intimate. He tells her his own nonetheless. Julian Bauer. He puts no military rank before his name. He does not even say *herr doctor*, though he mentions his profession and training when he inquires about Vivi, when he reports on Simone, when he asks about certain books, every chance he gets. She understands the ploy. I have sworn to first do no harm, he is telling her. You're in the Wehrmacht, she wants to scream back at him. The Wehrmacht killed my husband. The Wehrmacht drove my father into hiding. The Wehrmacht is occupying my country. The Wehrmacht has taken away my friend. No, he will tell her about the last. That was not the Wehrmacht. They were French gendarmes. I have no authority.

Nonetheless, he begins addressing her as if they are on friendly terms. *Bonjour, madame,* he says, *bon soir, madame,* always with a small bow. Funny about that bow. Slight as the gesture is, it manages to stir the air, and that particularly German military scent of leather and cleanliness, especially cleanliness—she is so tired of unwashed flesh and dirty hair and soiled clothing—is more dizzying than the most intoxicating perfume.

Then one day as he is taking another piece of cheese, two potatoes, and milk, always milk for Vivi, from his black leather bag, he asks her casually, as if they are both thinking about the food, which she is, where her husband is.

She does not answer. Of all the subjects she will not speak of with him, Laurent is first on the list, especially since she started having the dreams. Night after night, Laurent returns to her, but each time something goes wrong. He tells her he no longer loves her. He accuses her of infidelity. He says Vivi is not his.

"He is here?" the officer asks.

She is silent.

"A prisoner of war?"

She still doesn't answer.

As the realization dawns on him, the shop goes quiet except for the ticking of the clock that she has kept set to German time since the day he noticed it.

"I am sorry," he says, as the bell over the door jingles and a customer steps into the shop. She turns to put the food back in the doctor's bag, but he has already done it. He is protecting her. Her and Vivi. She tries not to think of what Laurent would say to that.

❦

He stays away from the shop for more than a week. She tells herself she notices only because of the food. She and Vivi have grown accustomed to eating again. Two nights earlier, Vivi spit out the turnips she made for dinner. Last night, she pushed the spoon away with her small hand and cried, but finally ate some.

Then late one afternoon, when a downpour has lowered the sky and draped the shop in shadows, when Vivi has gone down for her nap in the back room and Charlotte is sitting at the cash register struggling to read in the gloom, the bell above the door vibrates, the door opens, and he comes in on a gust of wet wind. She is relieved to see that he is carrying his black leather bag, and ashamed of the sentiment. She thinks of Simone, still in Drancy.

These days she prays that Simone is still in Drancy. Anything is better than deportation.

He puts the bag on the counter, takes off his cap, shakes it out over the floor, careful not to spatter the books, and smooths his dark non-Aryan hair. Then he removes his glasses, takes a handkerchief from his pocket, dries and polishes one lens, the other.

"I am sorry," he says. She thinks he is talking about the rain he has brought into the shop. Then he goes on. "I was sent home." He pushes the bag closer to her.

She doesn't understand his dejected air. It's kind of him, or wily she thinks again, to apologize for not bringing the food she has come to expect, but surely he can't be sad about having gone home on leave.

"You must have been happy to see your family."

"No one was there."

"You didn't have a chance to tell them you were coming?"

"I wired, but it was too late."

She does not ask too late for what. If they were on holiday, she will be furious. If they perished in an Allied bombing, she will be sympathetic, and that is even more dangerous. She refuses to feel pity. They brought it on themselves. But she cannot sustain the heartlessness. He may have lost people he loved. She knows how that feels. And are he and his family really responsible for the war?

Perhaps they had been no more eager for it than she and Laurent.

Again she pulls back from the thought. Sometimes she thinks he is too cunning for her. But why should he be cunning? If he is after sex, it's easy enough to find. The amount of food he brings would buy him a different woman every night or the same woman for as many nights as he likes. She is not thinking of prostitutes but of nice Frenchwomen, hungry like herself. Sometimes she thinks he is just lonely. Again she pushes the thought from her mind. She will not sympathize with him. She will not humanize him. But the memory of Laurent once again undermines her resolve, though there is no similarity between the husband she is trying to hang on to and this man she is trying to keep at a distance. What if Laurent had lived? What if the war had gone differently? She tries to imagine him in Berlin, walking the streets, going to concerts and the cinema, befriending a woman in a bookshop. She cannot. But then with all that's going on, with the constant struggle to survive, she finds she can remember less and less the way things used to be.

❦

The next time he comes to the shop he is not carrying his black doctor's bag. She tries to hide her disappointment. He says he has just been to tea with his superiors at the

Meurice. That's something else she wonders about but will not ask. How has he managed to remain in Paris for so long? As the fighting in Russia intensifies, more and more soldiers and officers are sent to the east. Parisians hear their grumbles, and witness their desperate clutching at pleasure in their last days and hours, and see, almost smell, the fear coming off them. One of the officials from the Propaganda Office was posted there as punishment for taking bribes to steer extra allotments of paper to certain publishing houses, or so gossip has it. But this officer, Julian (as she refuses to think of him), seems to have found himself a permanent perch. She can't help wondering what unholy act he has committed to earn it.

He begins drawing slices of lemon from his pockets. "There are no more oranges," he says, "but I managed to take these when no one was looking."

She pushes what he might have done from her mind and carries the lemon slices to the back of the store. When she returns, a man in a blue pinstripe suit that looks improbably new, a strange phenomenon these days, and a carefully brushed homburg is coming through the door. The German officer turns away, goes to the far corner of the shop, and picks up a book. There is nothing unusual about that. He is always discreet when others are in the shop. He knows how dangerous it can be to her if they seem on good terms. He even keeps his back to them now, as if somehow he can obscure his identity, as if the uniform doesn't give him away. It never occurs to her that he might be hiding for his sake rather than hers.

The man removes his hat to reveal a broad but low forehead, approaches the counter, and asks Charlotte if she carries a book called *Sterilization for Human Betterment*. She says she doesn't. He frowns.

"It is an important work."

"We have no call for it."

"I am requesting it now."

"I'm sure you can find it in another bookshop."

He goes on looking at her, as if he is studying her. "Are you the proprietor?" he asks.

"The proprietor is a prisoner of war in Germany." At least she hopes Monsieur de la Bruyère is still a prisoner of war and not a casualty of forced labor.

He goes on studying her. "Do you have another work, *Eugenics: The Science of Human Improvement by Better Breeding*? It was written by an American, Charles Davenport. Until recently, the Americans were ahead of us in sterilization and other eugenics measures, but thanks to the Führer, we have caught up and gone beyond them."

She tells him they don't carry that book either.

"Do you have *How to Recognize Jews*?"

"We have no call for it."

His frown deepens. "Do you have any books on eugenics?"

She shakes her head. "I'm sorry, monsieur. We have no call for them."

Now he is angry. He thinks she is making fun of him, and maybe she is. She wouldn't if he were wearing a German uniform, but he is only a Frenchman whose mind has been squeezed into a Nazi straightjacket.

"These are seminal works on the subject. It is essential that you carry them," he says, and stands staring at her, as if he expects her to put in an order for them while he waits. She walks to a table of books and begins straightening them. He goes on watching her, then finally puts on his hat, turns, and leaves the shop. The bell rings noisily as he slams the door behind him. Her gaze follows him, and when she turns back, she sees the German officer is still holding the book, but he is not looking at it. He is staring after the man.

He comes over to where she is standing. "Do you know who that is?"

She shakes her head. "He's not a regular customer."

"Professor Georges Montandon, the author of one of the books he asked for. *How to Recognize Jews*. According to him, he is an expert on the subject. He claims he is able to spot a Jew on sight."

"A talented man."

"He says it is not instinct but science."

She wants to ask if he believes that. He is a doctor, as he never lets her forget, a man of science, but she doesn't ask. She tells herself she doesn't want to engage him in any more conversation than necessary, but she knows it's more than that. She is afraid of the answer.

"The General Commission has hired him as a specialist to unmask Jews who are hiding behind false papers."

She wonders why he is telling her this. It doesn't come to her until later that night. She remembers his assumption that she and Simone are sisters. He thinks she, too, is a Jew, but one passing as a French gentile. He was trying to warn her to be careful of the man.

❦

They come bursting into the shop in high spirits, three university students, a girl and two boys, whom Charlotte recognizes from earlier visits. They want to know where the children's books are shelved. The girl is looking for a birthday gift for her nephew. Charlotte directs them to a nook in the back of the store. They have to pass the German officer, who is in the philosophy section, to reach it. They lower their voices only slightly as they push past. He has become that familiar.

One of the boys lifts out *Emil and the Detectives* and hands it to the girl. "This was my favorite."

The girl looks down at it. "No books by—"

The other boy catches her eye and nods toward the German officer.

She doesn't finish the sentence, but the first boy puts the volume back on the shelf.

Finally they decide on a French translation of *Winnie-the-Pooh*. They are still trading lines from it about bumping down the stairs, and bumping up the stairs, and climbing and climbing, as the girl pays and they leave the shop.

Charlotte closes the cash register and goes to the nook to straighten the books they have been looking at. As she is rearranging titles, she hears the voice behind her.

"'He could see the honey, he could smell the honey, but he couldn't quite reach the honey,'" he says in English. The words are whimsical, but his voice is somber.

She turns around to face him. "You've read the book to your child?"

"I have no child. I am not married. I read it to my sister when she was small. It was her favorite book."

She hears the undercurrent of grief beneath the words and remembers his response when he returned from his home leave. The telegram was too late. They were all gone. Now she knows they were not on holiday. The Germans brought the Allied bombing on themselves, but a young girl cannot be held responsible. She leans toward him, inhaling the smell of leather and cleanliness, and her hand, which knows more of human sympathy than she does, begins to rise to his arm. Horrified at herself, she checks the motion, but she is too late. He has seen it.

Eight

This time she didn't throw away the letter. Strictly speaking, she hadn't thrown away the earlier one. At least she hadn't meant to. She'd merely panicked and tossed it in the wastebasket, and by the time she remembered to fish it out, the cleaning woman had come through the office.

At first she didn't think this letter had anything to do with him, despite the Colombian stamp. She'd published translations of a handful of South American books. She turned the letter over. The name on the back was Rabbi Sandor de Silva. She sliced open the envelope with the steel letter knife, unfolded the piece of stationery, and started to read. The rabbi wanted to know what she could tell him about Dr. Julian Bauer during the years she'd known him in Paris.

She sat staring at the page. The real issue was what Dr. Bauer had told Rabbi de Silva about what she'd been up to during those years in Paris. She was so busy worrying the question that she didn't sense Horace's presence until he was sitting across the desk from her. Those rubber wheels could be silent when he wanted them to. Her eyes snapped up from the letter and, without meaning to, she shoved it under the blotter.

He shook his head and smiled. "Don't worry, Charlie. I can read upside down—one of the tricks you learn working with printers, as I'm sure you know—but I won't. It's like the definition of a gentleman. Someone who knows how to play the accordion but doesn't. Did you have a chance to look at that manuscript I gave you? The one that's been turned down all over town?"

"*The Red Trapeze*? I was going to write you a report today. You do realize there's a reason it's been turned down all over town, don't you?"

"Because my fellow publishers are a bunch of philistines who lack literary taste."

"I think that's redundant."

"Okay, because they're a bunch of cowards."

"For not wanting to tie themselves up in legal battles for God knows how long and possibly end up with a hefty fine, or even in prison?"

"But that's the point. It's been eight years since Doubleday brought out Wilson's *Memoirs of Hecate County,* six since the Supreme Court upheld the obscenity ruling. Mores are changing. It's time for another test."

"What if you're wrong? What if times haven't changed as much as you think?"

"That's okay, too. I can't lose. Either we make a serious dent in the censorship laws or we end up being raided by a bunch of detectives egged on by the American Legion. That's what happened at Random House several years ago. About a book of poetry. I can't even remember the title, but poetry has never sold as well as that collection did after word of the raid got around. But I asked for your opinion of the book, not legal advice."

"It's brilliant. I admit that. But even if you forget the sex scenes, the war parts are pretty raw."

He sat staring at her across the desk. She'd never seen his eyes so cold. "I think the word you're looking for is honest. But that won't get it censored. War doesn't offend them. Only sex and the struggle for social justice get under their skin."

"Then you're going to publish it?"

"You bet I'm going to publish it. I was pretty sure I was going to anyway, but your 'brilliant' is the stamp of approval." He wheeled around and started out of her office. "Now you can go back to that letter. I don't know what's in it, but from the way you slid it under the blotter and the guilty look on your face, it must be hotter stuff than this book."

🍃

He didn't know why he teased her, he thought on the way back to his office. No, that wasn't true. He knew exactly why he teased her. He was trying to make light of things. He had no idea what the letter she'd shoved under the blotter was about or whom it was from, but he did know one thing. It scared the hell out of her. Hannah had a term she used about her more fragile patients: She or he was not too tightly wrapped. Charlotte was too tightly wrapped. In the end, both conditions amounted to the same thing. The ones who weren't too tightly wrapped came unraveled. The ones who were erupted. Charlotte belonged to the latter group. He knew because he was on intimate terms with the condition.

🍃

She didn't go back to the letter after Horace left her office. She sat thinking about the book he was going to publish. Other houses wouldn't bring it out because they didn't want a fight. He was spoiling for one. If he couldn't get into the physical ring, he'd climb into the moral one. But she had a feeling it was more than that. The war scenes were, as she'd said, brutal, not just the blood and guts and physical toll but the mental horror. She'd never been in war, but she'd witnessed roundups and brutality and, once, a Nazi officer raking a crowd with machine gun fire just for the thrill of it. She'd seen bloodlust. That was what this book he was hell-bent on publishing was really about.

❦

This time she wasn't fooled. The same patient was standing in front of the mirror in the black-and-white-tiled foyer fixing her hat—a different one with a burst of spring flowers on it—but that's all she was, a patient of Hannah's primping, not a concierge holding an imaginary gun to her temple. The woman turned to Charlotte and nodded. Over the years, Charlotte had noticed that some of Hannah's patients acknowledged her when they passed in the hall; others averted their eyes and slid by as if they'd been caught red-handed. These days, one, a young man, sometimes stopped to chat, though she'd found out recently that he wasn't a patient but an analyst Hannah was training. Now Charlotte nodded back and started up the stairs.

Vivi was sprawled on the sofa, her brown oxfords on the floor beside her, her navy-blue-knee-socked feet on the armrest. She'd dragged the phone over from the end table in the corner. The sight still gave Charlotte pause. At Vivi's age, she wouldn't have dared sprawl on the sofas in the family drawing room, her mother's boudoir, her father's study, or anywhere else. Her parents would not have allowed it. And the single phone in the apartment on the rue Vaugirard had been attached to a wall, there for important adult matters, not teenage gossip. But she was not her parents, she was especially not her mother, New York in 1954 was not Paris in 1932, and she had made up her mind the day she'd walked up the gangway in Le Havre, clutching Vivi's hand because it would be so easy for a child to slip beneath the railing and plunge that dizzying distance into the black water churning around the hull, that they were going to become Americans. Paris was behind them. Nothing held them to France.

She dropped a kiss on Vivi's forehead, hung her coat in the closet, and headed to her room to get out of her high heels and suit. On her way, she noticed the light was on in Vivi's room and took a step in to turn it off. The habit was a holdover from the Occupation. She was incapable of leaving the lights on when she left a room, or letting water run, or wasting anything. She reached for the light switch. That was when she saw it. The article lay on Vivi's desk among her schoolbooks. Only one word of the title was visible. "Auschwitz."

Charlotte prided herself on respecting her daughter's privacy. They lived too intimately and, she feared, in too much isolation with only each other as it was. So she was careful not to open the pink leather diary Vivi kept in her night table drawer, even when she forgot and left it out. She did her best to tune out those endless phone conversations Vivi had with her friends. She even, and this was the hardest, refrained from asking what Vivi and Hannah talked about on the evenings she got home late and Vivi went down to spend time with Hannah after school or for dinner. But respecting privacy was one thing, turning a blind eye something else.

She moved the book to see the rest of the title. "From the VIe Arondissement to Auschwitz." This was worse than she'd thought. "By Simone Bloch Halevy" ran beneath the words. The sudden dizziness made her grip the back of the desk chair. She knew Simone had written about the Occupation. A few years earlier, rummaging through the used books at the Argosy—the inexpensive secondhand volumes on the stand outside the store, not the valuable first editions inside—she'd come across Simone's memoir. Picking it up carefully, as if it might detonate in her hands, she'd read the dedication.

IN MEMORY OF MY PARENTS
AND 75,000 OTHER FRENCH JEWS
AND FOR SOPHIE

That was as far as she'd got. She'd closed the volume and put it back in the trough carefully, though the explosion had already gone off. At least Simone and her daughter had survived, she'd told herself on the way home. It had made her feel better about them, but not about herself.

Looking at the piece on Vivi's desk now, she wondered what magazine it had been clipped from. There was no identification at the top or the bottom of the page. She didn't recognize the typeface or layout. The stock was not glossy. This was no *Life* or *Time* or *Saturday Evening Post* piece. It certainly wasn't *Seventeen*. So the question was not only where it had run but how Vivi had got her hands on it. She didn't think she could blame this on Mr. Rosenblum. For one terrifying moment, she thought Simone might have tracked them down and mailed the piece. But if that were the case, she would have sent it to Charlotte, not Vivi. Simone would never blame the sins of the mother on the daughter.

She picked up the clipping and began to read. The first paragraph was a description of a privileged childhood in Paris, of little girls playing in the Luxembourg Gardens in their proper navy-blue coats with velvet collars, brimmed hats with grosgrain ribbons around the crown, and kid gloves, all from Jones in the avenue Victor-Hugo. Despite their correct attire, however, they ran wild, braids flying from beneath those hats, ankle boots racing, or as wild as they could under the watchful eyes of their stern English nannies. The image stole up on Charlotte like a thug in the night and hit her hard. She paused for a moment to catch her breath, then went on reading. Some of the little girls were named Bloch and Kahn and Weil, others Aumont and Goderoy and Lefort. Nonetheless, they all played together, the same games, the same language, the same glorious French heritage, or so the little girls named Bloch and Kahn and Weil believed. But those little girls with the names that weren't really French, the ones who didn't go to mass, or decide for a week or two to become nuns, or fall in love with their confessors, had been hoodwinked. They had no glorious French past, only a grim future in a Polish town called Oświęcim.

Charlotte skimmed the rest of the piece. She knew where Simone was going. The article was a rant against the inhumanity of man. It was also a warning against the dangers of assimilation. She came to the author's bio at the bottom of the column. Simone Bloch Halevy was a journalist who ran an information network that tried to reunite deported Jews with surviving members of their families, if any existed.

She put the article back on the desk. She was not going to overreact. She was not even going to mention it to Vivi.

Vivi was the one who brought it up. After she got off the phone, she came into the kitchen, where Charlotte was chopping garlic, and held the piece out to her.

"What's that?" Charlotte asked.

"A magazine article. I thought it might interest you. It sounds a lot like the stories you tell about playing in the Luxembourg Gardens when you were little, and having an English nanny, and all that."

Charlotte wiped her hands, took the piece, and skimmed through it again. She felt Vivi's eyes on her as she read. "Interesting." She handed it back to Vivi and returned to the cutting board.

"She sounds a lot like you, right?" Vivi insisted.

"Her childhood sounds similar to mine, if that's what you mean."

"More than that. She needed Hitler to teach her she was a Jew, too."

The paring knife nicked her nail but didn't pierce the skin. "Is that a taunt?"

Vivi shrugged. "You send me to a good school to learn reading comprehension."

That was a taunt, but Charlotte decided to let it go.

"Where did you get it, anyway?"

"Aunt Hannah. She clipped it from a magazine. She said it raises some interesting questions I ought to be thinking about. She said I'm at an age when I'm wrestling with my identity."

"Doesn't sound like much of a wrestling match to me. You're Vivienne Gabrielle Foret, French born, American

156

bred, New York City situated, Endicott School educated, and one extremely nice girl, in my humble opinion, and lots of other people's, too."

"And Jewish. You forgot Jewish."

"And Jewish," Charlotte conceded and slid the garlic into the skillet.

Nine

❧

As the Germans begin to suffer military reversals in Russia and North Africa, they turn crueler and more sullen. The French become more fearful but also more defiant. Paris is a tinderbox. A slight incident can turn into a confrontation, a confrontation into a bloodbath. Twenty hostages, chosen indiscriminately, are shot in exchange for one German murdered by the Resistance. Examples must be made. Though executions are no longer public, as they were in the beginning of the Occupation when nine Resistance fighters were guillotined on the grounds of La Santé Prison, posters announcing them become as chillingly common as advertisements for plays and concerts and exhibitions. The singing of "La Marseillaise," forbidden by both the German and the Vichy regimes, can be heard more often, especially from the trucks carrying the condemned to the killing grounds. The forbidden word "boche" is whispered a little louder and more often. The rumor mill cranks up. The gendarmes snatch a three-year-old girl—Vivi's age, Charlotte thinks when she hears the story—from the gentile family who took her in when her parents were arrested, intern her at the Pithiviers camp, and put her on a transport to the east alone, if you can call being packed into cattle cars with 999 other human beings alone. A woman in the Twentieth Arrondissement throws her two children out the window to save them from a slower, more torturous death. In some accounts of the incident, the arrondissement is different and there are three or four children. Perhaps this is embellishment or perhaps more mothers are resorting to the unthinkable. The roundups accelerate. The Germans and the gendarmes cordon off neighborhoods, block Metro entrances, and snare the inhabitants like animals in a net. Occasionally a sympathetic gentile will try to help. A policeman cautions Jewish acquaintances not to go out on a certain day for fear of being arrested on the street. A concierge tips off her Jewish residents not to stay home because the building is to be raided. Which chance do they take? A woman who lives in an apartment building that opens onto the same courtyard as the bookshop is rumored to be taking in Jewish children whose parents have been deported. Charlotte doesn't know if the story is true and doesn't try to find out. The less you know these days, the safer you are. But once she looks up at the flat from the courtyard and sees three pairs of eyes just above the sill, wide and staring and, it seems to her, terrified. A curtain closes quickly.

French men, and women, fight back. Grenades fly, at a hotel appropriated by the Germans near the Havre-Caumartin Metro station, at a restaurant reserved for Wehrmacht officers, at a military patrol crossing the rue de Courcelles, at a car carrying Kriegsmarine officers. One after another, trains leaving the Gare de l'Est on their way to Germany and who knows where beyond are derailed. The general responsible for drafting Frenchmen between the ages of eighteen and twenty-two for forced labor in the Reich is assassinated. Closer to home for Charlotte, a hollowed-out copy of Karl Marx's *Das Kapital,* stuffed with dynamite, is left on a table in the *collabo* bookstore, Rive-Gauche. Destruction of books is no longer the tactic of only one side.

Combustible as the city is, the German officer continues to visit the shop and bring food. He does not seem troubled by the turning tide of German fortunes, but then perhaps the tide is not turning as dramatically as the French want to think. Vivi, who has grown accustomed to his presence, tugs on his hand or trouser leg as he stands paging through books. At first Charlotte tries to stop her, but he says he enjoys her attentions. "She reminds me of my sister when she was little." She ignores the comment. He probably doesn't even have a sister, despite the lines he quoted from *Winnie-the-Pooh*. One afternoon, he takes a book from a shelf and carries it to the old leather chair. She thinks of it as the professor's chair, but she cannot stop him from sitting in it. She's not even sure she wants to in view of the fact that he sat there when he gave Vivi the bottle. Perhaps some part of Vivi remembers, because she climbs into his lap and curls up quietly, her head against the rough cloth of his despised uniform. Can a child that young miss a father she has never known?

❦

She decides to sleep in the shop that night. She has begun to do that more and more often. She is not the only one. Half of Paris is sleeping in the wrong place these days. It has nothing to do with sex, only with survival. When the roundups started, Jewish men began leaving their families just before the curfew, though that is constantly changing, to spend the night elsewhere so they would not be at home when the gendarmes or, less often, the Germans came to arrest them. Now that they're taking away women and children as well, whole families split up each evening and head for what they pray are different safe houses. Sometimes Charlotte thinks about the choice. Is it preferable to suffer and perhaps perish together or to hope that at least one member of the family will survive?

She has her own reasons for sleeping in the room behind the shop. The rear wheel of her bicycle has been patched so many times it is beyond repair. With no automobiles or petrol, the Metro is packed, and since the Germans close down lines and stations at will, or is it whim, the trains are likely to land her and Vivi in some distant and unknown part of the city. The blackout makes walking treacherous. The handful of automobiles that remain must shroud their headlights with a blue material so effective that the only way a driver knows a pedestrian is there is the thud and shudder of car and body colliding. Even if she could use a flashlight to light the way, batteries are impossible to get. Besides, the flat is no more comfortable than the shop and certainly no warmer. When she and Vivi are there, they live in the kitchen, close to the stove, leaving it only to race to bed and huddle beneath the eiderdown quilts. They are not the only ones. She has heard of people shrinking their eight- and ten- and twelve-room apartments to one small barricaded chamber. The back room of the shop is like a cave, shielded from the wind by the courtyard, warmed by a furnace pipe that goes through a cramped closet under the eaves, when there is fuel for the furnace. The sofa is perfectly adequate for one person, she has a small cot for Vivi, and she doesn't have to sit in the dark all night because of the blackout. The windows in her flat are tall, and the light escapes even when she tries to cover them with blankets. The week before, when one of the blankets slipped, the gendarmes spotted the light, and the concierge, who has a bad leg, came clomping up the stairs to reprimand her for getting the entire building in trouble. Here, she can close the door to the front of the shop, cover the single small window in back with a heavy curtain, and read in the light from a small lamp, if there is electricity. She can also put her ear against the radio and listen to the forbidden BBC. It's propaganda, but superior to the propaganda the German Radio-Paris and the *collabo* Radio-Vichy broadcast. She doesn't feel safe in the shop. Where in Paris can anyone feel safe these days? But she feels easier. Until the sounds wake her.

At first she thinks the rustling is coming from animals in the night. Cats and dogs that have been abandoned by owners who can no longer feed them, but not yet eaten by starving city dwellers, prowl the courtyard after dark. Rats scuttle. Mice race through the shop. But as she lies there listening to the sound, she realizes it isn't coming from the courtyard or the building. It's more distant and more mechanical.

She turns on her side to make sure Vivi is all right. Innocent and fed, thanks to the German officer, she sleeps a deep childish sleep. Charlotte lifts her arm to look at her wristwatch, but it is too dark to make out the time. She tells herself again that the sound is only stray cats and dogs turned feral by starvation and rotates onto her other side, hoping for sleep. Sometimes she is so exhausted by the cold and hunger and struggle for survival that she falls unconscious as soon as she puts her head on the pillow. Sometimes the worry and horror of that struggle keep her up half the night.

The sound is getting louder now, closer, and more violent. Even animals turning over trash cans or fighting or howling at the moon do not send up so much noise. She makes out the growling of trucks; then the engines go silent. She thinks of getting up and creeping to the front of the shop to see what's going on, but she fears she will be asking for trouble. The shop is closed. No one knows they're here.

Some sort of heavy equipment is being dragged over pavement and cobblestones. Perhaps this is what war sounds like. If the city is going to be a battle zone, should she take Vivi and run or stay and hide?

She decides to get out of bed after all, and quietly, moving slowly on bare feet, careful to avoid bumping into things, she makes her way through the darkness of the shop. As she gets closer to the window, she drops to her knees, crawls the last few feet, and, keeping her head down, peers out into the street. Soldiers and policemen are setting up barricades. Some are mounting machine guns. They're all heavily armed. Do they need that much force to round up Jews?

Again she thinks of grabbing Vivi and fleeing. She knows every street and alley of the neighborhood, and they've only begun putting up the barricades. She will find a way out. But again the uncertainty sets in. Are they in less danger out on the street or hiding here? She crawls back to the room behind the shop. Vivi is still asleep. She sits on the sofa and tries to think. She and Vivi have nothing to fear. Their papers are in order. She remembers the clock set to French time, the banned book written by a Jew about a Jew, the documents Simone carried as a courier when she flirted with the Germans on the train. Simone was careful not to tell her what she was up to, and she refused to ask, but that doesn't mean the Germans are similarly uninformed. *Collabos* are everywhere, eager to swap information for food or cigarettes or their own skin, keen to prove their patriotism to the newly purified France by turning in the dregs of the old. Minutely detailed dossiers, kept with German precision, fill drawer after drawer of official file cabinets. Even formerly slipshod gendarmes, inspired by the example of their German masters and their own anti-Semitism, have become more efficient. And if there is no reason for an arrest, one can always be drummed up. Simone was sent to Drancy not for couriering forbidden papers, or even failing to wear a star, but for attaching her star improperly. On the other hand, she reminds herself again, no one knows she is here. The shop is closed. They will assume it's empty. But perhaps they will assume nothing. They are thorough, these Germans.

She makes out the noise of running boots. No, the roar of running boots. There are too many of them to distinguish individual steps. Voices are shouting in French and German. At one end of the street they're ordering people to come out; at the other they're warning people to stay inside. Oh, they're methodical, all right. They will go from house to house, taking their time, making sure not to miss anyone.

Suddenly light pours into the room. It is so intense that even the blackout curtain cannot dim it. The courtyard is bright as day. No, whiter than day. It is scalding. They must have set up searchlights. She'd thought darkness made the world more threatening, but the searing glare of illumination blinds her into helplessness. Even if she dares to lift the curtain and look into the courtyard, she will be able to make out nothing.

Boots are running through the courtyard, and men

are shouting, and people are screaming. Vivi has begun to cry. Charlotte pulls her from her cot to the sofa and holds her close beneath the covers, pleading with her not to cry, telling her everything is all right, trying to lie her into silence, not that anyone could hear the sobs of a single child in the uproar going on outside.

They are banging on doors, the dull thud of fists, the sharper sound of rifle butts, the crash of wood splintering. Men are shouting, and women are screaming, and children are wailing. She clutches Vivi to her and prays to a God she does not believe in. Across the courtyard a scream rises to the sky, then ends suddenly with a thud. It takes her a moment to interpret the sounds. Someone has been pushed from a window, or jumped.

Another door crashes. It is so close it must be the boulangerie next door. She has told herself they won't bother with shops at this hour. That is why they come before dawn, to catch people at home, barely awake, still undressed, vulnerable. She reassures herself that a boulangerie is different. The workers will already be at their jobs. She can see her watch in the glare from the courtyard. It says five o'clock. That means it's four o'clock here. She has become such a coward that she keeps her watch as well as the clock in the shop set to German time.

In the courtyard, the high-pitched scream of a child

makes her clutch Vivi closer. It stops suddenly. A woman begins to wail. Again Charlotte interprets the sequence.

The banging has moved closer. They are at the door to the bookshop. If she doesn't open it, they will shatter the glass and force their way in. She clutches Vivi to her. Once again her mind races back and forth between the options. The closet in the corner under the eave, the one warmed by the furnace pipe, is barely noticeable. But barely is not good enough. They will see it. If she and Vivi are found hiding, that will mean they have something to hide. Perhaps it is better to cooperate. She will open the door, they will storm in and demand her papers, she will produce them, and they will move on to the next flat or shop. But it does not work that way. In the years since they marched in, she has witnessed her share of confrontations and roundups. She has seen the intoxicating effects. The more they shout and bully, kick and club, the more they want to. It is bloodlust. It cannot be stopped, only spent.

Suddenly the banging on the door ceases. The shouting in the courtyard continues, but the front of the shop has gone quiet. Even Vivi has stopped crying and is listening.

Charlotte puts her on her cot, places her finger over her lips to warn her to be quiet, and creeps again to the

front of the shop. Through the glass, she sees the back of a
Wehrmacht officer and three gendarmes facing him. Even
without seeing his face she knows the officer is her officer.
She can't hear what he's saying, but she can see the way
the gendarmes are listening. They nod, look from one to
another, nod again, and move off.

The officer goes on standing in front of the shop. Another group of gendarmes approaches. Whatever he tells
them works again. They move on. This end of the street
has quieted. Even the noise in the courtyard is dying. Now
the racket comes from the buses parked beyond the barricades. People are screaming and crying and begging. She
moves closer to the door. The officer is still blockading it.
As she crouches there watching him, he takes a few steps
into the street. It is littered with the shards of lives, torn
from hands in rage, dropped in terror—hats and shoes, a
woman's handbag, a framed photograph, a string bag of
food. He bends, picks up a child's teddy bear, brushes it
off, stands holding it for a moment, then crosses to the
other side of the street and props it against the building.
He comes back and knocks softly on the door. "Madame
Foret," he whispers.

She stands, makes her way to the door, and opens it a
crack. He slips in and closes it behind him.

"How did you know I was here?" she whispers.

"Vivi tells me her secrets. She says you often spend

the night here. When I heard about the roundup . . ." His voice trails off.

"Thank you."

"Are your papers any good?"

"Do you mean are they in order?"

"I mean are they good forgeries."

"They're not forgeries."

He stands staring at her. "You still do not trust me."

Before she can answer, she hears boots crunching toward them in the street again. This time the shouting is in German. This is Wehrmacht or Gestapo, not gendarmes.

"Go to the back," he whispers. "And keep Vivi quiet." He slips out the door and closes it behind him.

In the back room, Vivi is sitting up on her cot, her eyes wide, the whites shining with fear. She starts to ask what's happening. Charlotte shushes her and takes her on her lap. She starts to ask again, her voice rising. Charlotte puts her hand over her daughter's mouth. "It's a game," she whispers in her ear.

Vivi shakes her head and tries to pull away. Charlotte holds her tighter. "It's hide-and-seek," she whispers.

Vivi knows it is not a game, but she also knows her mother means business. She stops wriggling. Charlotte hears the bell over the door. He has let them in. You still don't trust me, he'd said. She was beginning to, but now she wonders.

She sits listening to the voices in German. The men he has let in—she can't tell how many; at least two, she thinks from the conversation—say they have to search the premises. He tells them he already has. "There's no one here," he insists. "It's a shop, closed for the night."

They demand to know who he is. He insists on their credentials. It would be ludicrous, a comedy sketch, if it weren't so terrifying.

One after another, the lights are going out in the courtyard. The darkness should make it easier to hide, though she can't imagine where.

She hears them pushing past him, listens to the creaking of the old wooden floor as they move through the shop. She has left the door to the back room open a crack to listen. She doesn't dare get up to close it. Carrying Vivi, taking one step at a time, she walks to the small closet. The door squeaks as she opens it, but their loud voices and heavy boots drown out the sound. As she closes the door to the closet behind her, she hears them entering the back room. There is a shelf a third of the way up the wall, another toward the top. The wood is old and fragile. For the first time she is grateful for the hunger that has ruined her figure and turned her into little more than bones. Using the first shelf as a step, carrying Vivi in one arm, she manages to climb to the top shelf. She pulls her legs up after her and puts her hand over Vivi's mouth again.

They are moving about the back room. One of the men mentions the bedclothes on the sofa and cot. The officer, her officer, explains they were left behind when the gendarmes arrested the inhabitants in the sweep through the area.

Boots move, stop, move again, come to a halt in front of the closet. The knob on the door turns. The door opens. She forces herself not to move, not to try to make herself smaller. She holds her breath in the darkness. The door closes. The boots move away, across the room, into the shop. The bell over the door jingles, then goes silent. She wonders if it's a trick. She doesn't dare come out to see.

Vivi tries to twist her face away from her mother's restraining hand. Charlotte holds her tight. Her small body squirms. Charlotte's grip is like a vise.

A single pair of boots enters the room. Then there is silence. He must be looking around. The sound approaches the closet. The door opens. He squints into the darkness, then holds up his arms for Vivi. She hands her daughter to him.

Still holding Vivi in one arm, he reaches up to help Charlotte down. For a moment they are pressed against each other in the cramped closet. He steps back to let her out, carries Vivi to the cot, and puts her down. Charlotte follows him, covers the child, strokes the hair back from her forehead, tells her what a good girl she has been.

Vivi lies there looking up at both of them. Charlotte sees the terror begin to drain from her daughter's eyes. Then he does something extraordinary, more extraordinary, she thinks, than interceding for them. He sits down on the side of the cot and begins to sing. Vivi doesn't recognize the words—he is singing in German—but she knows the tune. Brahms's lullaby. His voice is thin and a little flat, but Vivi doesn't seem to mind. Her eyelids begin to droop. He comes to the end. Vivi's eyes open. "Again," she says, and her voice is childishly imperious, no longer frightened but demanding. He begins to sing again. By the time he finishes the second time, she is asleep. Who is this man?

"Thank you," Charlotte says for the second time that night. She is whispering, but he nods toward the shop and leads the way to the front room.

The world is dark and silent again. They have taken the lights from the courtyard. The buses and trucks have rolled off. The quiet is eerie. It is, suddenly, a ghost neighborhood, except for the occasional clatter of running feet. She remembers her own plan of escape earlier that night and thinks it's the sound of people fleeing, then realizes it's probably the first wave of looters, rampaging through the abandoned apartments, taking anything of value, and some things that are not. The opportunistic greed is not unlike the bloodlust. Once people start they cannot stop.

A police car careens down the street. The siren is silent, but the headlights rake the shop. He shoves her into the alcove in the back of the shop, behind the old leather chair. It is too late for that car, but if another comes through, all they will see is the back of a Wehrmacht uniform.

They go on standing that way, her backed against the shelves of children's books, him looming over her, waiting. After a time, she has no idea how long, she starts to slide away from him, but he puts a hand on her shoulder to stop her.

"There may be more," he says, but she can tell from his voice that he's not thinking of police cars. She feels the roughness of his beard against her forehead, then his mouth moving toward hers. She tells herself to move away, but she can't. The lurch in the pit of her stomach is too familiar, and too insistent. She is ashamed. She is shameless. She has no will, but her body does. It is fighting back to life. She feels herself sinking against him and lifts her face to his. He is unbuttoning the sweater she has taken to sleeping in, then reaching inside her nightdress. She manages to stifle her moan, but she has no control over her hands. They are undoing his tunic, pulling off the hated uniform. She begins to tremble again. It is the terror of the night, and the release, and the touch of skin. Oh, how she has missed the touch of skin. It's that memory, the feel of Laurent's skin, that stops her. She twists away, pulls her nightdress up over her breasts, hugs her sweater to her. She doesn't say anything. She doesn't have to.

He stands looking down at her. Only his eyes are visible in the darkness. She expected anger. She sees sorrow.

He buttons his tunic, tugs it into place, turns and starts for the door. His boots squeak on the wooden floor. His shadow ghosts through the darkness. He reaches the door. The bell shatters the silence. And something in her.

She is across the shop. "Julian." It is the first time she has spoken his name.

Later, the shame will return. How could she make love to the enemy? The enemy lover. It is unconscionable. She is unconscionable. But all that will come later. She straddles him in the chair. The chair makes it worse, she will think later, but not now. Arms and legs gripping, mouth hungry, body and spirit starving from years of loneliness and fear and denial. Driven by the same loneliness and hunger and, though she doesn't know it at the time, an even more insistent fear and shame, he rises into her. They are locked together, mouth to mouth, skin to skin, prick to cunt. By the time they finish—no, they will never finish—by the time they stop, the windows of the shop are turning gray with the dawn and a thin finger of light reveals the street littered with the detritus of last night's raid. The sight is like a slap to her soul. She climbs off him, turns away from the sight, pulls on her nightdress, slips into her sweater, and buttons it. He is still sitting in the chair, that chair. She wants to pull him out of it and hurl him into the street. It is not only that someone might pass and see them. It is her own horror at what she has done. The words "enemy lover," so erotically charged in the darkness, now give off a sordid stench.

She picks the pile of his clothes up off the floor and holds them out to him. He takes them from her and stands. That's when she sees. It had been too dark and she had been too hungry to notice before. Now, in the gray light and the cold glare of her conscience, she notices. He is not like Laurent. Laurent's penis was smooth. Her hand curls at the memory of it. His penis has a ridge around it near the tip.

His eyes follow hers. "As a child, I had an infection," he explains.

She turns away. They are strangers again. No, they are enemies again. She wants no confidences.

She tells him to hurry. He finishes dressing and takes a step toward her. She moves away, crosses the shop to the door, and opens it. He follows her, puts his hand on the door, and closes it.

"I do not want to lie to you. I cannot lie to you."

She doesn't know what he's talking about. They spoke

no words of love. They spoke no words at all. And if he had tried to say he loved her, she would have stopped him.

"I had no childhood infection. That is the story I keep ready for the other officers and doctors. In case they ask."

She doesn't know what he's talking about. She doesn't want to know. She reaches for the door again. He holds it closed.

"I am a Jew."

The hatred for him rises in her again. "That's not funny."

"I am serious. I am a Jew."

She stands staring at him. "You're a Nazi soldier."

"I am a German soldier. A Jewish German soldier."

She shakes her head. "That's impossible."

"There are thousands of us. Mostly half-Jews, but plenty of one hundred percent Jews like me."

"Just leave. Please," she says, and walks away from him to the other end of the shop.

He follows her. "I was drafted before the war. Then in 1940, the order came down that all Jews, even half-Jews and those married to Jews, must turn themselves in."

"In that case, why are you still in that uniform?"

"Some did turn themselves in. I had one fortunate friend whose commanding officer said he was a good soldier and simply managed to lose his papers."

"Now I understand. You're such a model soldier that you're invaluable to the Reich?"

"Please do not make fun of me. I am trying to explain. I have to tell someone."

Not me, she wants to scream but knows she has no right to, not after the act she committed in that chair, perhaps not since before that.

"I had another colleague who followed the order, went to his commanding officer, and told him he was a Jew."

"And was he forgiven, too?"

"His commanding officer took out his service revolver and shot him in the head. After that I decided the wisest thing to do was ignore the order and go on as I was, but even more carefully. My commanding officer at the time was not a model of Germanic efficiency. He drank too much. Somehow, several papers in my file disappeared. And one new one appeared. It is called an *Ahnenpass*. That is an ancestors' passport that the Nazis dreamed up. It proves Aryan heritage. Mine is a very good forgery. If you are important enough, the Führer takes care of the matter himself. He declared Field Marshal Erhard Milch, who is half Jewish, an Aryan. But I am too insignificant for that. After I took care of the matter of my papers, I came up with the story of the childhood infection."

"Do you really expect me to believe this?"

He stands inches away, holding her gaze. "It is all true."

"So you just went on serving in Hitler's army, helping to kill other Jews."

"I have killed no Jews."

"What about the professor?"

"What about you and the child tonight?"

"My daughter and I aren't Jewish."

He shook his head. "I trust you with my secret, but you still do not trust me," he said again.

"I don't know if I trust you or not. How can I trust a Nazi soldier—"

"I told you, I am not a Nazi."

"—a German soldier who says he is a Jew? All I know is that I'm not a Jew."

"But your sister, Madame Halevy."

"Simone isn't my sister."

He backs up, sits on the tall three-legged stool, and begins to laugh. It's a nervous ragged sound, closer to hysteria than mirth. "Now do you believe that I am not a Nazi? I cannot even tell a Jew from a gentile."

She goes on staring at him. She is finally beginning to believe him. "But I still don't understand how you can go through with it."

"How I can go through with it? Think about it. In the Third Reich, where is the safest place for a Jew? If I were not in the Wehrmacht, I would be in a camp." She watches his face change. He is no longer laughing. "Like my parents and sister. If they are still alive."

She doesn't know if she blames him or pities him, hates him or loves him. All she knows is there is enough shame to go around.

Ten

꧁❀꧂

She scrawled her initials on the mock-up of a book jacket, put it in her out-box, and stood. The office was silent. On the desks in the large common area beyond her cubicle, the secretaries' typewriters dozed under their black plastic covers. Around the perimeter, the offices and cubicles were dark. She rarely got to stay late at the office, but tonight she'd taken advantage of the fact that it was Friday and Vivi had a sleepover at Alice's with two other girls. She liked being the last one in the office, not only the feeling of accomplishment that came with cleaning up her desk but the eerie solitude. She'd had similar sensations some nights in the shop on the rue Toullier. She couldn't be certain she was alone. Someone might be lurking back in advertising or publicity. A cleaning woman could be working her way toward the editorial offices. Nonetheless, the sensation of being on a desert island surrounded by a sea of books was heady. Everywhere she looked, there were boxes of new books smelling of ink and hope, and shelves of old award winners and bestsellers radiating dignity and success, and stacks of galleys waiting nervously to be sent out to reviewers. It was a world of infinite adventure, experienced at a safe and painless distance.

She put a manuscript in her briefcase, slipped into her coat, and started down the hall toward the elevators. The light was on in Horace's office. It hadn't been visible from her cubicle, but she'd been right. She wasn't alone. She wondered if he'd been waiting for her, then decided that was ridiculous. The man ran a publishing house. He had work to do.

"People who are trying to sneak past the boss shouldn't wear high heels that click like goddamn castanets."

She stopped in the door to his office. "I'm not trying to sneak past the boss. I'm showing off for burning the midnight oil."

"In that case, get yourself in here."

She stepped into the room, slipped out of her coat, put it on one of the chairs in front of his desk, and sat in the other.

He leaned over, opened the bottom drawer of his desk,

took out a bottle of scotch and two glasses, and put them on the blotter. "My late mentor and partner, Simon Gibbon, kept a silver tray with cut crystal decanters of bourbon, rye, scotch, and gin on a breakfront in his office."

"Those must have been the days when publishing was a gentlemen's profession."

"I resent that."

He poured a couple of fingers of scotch into each glass, handed her one, and gave her a smile she'd never seen before. No, that wasn't true. She'd seen it on that tall, rangy publishing wunderkind in the picture in *Publishers Weekly*, the one from before the war. It was wickedly boyish.

"I just got the damnedest call."

She waited.

"Aren't you going to ask from whom about what?"

"If I ask, you'll just make me work harder to pull it out of you. I figure silence will do the trick."

"No one likes a smart aleck. From *Newsweek*. They got wind of the fact that we bought *The Red Trapeze* after it was banned in England and turned down all over town."

"Gee, I wonder how they found out."

"You have a Machiavellian mind."

"I work for the prince himself. Which eager reporter did you mention it to, in the strictest confidence, of course?"

"A writer in the 'culture' department, if you'll excuse the expression. They're going to run a couple of columns on the publication. How we got our hands on the smuggled French edition. Whether we think it will go all the way to the Supreme Court. What makes it so shocking. We're going to beat the censorship bastards and sell a couple of hundred thousand, make that a million, copies in the bargain. This calls for a celebration."

She started to say that he hadn't won yet, but he was in such a good mood she didn't want to ruin it. She lifted her glass toward him. "We are celebrating."

"Hell, this isn't a celebration, just an evening occurrence. At least it is for me."

"Take Hannah out to dinner."

"Hannah is already engaged for dinner. Her regular Friday session with young Federman."

"Young Federman?"

"You must have seen him coming and going in the house. Dashing young chap with a head of romantic, or so Hannah tells me, dark curls. She's his training analyst. Makes her sound like a pair of wheels on the back of a bike, if you ask me."

"Okay, I'll take you out to dinner. Where would you like to go?"

"'21,' and you can't afford it. I know how much I pay you. Besides, I don't want to go out for dinner. I go out for dinner with writers several times a week. Even the glow of '21' dims after you've spent enough nights there listening to unappreciated writers, or writers who think they're not sufficiently appreciated, cry in their martinis."

"Then what do you want to do?"

"Go for a ride."

"Is your car downstairs?"

"For Christ's sake, Charlie, where's your imagination? I'm not talking about a ride in that hearse behind that sullen driver."

"The New York City subway system? A hansom cab? The bumper cars at Coney Island?"

"You're getting closer."

"I give up."

He sat looking at her for a beat, then another. She was beginning to feel uncomfortable. He lifted his glass and finished it in a single gulp. Later she'd realize that was for courage. He put the glass down, gripped the wheels of his chair, backed away from his desk, pivoted, and came around until he was beside her chair.

"Hop on."

"What?"

"I said hop on. I'm going to take you for a spin."

"Where?"

"Right here. The hallowed halls of G&F. Where great literature will not be cowed by small minds."

She went on staring at him. "Are you serious?" she asked finally.

His face was immobile, all cold stare and challenge, except for his mouth. A tic so small it was almost imperceptible pulled at the side. "To coin a perfectly new cliché, I have never been more serious in my life."

She went on looking at him. The invitation was absurd. But a refusal of it would be insulting. As if she were afraid of him. Worse still, as if she found his condition offensive. She remembered the conversation she'd overheard on the stairs the night Vivi lighted the menorah. You're lousy at hiding disgust, he'd shouted at Hannah. She leaned forward, put her glass on the desk, and stood, then went on standing because she wasn't sure what to do next.

He lifted his hands and put them on her hips. For years she'd sat in meetings and across desks and in other venues and noticed his hands. The palms were wide and the fingers thick and strong from years of propelling him through the world. They weren't graceful or beautiful, not a pianist's or surgeon's, but they were admirable. They were also strangely gentle. She'd seen him break pencils in frustration and wrestle impatiently with those wheels, but except once when she'd watched him paging through a valuable first edition of *The Red Badge of Courage,* she'd never seen them so delicate of touch. No, not seen them delicate of touch, felt them.

Then slowly, with the slightest pressure, he turned her until she was standing sideways to him and drew her onto his lap so they were sitting at right angles. His arm went around her waist. She didn't know what to do with her hands. She folded them in her lap. She unfolded them. She crossed her arms in front of her chest. She put her hands back in her lap. With his free hand, he took one of her arms and placed it around his neck.

"Pretend we're dancing," he said, then gripped the wheel with his free hand and propelled them out of the office and into the maze of secretaries' desks running up and down the common area. He hooked right around one desk, left around another, took his hand from around her waist to grab the other wheel to keep them on course, then put his arm around her again and headed straight and fast down the middle aisle. At the end, he spun around and raced up the side, narrowly missing chairs and desk corners and wastebaskets, propelling them faster and faster. He swerved in another sharp turn, almost toppling the chair, and let go of her again to regain control. "Watch out," she shouted.

"No backseat driving," he shouted back.

The euphoria in his voice was contagious, and heartbreaking. That this passed as abandon . . .

He whizzed down the hall, into Carl Covington's office, around his desk once, a second time. Beyond the darkened windows, the crown of the Chrysler Building sped by in a phantasmagoric blur of streaking light. The sight made her giddy. She clung to his neck. His arm tightened around her waist.

Then they were out in the hall, turning left, then left again, into Faith Silver's office. The photographs of women in long slinky thirties dresses and cloche hats, and men in bow ties and sardonic smiles, and groups sitting around a table mugging for the camera went by so fast they might have been a moving picture.

They sped into Bill Quarrels's cubicle, around his desk, out again, down the hall to the copyediting department, in and out of the four desks there, down the hall, and into the sales manager's office. Every now and then he took his arm from her waist to keep the chair on course, but his hand always found its way back.

"Watch out," she shrieked again as he nearly collided with a bookcase.

"Relax, you're with the Stirling Moss of the wheelchair set," he practically sang, and again she was struck by the desperation beneath the joy.

They raced across the open space in front of the elevators, past the receptionist's desk, down the hall, and back into his office.

He stopped. His breathing sawed the sudden silence. Her own was almost as sharp. He had an excuse. He'd been propelling the chair. She'd been doing nothing but holding on for dear life. She started to stand. His arm tightened around her waist again. They sat that way for a moment, waiting. She could feel his eyes on her face. Her own were focused on the window, the Chrysler Building again, but from a different perspective, and steady, not a blur but a luminous tiara burning in the night. It struck her that until now the passionate moments of her life had all played out in the shadows of war and fear. She turned her face to him.

He tasted of scotch. Or maybe that was her own tongue. She twisted more toward him. He took his other hand off the wheel and held her. It should have been awkward there in that chair, but it wasn't. It was the most natural thing in the world.

She'd never be sure what stopped her. There was no deus ex machina, at least not a real one. No cleaning woman came through the door. Hannah didn't come by to collect her husband. The phone didn't even ring. The deus ex machina was in her head. How could she lecture her daughter about moral compasses when her own was so unboxed?

Somehow she managed to pull away. He tried to hold on to her for a moment longer, then let her go. She stood and began smoothing her skirt. He sat watching her. She turned away. She didn't want him to see her face. She had a feeling it was giving away everything that was racing through her mind. It shouldn't have happened. She would not let it happen again. In any event, it didn't mean anything. The sentences kept chasing after one another, and she didn't realize she'd spoken aloud until he answered her.

"It didn't mean anything," she said.

"Don't you believe it," he answered.

Eleven

Charlotte let herself into the apartment, then stopped when she saw the framed photograph on the mantel. It must be another hallucination. Or else a picture of someone who looked like him. She crossed the room, picked up the frame, and brought it closer. It wasn't a hallucination or someone who looked like him. It was Laurent.

She felt Vivi standing behind her in the archway between the hall and living room but didn't turn, not yet. She wasn't ready to face how the photograph had got there. She just wanted to go on looking at him.

He was so young. It came as a shock. She was older now than he'd been then. She was older now than he'd ever be.

The rest was rushing back, too. She'd remembered the

thick lashes and beautifully shaped brows, she'd even remembered the nose that was a little too short, but she'd
forgotten the mouth that gave him away. It could curve
in pleasure at some joke or absurdity, or open easily to
let out the laughter, or curl with disdain. And it was soft.
She remembered that, too. She wiped her eyes with the
back of her hand.

Vivi crossed the room and put her arm around her
mother's waist. "I didn't mean to make you cry, Mom. I
thought you'd be glad."

"I am glad," she said, and wiped her eyes again. "But
where on earth did you get it?"

"From someone who'd been at the Sorbonne with
him. With my . . . dad." Again she pronounced the word
tentatively. "It was Aunt Hannah's idea. When I told her I
didn't even have a picture of him, she said there had to be
a way to get one. So we started talking about where he'd
gone to school and stuff like that. Then she remembered a
colleague she'd corresponded with about some psychiatric
study. He'd gone to the Sorbonne, too. So she wrote to
him, and he wrote back and said he'd never known Laurent Foret himself. He'd been older. But he knew someone who he thought had been a friend of Dad's." She
was getting more comfortable with the word. "So Aunt
Hannah and I wrote to the friend, and he wrote back
and said he'd known Dad well, they'd even tried to start

a student magazine together. That's why he had a picture of him behind a desk. Isn't that amazing?"

"Amazing," Charlotte agreed. "Who is this friend?"

"Somebody called Jean Bouchard. He said he never met you. He knew about you, because Dad talked about you, but he'd never met you. Isn't this amazing?" she said again. "Aunt Hannah said the world isn't as big as people think."

"Apparently."

Vivi took the photograph from her mother, and they went on staring at it together.

"He was handsome," Vivi said.

"That he was."

"And I think I do have his eyebrows."

"And lashes."

"He looks nice."

"Oh, sweetheart, he was. He really was."

Vivi glanced sideways at her mother. "I bet he'd never scold me." She was kidding, but only partly.

"Of course not. He'd be the perfect parent. Not like the one you're stuck with."

"I'm not so stuck," Vivi said, and put the photograph back on the mantel. "It can stay there for now. Though I suppose we'll have to let it out of the apartment to have a copy made. Then you can put that here or in your room or wherever. But this one goes on my dresser. Just like Pru

McCabe's father is on her dresser. So everyone can see it when they come to my room. Alice is going to be so jealous. Her father is fat and bald. I mean, Mr. Benson is nice and all that, but he's not handsome. He's not like my dad."

꒰

Charlotte couldn't decide whether to thank Hannah for helping Vivi find the photograph or tell her to mind her own damn business. In the end she thanked her. She even went downstairs to do it. A note or phone call seemed too chilly.

Horace answered the door. She couldn't make up her mind how she felt about that either. They'd seen each other at work, but neither of them had mentioned the ride through the empty office. Fortunately—did she really think it was fortunate?—Hannah came up behind him before either of them could say anything.

Hannah invited her in, but she said she had only a minute. The cassoulet left over from the weekend was already in the oven. She just wanted to thank her for helping Vivi track down the photograph. "She's thrilled."

"I'm surprised you didn't think of doing it yourself."

"I did. I wrote to a few friends. But after the bombing—"

"I thought Paris was spared bombing."

"There was some. Mostly it was street battles and looting and chaos. Pretty much the same end results. No one I wrote to had anything."

"That was tactful," Horace said after Charlotte had gone back upstairs.

"Helping Vivi get the photograph?"

"Contradicting Charlotte about the bombing of Paris."

"From what I've read, there wasn't much."

"How much is enough?"

"All right, that was tactless of me, but I don't believe she wrote to friends at all. I don't believe she lifted a finger to find a photograph."

He didn't answer.

"It's not fair to Vivi," she insisted. "It's sad enough she never knew her father. She deserves at least some idea of him."

"Whether she does or doesn't is none of our business," he said as he started toward his study.

She followed him. "I disagree. I cannot stand by and watch a child suffer. Maybe the match was a mistake— people must have been rushing into marriage before the war over there just as they were here—but she has no right to visit her bitterness on Vivi."

He stopped and rotated the chair to face her. "Maybe she's not bitter. Maybe it has nothing to do with her late husband. Maybe she just doesn't want to dredge up old memories. It wasn't a pretty time."

She stood staring at him. He managed to hold her glance. He knew what was coming.

"That is what we call projection," she said.

"Save your instruction in analytic terminology for Federman. That's what I call respecting privacy."

❦

Charlotte had a copy made of the photograph. Now Laurent stood on her dresser as well as Vivi's. Vivi said good night to the picture faithfully. Charlotte didn't exactly avoid it. Sometimes she found herself apologizing to it silently. I did it for Vivi, she explained. She could swear the lip in the photograph curled.

Once she walked into Vivi's room to say good night and found Vivi sitting on the end of her bed staring at it. "I like this one, but it would have been nice to have one from the army, too. In his uniform."

"Like Pru McCabe's father?"

Vivi shrugged.

"I prefer this," Charlotte said. "He was never a militarist."

Vivi stood and started unbuttoning her school uniform. "Did you know Uncle Horace was recommended for the Congressional Medal of Honor?"

Charlotte, who had started out of the room, turned back. "What?"

"Aunt Hannah told me when we were writing letters to get the picture. I was telling her about Pru McCabe's father, and she said Uncle Horace defended a bunker and killed lots of Japanese all by himself. That was how he was wounded. It was in something called the Battle of Buna. After it, his company commander recommended him for the medal, but he didn't get it."

"Why not, if he killed so many Japanese singlehandedly?" There was an undercurrent of skepticism in her voice. She was suspicious of heroism, even Horace's heroism.

"Because he's a Jew."

Charlotte shook her head. "You have got to stop seeing everything through the prism of religion. You're getting as bad as Eleanor Hathaway's grandmother."

"I don't see everything, but this does have to do with religion. Aunt Hannah says it's a well-known fact. She says Jews don't get the Congressional Medal of Honor. Neither do Negroes. No matter how brave they were. She said she read an article where they questioned some general about it. You know what he said? 'A Jew or a Negro for the Congressional Medal of Honor? Don't make me laugh.'"

"Don't believe everything you hear, or read."

"But Uncle Horace is proof. His commanding officer

recommended him, and a group wants him to fight for it, but he refuses."

"Now you're talking. Horace's refusing to fight to get a medal sounds like the first true part of the story."

❦

Charlotte had no intention of mentioning the Medal of Honor to Horace. You didn't go around asking a man about his war experience, even if you had taken a ride on his lap. But firm resolutions are funny things. The more determined you are not to say something, the more likely you are to blurt it out. The phenomenon reminded her of an anecdote she'd read in a biography of J. P. Morgan. A woman who had invited Morgan to tea told her young daughter again and again that under no circumstances was she to mention Morgan's grotesque nose or even look at it. Morgan suffered from rhinophyma. The girl was scrupulous, until her mother poured the tea and handed it to her to serve the great financier. "Do you take one lump or two in your nose, Mr. Morgan?" she asked. That was the way Charlotte felt in the back of Horace's car that night.

He'd offered her a ride home. This time she didn't refuse. It was snowing. And what did it matter what people thought? They probably already thought a great deal. Neither of them had mentioned that nighttime ride through the office, but their behavior had changed. In front of others, they'd become circumspect. He called her Charlotte, not General, or Charles with a French accent, or Charlie. They were careful not to exchange glances, as they used to, when Carl Covington said something particularly pompous or Faith Silver retold another anecdote about the time she'd lunched at the Round Table. There was no more accidental running over Bill Quarrels's foot, though a few days earlier when Bill had come into her cubicle on some pretext and sprawled in the chair on the other side of her desk as if he were there for the duration, Horace had wheeled by and told him he was still waiting for those sales figures.

Their behavior when they were alone had changed, too. They'd become uneasy; no, not uneasy, overly attuned, as if an accidental touch of fingers could set off sparks. Fortunately, there was plenty of room for them to keep a distance in the back of that big black Cadillac. She even put her handbag and briefcase between them on the seat as they sat waiting for the chauffeur to fold the chair Horace had swung himself out of, put it in the trunk, and come around to get behind the wheel. If the delay struck her as awkward, it must have been agony for Horace. She remembered him careening through the office that night. He wasn't meant to be sitting in the back of a stately hearse while someone else did the driving.

He should be tooling around town and speeding over country roads in a nifty little Triumph or a fire-engine-red Austin-Healey. The image broke her heart. And she didn't even care about automobiles.

As the driver pulled away from the curb and inched into the traffic, slowed and snarled by the snow, she asked how the campaign for *The Red Trapeze* was going.

"I was right. The times are changing, thank you, *Ulysses, Lady Chatterley,* and various *Tropics of.* We're not likely to have trouble after all, or rather just enough talk about possible trouble to boost sales. The author helped. After the piece ran in *Newsweek,* he lined up a slew of what are known as leading literary figures to sign a letter to the *Times.* Wait till you see it. It's quite a list. Maybe the book isn't fiction after all. Maybe he really has slept with half the literary establishment, of both sexes. The letter swears that the novel is art with an upper-case *A* and preventing publication of it would be a crime against humanity. The kicker is a line about how Flaubert and Joyce are revered today, but no one remembers the philistines who tried to silence them."

"If Henry Garrick ever gives up writing books, you ought to hire him as publicity director."

She saw his smile flicker in the snow-muffled light from the streetlamps. "My thought exactly."

She could have sworn his hand moved toward her on

the seat. She rearranged the barricade of her handbag and briefcase between them.

A taxi swerved in front of the car. A horn sounded. The windshield wipers thumped back and forth. The silence between them grew longer. Conversation had never been a problem before that nighttime ride.

"How's Vivi?" he asked finally.

"You know those antennae you said I didn't have? The lack of which meant I wasn't preparing her for the world. She's growing an impressive set of her own. The other night I got a lecture on various slights to Jews. Honors they don't get. Medals—" She stopped.

He turned to look at her in the eerie light. "Why do I get the feeling Hannah has something to do with this?"

"Not really. Anyway, I was just nattering on about Vivi's antennae. In answer to your question of how she is. Forget I mentioned it."

"But you did."

"It's not really the antennae you meant. She was talking about prejudice in general. Against Jews. Against Negroes. Against Eskimos for all I know."

"Let's forget the Eskimos. Against Jews and Negroes? Don't tell me. Let me guess. Hannah started in on that cockamamie story about the Congressional Medal of Honor again?"

"I believe she was speaking hypothetically."

"The hell she was." He turned to look out the window on his side. The car inched forward. The windshield wipers went back and forth. He turned back to her. "Hannah has a rich fantasy life. If she has to be married to a cripple, he damn well better have got that way by being a hero. I'll tell you a secret, Charlie. Millions of men got shot in the war. Almost half a million of them died. So let's not get melodramatic about a single wound, which was debilitating but not terminal. In other words, I do not deserve any medals. I wasn't a hero. I was just in the wrong place at the wrong time."

She didn't know what to say to that, but she didn't have to say anything. He'd already turned to look out the window again. This time he didn't turn back until the car pulled up in front of the house. Then he barely said good night as the driver brought his chair around and he heaved himself into it.

Twelve

She swears she'll never let it happen again. How could it happen again? She hates him. Almost as much as she hates herself.

Besides, she is terrified of the immediate consequences. What if she is pregnant with a little Fritz, as those off-spring of shame are called? She remembers the stories of abortion whispered behind closed doors before the war. Dirty hovels on back streets. Cold-eyed men and women of dubious skill and certain greed. Since Vichy and the Occupation the penalties have become only more dire. The guillotine is not out of the question. Then she realizes that is one worry she doesn't have to face. She has not had her period in months. She is not ovulating. Saved by malnutrition. Even the food he brings, most of which she gives to Vivi, is not enough to make her a woman again.

So what she has sworn will not happen again does. And again after that. It has nothing to do with the food, though the shortages are getting worse. This is a different kind of hunger.

What strange lovers they make, either locked together in desire or circling each other with suspicion. He is the conqueror and can do as he likes with her. The knowledge of his secret makes her equally dangerous to him. Sometimes she thinks the mutual fear binds them closer; at other moments she's certain it drives them apart.

Then something strange happens. Tenderness begins to creep between them. That has to do with Vivi. His affection for her is palpable. But it has to do with more than Vivi. Another hunger stalks the cold blacked-out city, perhaps even stronger in these hopeless times than those of the body. They are both starved for a human connection. As they lie together on the narrow sofa in the room behind the shop, as they say good-bye in the murky predawn light, he is no longer the enemy or a Wehrmacht officer or a craven Jew in hiding. He is only Julian. Under other circumstances they might have become different lovers. But she does not love him.

They tell each other the stories of their lives, as if the

shared knowledge is a nugget of amber that can preserve that easier, less complicated time. Or rather, he tells the story of his life and asks about hers, and gradually, as she begins to let her guard down, she asks about his.

One night, lying on the narrow sofa after they have made love, her head on his chest, his arm around her, she feels his fingers moving on her back. She can tell it is the same intricate pattern she has seen him perform as he reads or browses in the shop. She asks him what he is doing.

"Tying imaginary surgical knots. In the beginning I did it for practice. Now it has become a habit. A nervous habit, I suppose."

"Did you always want to be a doctor?"

"For as long as I can remember."

"*Primum non nocere.*"

"Please do not make sport of me."

"I'm not making sport of you. I'm admiring you. I admire people with a purpose. Especially an altruistic purpose."

He lifts his head to get a better view of her face. "That is the first time."

"The first time what?"

"The first time that you have commended me."

She doesn't say anything to that.

"Being in the Wehrmacht must be difficult," she goes on after a while. "In view of your desire to first do no harm."

"It was my duty. I would have enlisted even if I had not been called up. My father was a captain in the First War. His brother died at Verdun."

She stiffens at the undercurrent of pride in his voice, but when he speaks again, there is only shame.

"Then, as the anti-Semitism grew worse, it was my safe haven."

The shame, as much hers as his, makes her want to soothe the wound. "You must be a very good physician to have them keep you here in Paris." She has changed her mind about his having committed a vile act.

He lifts his head to look at her again, and this time he is smiling. The expression is rare. It is also magical in its transformative power. He is no longer the ascetic saint but a man who has once been, and perhaps might again be, happy. "I am a good physician," he admits. "I am also fortunate."

"In what way?"

"Early in the Occupation, a high-ranking official—I will not say how high—brought his six-year-old son to Paris. He thought it would be a good experience for the child. A few days after the boy arrived, he was taken ill with terrible stomach pains and nausea and vomiting.

Also a high fever. The doctor in charge was a better officer than physician. He could not diagnose the problem.
They called me in. I was junior, but they were desperate.
As soon as I examined him, I realized it was a case of
appendicitis."

"That doesn't sound as if it would be hard to diagnose."

"The child's pain was on the left side of his abdomen."

"Isn't the appendix on the right?"

"In most cases, but the boy was suffering from situs
inversus. That is when the major visceral organs are on
the opposite side of the body from their normal position.
I performed surgery, the boy came through nicely, and
the high-ranking official remains grateful."

"So you really are a good physician."

"That is the second time," he says.

"Are you keeping score?" she asks, and realizes this is
the first lighthearted exchange they have had. Then a moment later it turns dark, as everything must these days.

"There's one thing I don't understand," she says. "You
say the first doctor was a better officer than physician.
But surely the boy had been examined before, at birth or
in infancy. Surely someone had discovered the, what is it
called, situs inversus."

"A physician had."

"Then why didn't the father know?"

"Because the mother did not tell him. I learned this when she arrived in Paris. She thanked me for the boy's life and begged my discretion. Her husband is a high-ranking member of the Nazi party. By his lights, by Nazi doctrine, the boy is damaged, a stain upon the Aryan race, useless to society, unworthy of life. She was afraid of what her husband might do if he found out about the boy's condition."

She pulls away and sits staring at him in the darkness. "And this is the country you're willing to fight for?"

"Germany was not always like this." It is his constant refrain. "And before you condemn me, remember what the professor who came into the shop asking for books on eugenics said. For years the United States was ahead of Germany in euthanasia and racial purification. It is only thanks to the Führer that we have caught up and outstripped them."

She hears the irony in his voice, but it is not enough, and he knows it. He sits up, puts his feet on the cold floor, and reaches for his uniform.

"If it is any consolation," he says, "and I realize it is not, I adhered to the mother's wishes. I never told the father of the son's condition. I even explained that the position of the scar so far to the left was the result of a new surgical technique."

She reaches out and puts a hand on his back, the delinquent consoling the criminal, or the other way around.

But she does not love him. On that point she is adamant.

Nonetheless, a kind of domesticity sets in. Once, he infuriates her—infuriates her about a book, as if they were living a normal life in normal times—by pronouncing Emma Bovary a neurotic. Then he redeems himself with his sympathy for Dorothea Brooke. Books are important to them. Words are important to them. He is the one who teaches her the phrase "Hitler made me a Jew."

꙲

Holding Vivi's hand, Charlotte comes out of the apartment building, then stops and stands staring. The woman across the street looks like Simone. She goes on gawking at the emaciated, unkempt figure. It is Simone.

Simone sees her at the same moment. They start toward each other and meet in the middle of the street. A few years ago that would have been dangerous, but there is no traffic. They stand for a moment torn between laughter at the miracle of it and tears at the joy. Then, as Charlotte takes a step closer to embrace, Simone takes a step back. Charlotte is stung, and shamed. Simone knows.

"I need delousing," Simone says.

Charlotte exhales in relief.

Vivi tugs on the skirt of Simone's filthy dress and lifts her arms to be picked up. "Soon, my darling, soon," Simone says.

"You're free!"

"For the moment."

"How did you get out?"

"Don't try to fathom the Nazi mind. First things first. Do you have anything, vinegar, olive oil, mayonnaise?" She runs through the home remedies for getting rid of lice. Charlotte says she can't remember the last time she had any of those things, then remembers the tube of petroleum jelly Julian brought for Vivi's rashes. They turn and go back into the apartment building.

On the way up the stairs, they encounter the concierge coming down, her bad leg thumping heavily on each step. Simone turns and flattens herself against the wall. The concierge puts her hand on Simone's shoulder and gently turns her away from the wall.

"Welcome home, Madame Halevy," she says, and her voice is kind, though in the old days, she hadn't approved of Simone. She'd found her too bold.

"Why were you avoiding Madame Rey?" Charlotte asks as they continue up the stairs.

"I wasn't. It was a reflex. In the camp, we were forbidden to look directly at the guards. If we passed one of them in a hall or on a staircase, we had to flatten ourselves against the wall. If you didn't . . ." Her voice trails off.

"How on earth does Madame Rey know something like that?"

"Radio-Loge," Simone says, using the term for the concierge rumor mill. "I'm not the only one who was released from Drancy. Remember Monsieur Bendit, the proprietor of the café in the rue des Écoles who used to try to flirt with us? They arrested him, they released him, then they arrested him again. They do that sometimes. I think it's part of their sadism."

"Have you had word of Sophie?" Charlotte asks as she unlocks the door to the flat.

"She and my mother didn't know I was arrested, thank heavens. And thank you for not telling them. Last I heard, they were both safe in the south."

Charlotte goes into her bedroom and returns with the petroleum jelly, clean underwear, and a dress and hands them all to Simone.

Simone takes everything and looks at the tube of petroleum jelly. "How on earth did you get your hands on this?"

"Luck," Charlotte answers too quickly. "And an endless queue. I also have some black bread and a few mouthfuls of sausage," she adds as she starts toward the kitchen.

"Bread, sausage, petroleum jelly. Tell the truth, Charlotte, you have a lover in the black market."

"Dozens. But come eat."

"First the delousing. I can't feel human until then." She takes the petroleum jelly and clean clothes from Charlotte. "I'm headed for the public baths." She hesitates. "They're still open, aren't they?"

"And crowded."

"Then I'd better hurry. I'll come by the shop when I'm a new woman."

An hour later, Charlotte looks up from the accounts she is trying to balance and sees Simone standing outside the shop. Her long dark hair is still wet, and the dress hangs on her as if on a scarecrow. Before the Occupation they were the same size. Now Charlotte is gaunt and Simone is skeletal. She is peering into the shop, trying to make out who, if anyone, is inside. When she sees there is no one except Charlotte, she opens the door and steps in. She used to be fearless. The camp has made her wary.

Charlotte makes a pot of what has become known as acorn juice, one of the names for the ingenious but awful-tasting ersatz coffees, and they perch on stools behind the counter, talking quietly, falling silent when customers come into the store, though a few of the regulars stop when they see Simone, as if they're seeing a ghost. Then they cross the shop to her. Some embrace and kiss her; others take her hands and say how happy they are to see her. No one asks where she has been. They know. No one asks what it was like. They do not want to know.

Charlotte does not want to know either, any more than Simone wants to talk about it, but she cannot help herself, and Charlotte has no choice but to listen to the stories of crowding and hunger, squalor and disease, the minor indignities of overflowing slop pails and women serving as human shields to afford a modicum of privacy for other women who are menstruating, and the inescapable gratuitous violence. But worst of all, Simone says, is the inhuman sorting of human beings for the transports. The memory of that makes her fall silent.

"I went by my old apartment," she says after a while. "Strangers are living there. The worst part is they're French." She shakes her head. "Not that it would be any better if the boches had requisitioned it."

"Come stay at the flat with Vivi and me." Charlotte does not want to think of Simone moving into the room behind the shop. There are no traces of Julian. She is careful to see that he leaves nothing behind. But the room seems to her to be redolent of him, to reek of their passion, to give off a stench of their illicitness. She is sure someone, especially someone as attuned to her as Simone, will sense it.

Simone thanks her but says she can't stay in Paris.

"They let me out now, but that doesn't mean I won't be arrested again. And the second time, you're even more likely to end up on a transport."

"Where will you go?"

Before Simone has a chance to answer, the bell above the door jingles, and Julian steps into the shop. He stops when he sees Simone, as some of the regular customers did, but unlike them, he does not rush over to welcome her. He glances at Charlotte. She meets his gaze, then looks away quickly. That is all it takes. Charlotte recognizes the phenomenon because she has had experience with it, though not in such dire circumstances.

Shortly before she and Laurent were married, his parents gave a party for them. The world was hurtling toward war, but the formalities must be observed. With the world hurtling toward war, it was more important than ever to observe the formalities. She still remembers the city beyond the open doors to the balcony turning a smoky blue as it does at that hour and the aroma of exhaust from the traffic below mingling with expensive perfumes. A woman, slightly older, wearing a Chanel suit she also remembers, came over to Laurent and kissed him on both cheeks. There was nothing unusual in that. But something about the way her hand lingered on his arm and his discomfort at the introduction gave them away.

"You were lovers," Charlotte said after the woman moved on.

He shook his head, but the gesture was not persuasive. That was how well she had known Laurent then. And that is how well Simone knows her now.

Simone is silent, watching Julian as he picks up a book, barely glances at it, puts it back, picks up another, repeats the gestures, and leaves the shop.

"Now I understand the petroleum jelly and the bread and sausage," she says when he is gone.

Charlotte does not try to deny it. That will only make matters worse. She knows she shouldn't try to explain either, but she cannot help herself. "Vivi was sick and hungry."

"Do you know anyone in Paris who isn't? Except for the filthy boches and their *collabos*."

"He's the one who bribed the guards to get the packages to you."

"He's the one who put me there in the first place."

"He's a doctor in the army, not a guard or Gestapo or SS."

"He's a boche."

Charlotte has one more explanation, but she cannot use it. It would be a betrayal of Julian's secret. And it would only make Simone hate him more.

Simone stands.

"Where are you going?"

"I told you. I can't stay in Paris."

"Yes, but where will you go?"

Simone smiles. The expression is anything but kindly. "I couldn't have told you before. It would have been too dangerous, for you as well as for me. I certainly won't now."

"You can't think I'd give you away?"

Simone goes on staring at her for a long moment. "I don't know what to think. I thought I did, but I don't. Not anymore."

⁊

She hears of Simone twice more before the end of the war. Monsieur Grassin, her father's ethnographer friend, tells her on one of his visits to the shop that Simone is in hiding somewhere in the south. He doesn't say where in the south. Charlotte tells herself that is ordinary discretion, not personal distrust. Then later, in the camp, a woman who knew both of them before the war reports that Simone was arrested again. This time she was not so lucky in the deportation sweepstakes.

⁊

She tells Julian he must stop coming to the shop. It has nothing to do with Simone. Well, perhaps something to do with Simone. But mainly she is afraid. It is too dangerous, she insists. He doesn't argue with her. He doesn't even try to say good-bye. At least not to her. But he picks up Vivi, holds her for a moment, and tells her to be a good girl and listen to her *maman*. When he tries to put her down, she clings to him. He peels away her arms reluctantly.

"If things were different . . . ," he says, and strokes Vivi's head.

"But they're not."

The harshness of her words shames her. Again and again he has talked of the children he dreams of having someday. It is not a question of carrying on his name, he explains, though he doesn't have to. She is coming to know him. He is one of those men whose sweetness comes out with children. He is, she suspects, fonder of them than she is. She loves Vivi, her own, but she does not revel in children in general.

Once, late at night, talking in the room behind the shop—it is not all sex—she asked him why he never married.

"I was engaged to marry."

"What happened?"

"The Law for the Protection of German Blood and Honor happened."

"They took your fiancée away?"

He shook his head and smiled, not the smile that shows he was happy once and might be again but a terrible grimace. "Let us say, she absented herself. I do not blame her. I am not in a position to blame anyone. The Law for the Protection of German Blood and Honor criminalized sexual relations and marriage between Germans and Jews. She is a good German. I am a deracinated Jew."

She tells herself the memory of the fiancée's callousness makes her relent, but she knows it's her own need. He can come at night, she says, when no one is in the shop to see him.

Several nights a week, she locks the door at closing, then unlocks it when the city has gone dark. He is discreet slipping in, more than discreet, stealthy. Once as he is about to open the door, a man turns the corner onto the street. Julian lets go of the door and begins making his way down the street, trying the other doors, doing his best to look as if he is on official duty, checking doors to make sure they are locked for the night. A little while later, huddled in the back room, she hears the doorknob rattling again and waits for the sound of his steps in the shop. There is only silence. A moment later, someone knocks on the door. Hugging her sweater to her, she goes into the shop. The man with the unmovable face is on the other side of the glass. She tries not to recoil and points to the sign that says CLOSED. He opens the door nonethe-less, sticks his terrifying face into the shop, and tells her she has forgotten to lock up for the night.

"You're lucky," he says. The words, smashed by his rigid lips, come out mangled. "A boche just came down the street checking doors. Fortunately, he wasn't one of the efficient members of the master race."

She thanks him and starts to close the door, but he stops her.

"The child is in the back?" he asks.

She nods.

"Good. I'll tell Madame Rey that you're both safe. The concierge worries when you don't come home."

She explains about the blackout and the Metro clos-ings and her broken bicycle, and even while she's speaking, she knows it's a mistake. She owes him no explanation, especially not one this elaborate.

After he leaves, she locks the door. A while later she hears it rattling again. This time she does not get up and go into the shop. It could be the man with the terrible face, but she knows it's not. It's Julian. She lies rigid until the noise stops, hating herself for her cruelty, but hating him, too, for the compromised position in which he has placed her. Only she knows he has not placed her there. She has put herself in that position of her own free will.

The next night she goes home to the flat to sleep. The

concierge is waiting for her. She has not yet begun hold-ing her finger to her temple and murmuring about *les boches*. She simply observes how well little Vivi is looking and pinches her cheek. Vivi's small fist tries to swat away her hand.

The concierge and her friend with the grotesque face are not the only ones Charlotte fears. French men and women are still turning in their Jewish neighbors, but now other French patriots are fingering their fellow citizens for other crimes, some real, some imagined, some fabricated to settle old scores. And just as there is no denying being Jewish, there is no court for contesting these accusations. Men and women are tried behind closed doors, judged in secret, found guilty in whispers, executed in stealth. Freelancing revenge, Monsieur Grassin, her father's friend from the Palais de Chaillot, will call it, but that chilling phrase is still in the future.

Rumors of the coming invasion race through the city. The closer the Allies get, the more certain German de-feat becomes, the more explosive the situation grows. Anti-Semitic propaganda blares louder and more violently from signs and newspapers and broadcasts. The Resistance escalates its sabotage and steps up reprisals against the occupiers and those who cooperate with them.

One morning, walking with Vivi along the river, she sees a crowd gathered on the quay. Holding Vivi's hand, she changes her course to give the group a wide berth. One way or another, gatherings mean trouble. But she isn't quick enough. Before she veers away, she sees two gendarmes hauling a body from the water. His hands and feet are bound. A limestone block is tied to his neck. She does not have to go on looking to know there will be signs of torture.

"Gestapo pigs," a man on the edge of the crowd spits out. A woman standing nearby shushes him.

Then Radio-Loge kicks in. The Gestapo cannot be responsible. The victim was a well-known collaborator. He and his wife were often seen tucking into tournedos of beef and bottles of Saint-Émilion with German officials at Le Grand Véfour, the restaurant below the flat where everyone knows Colette lives and hides her Jewish husband.

Reprisal is in the air. Charlotte never learns how the concierge finds out. Perhaps the man with the waxy immovable face wasn't there by chance the night he caught Julian entering the shop. Perhaps he has been watching her. She sees him in the neighborhood, a one-man vigilante group, reprimanding women who return a boche's glance, harassing men who take or give a light for a cigarette, even scolding children who stare in fascination at the guns and uniforms, cars and trucks of the occupying forces. Or perhaps Simone has said something to someone, and the word has spread. "Après les boches," the concierge hisses as

Charlotte passes. The first time, there is no accompanying gesture. The next time, she holds her hand to her temple and pulls the trigger finger.

Charlotte tells Julian he has to stop coming to the shop at night as well as during the day. Again he doesn't argue with her. He knows what it is like to live in constant fear of being found out.

A few mornings later, she arrives at the shop to find a box in front of the door. She assumes it is a delivery of books. Strange how the cultural life of the city goes on. A production of *Traviata* is running at the Palais de Chaillot. At an art auction at the Hôtel Drouot, a Matisse is sold for more than four hundred thousand francs, a Bonnard for more than three hundred thousand. Confiscated or stolen, people whisper to one another, but that doesn't stop them from raising a paddle or calling out a sum. Publishing houses continue to thrive not only on current titles but on French translations of German classics and Nazi propaganda. Even the sporting life continues, though the programs at the racetrack have been reduced from four a week to two. She unlocks the door, takes Vivi into the shop, then goes back for the box. It feels too light for books. She carries it inside and opens it. Inside are three potatoes, a loaf of bread, a minuscule amount of cooking oil, and milk. On her knees, stooping over the bounty, she begins to cry. That night, she leaves the door unlocked. It has nothing to do with the food, only with his leaving it there despite the fact that she has banished him. Perhaps there is something of love between them after all.

But that cannot be. In less tender moments on that narrow sofa, sweat-slicked from sex, guilt-riddled from pleasure, she looks at him and sees the reflection of her own weakness. They are both compromised. More than compromised, damned.

Other times when she looks at him, she is overwhelmed with pity for his impossible situation. The torment haunts him. She hears it in his voice when he mentions his country and his compatriots. She senses it in the way his body stiffens as he slips back into the hated uniform. Once, in the darkness, he whispers to her that he is waiting for the day the Allies triumph. Only then will Germany return to sanity. More than once he has told her that she and Vivi are his only salvation. He has lied to the world, betrayed his family, done terrible things. Only his connection to them leaves him a shred of humanity. Then she holds him and reminds him that he has rounded up no Jews, could not have saved his family, is not lying to her. She is not sure any of that is true, but she knows his pain is real, as genuine as her shame. Sometimes after he puts on that despised uniform and leaves, she looks at herself in the cracked mirror and mouths the words she swears she is not. *Collabo horizontale.* Is it any wonder they cling to each other?

Then, in the early hours of June 6, what all of Paris, all of France, everyone, even Julian in secret, has been waiting for, some with hope, some with terror, happens. The Allies land on French soil. The news reaches Paris the following day. Radio-Paris reports that the Allied Forces have been repulsed almost everywhere, but no one believes the German-run station anymore, if they ever did. The Liberation is imminent. Julian confirms the prediction. He senses panic in the hospital, among the troops, from the other officers, while he, he whispers to her in the dark privacy of the back room, feels only joy, which he has to hide behind a mask of gloom and a façade of bravado. But then he is a master of the masquerade.

Isolated acts of sabotage spring up like mushrooms after the rain. Railroad tracks are dynamited, telephone and telegraph lines cut. The Germans repair the damage. The Resistance repeats it. In retribution, or perhaps only in fear, the Germans accelerate their arrests, roundups, hostage taking, and executions.

Even casual observers and those determined to stay out of trouble begin to notice something. The German presence in the city is shrinking. Truckloads of able-bodied men, and those who are barely that, lumber past the populace, headed for the front. Julian remains at the hospital, but there is no saying for how long. Even the high-ranking official whose son he saved cannot help him now. The gray mice in their drab shabby uniforms hurry to trucks and trains carrying suitcases. When one of them drops her bag and it springs open revealing several silk scarves, a fashionable hat, and a china tea service spilling out of the newspaper it has been wrapped in, a crowd begins to gather, and the mouse runs, leaving the suitcase with her war spoils behind. An official trying to hustle a painting into a waiting automobile is set upon by a crowd who wrests it from him. As the story spreads, the picture becomes more valuable and the artist better known with each retelling. By the end, people who have never seen the painting and don't know its size are swearing it was Géricault's *Raft of the Medusa*. The German official was trying to make off with a piece of France's patrimony.

To prove to the Parisians that it is still a force to be reckoned with, the Wehrmacht stages a parade of uniformed men, vehicles, and artillery down the avenue de l'Opéra—the last German parade in Paris, though no one knows it at the time—but its forces are so depleted that the first lines of troops must loop back and march down the avenue a second time in an attempt to fool the Parisians.

Julian veers between optimism and despair. Much as he looks forward to Germany becoming Germany again, as he puts it, he knows he is in for a bad time. His countrymen, starved, bombed, brutalized, and humiliated, will blame the entire army for their defeat. His coreligionists will condemn him for his betrayal.

On Bastille Day, Charlotte comes down from her apartment to find the concierge's loge draped in blue, red, and white. "*Vive la France,*" she says with a grin. Her finger comes up to her temple and the grin turns into a snarl. "*Après les boches,*" she hisses.

Charlotte hurries past and comes out into a carnival of blue, red, and white. Buildings are draped in the colors; people wear them, women's scarves and men's ties and children's shirts and pinafores. She thinks of going back to her flat to change her clothes and Vivi's—they are as French as their neighbors—but she doesn't want to pass the concierge again. No, it's more than that. She doesn't feel she has a right to the colors, not anymore. Like Julian, she swerves between joy and hopelessness.

At the corner, an accordionist is playing "La Marseillaise." A crowd has surrounded him. Tears stream down faces as they sing. At the next corner, another accordionist and another crowd, and so on as she and Vivi make their way toward the shop. In the Place Maubert, near the Sorbonne, a crowd of hundreds, perhaps thousands, is singing and waving flags. Had they been hiding them since the Germans marched in? Had they made them overnight? It is almost enough to make her forget her fear. Further on, at the Porte de Vanves, Hitler is being burned in effigy. The terror returns. She hates the Führer as much as her neighbors, but she also recognizes the dark underbelly of the euphoria. Celebration will turn to vengeance. She knows that as certainly as she knows her own guilt.

A few days later, two more bodies are fished from the Seine, hands and feet bound, a limestone block weighing each of them down. The sickening irony is that the stones are not heavy enough to keep the bodies below the surface for long. Within days, sometimes within hours, they float to the surface. It occurs to Charlotte, and she's not the only one, that perhaps the blocks are not meant to prevent the bodies from bobbing up like macabre harbingers of France's future. Perhaps the good French men and women who are evening the score are impatient. They cannot wait a year or even a month for their handiwork to be discovered. They want to parade their vengeance now.

Mentally Charlotte prepares her defense. She has transgressed, but she has not collaborated, not really. She did not turn in Jews, or provide information to the authorities, or betray anyone but herself. She is to be blamed but not condemned. The excuses are similar to the ones she trucks out to console Julian, and, she knows, just as bogus.

She tries to beat back the fear as she goes about her

229

life, taking care of Vivi, running the shop, walking the boulevards with her head up and a smile on her face, because she, too, is French, and soon she, like the rest of her country, will be free. Only she knows she won't. The nightmare is over. Long live the nightmare.

One night she comes home to find the concierge lying in wait for her. She is smiling again, that mocking death's-head grin Charlotte has come to hate, but she doesn't raise her hand to her temple or murmur about *les boches*. She merely hands Charlotte an envelope and stands waiting for her to open it. Charlotte will not give her the satisfaction. Holding the envelope in one hand, Vivi's small fist in the other, she climbs the stairs. Only when she has closed the door to the flat behind her does she pry open the flap.

The photographs are murky. She has to carry them to the stream of setting July sun pouring through the window to make them out. Vivi follows and reaches up to take whatever her mother is holding. She does not want to be left out. But Charlotte has already glimpsed the first picture. She pushes her daughter's hand away. "No!" she snaps.

Vivi begins to whine. Charlotte barely hears her. She stands staring at the photograph on top. In it, a group of men stalks a woman down a country road. A sign is dimly visible in the distance. She tilts the picture to get more light on it. The sign says RENNES with an arrow. She can't read the number of kilometers, but it doesn't matter. This is clearly recently liberated territory. She slides the top picture off the pile. The second photograph shows the men grabbing the woman. In the third the woman is sprawled in the road, while two of the men hold down her legs, spread to allow the camera to capture the view up her skirt. In the fourth, another man is pulling off her dress. Charlotte turns to the last photograph. The woman's naked body is hunched on the dirt road, her ankles bound by her panties, her wrists by her brassiere, her head burrowing into the ground, her rump raised. A large black swastika is scrawled on her back, a smaller one on each buttock.

Charlotte tears up the photographs, but the images are seared into her brain. She thinks of fleeing. Surely she'll be able to slip away in the chaos, especially since, unlike at the beginning of the Occupation when everyone was leaving Paris, refugees are flooding in, hoping for a safe haven. Radio-Loge insists that the Germans will not destroy the city as they leave, and the Allies will not bomb it in preparation for their arrival. Paris is, after all, Paris. But how can she leave? The trains are barely running. She doesn't even have a bicycle. And where will she go? A cousin of Laurent's has written from Avignon to say his parents died in the massive bombing in May. She hasn't had word of her father, and now that the Germans have taken over the Italian-occupied zone where he was the last she'd heard, she is more worried than ever.

Two weeks after Bastille Day, she arrives at the store to find another box. This one is heavy enough to be books. She unlocks the shop, drags the box inside, and settles Vivi in the children's alcove with a picture book and a dog-eared doll. There is enough to do that she doesn't get to the box for some time. Worn with use and reuse—shortages of everything—it opens easily. She turns back the flaps. The box does not contain books. Inside is only a limestone block. No, wait, there is something else. Beside it lies a smaller limestone block. An adult's limestone block and a child's limestone block. For a moment she thinks she is going to throw up. Though the nausea passes, the fear remains. Surely they wouldn't kill a child. Unless they thought she was a little Fritz. The timing is impossible for that, but people out for revenge don't check birth certificates.

She doesn't mention the delivery to Julian, or the concierge's threats, or the photographs. He cannot help. He is the problem. Besides, she doesn't have to tell him what's going on. He knows. He knows better than she does. She hears rumors. He has access to information. Reports still come in, files are still kept, though the Germans no longer pay attention. They are too busy trying to save their own skins. But not Julian. He is determined to save them. Perhaps he is trying to assuage his guilt for his own survival. Perhaps he is simply a decent man. Or perhaps, and she pushes the thought from her mind, he loves her. He begins coming up with ideas, each more outlandish than the last.

One night in the back room, he outlines a plan to take her and Vivi with him when he is evacuated. It will be difficult but not impossible, he explains.

"I know what you think now, after this." He gestures around the room as if it is all Paris under the Occupation. "But this is not the real Germany. The occupiers are not the real Germans."

"You're an occupier."

She feels his head move against her shoulder as if he has been slapped.

"I'm sorry," she says.

"We could go to another country. It would not be so difficult to slip into Switzerland or Portugal."

"It would be impossible. You'd be shot for desertion before we reached the border."

They have both heard her use the word "we." She has, if only for a moment, considered the plan.

He tells her he cannot imagine the future without her and Vivi. They have kept him human. They give him hope.

She does not tell him she cannot imagine the future with him. For the rest of her life, every time she looked across the table at him or turned to him in bed, she would be face-to-face with her shame. She still thinks she can outrun it.

There is nothing she can do but wait, and hope. At least no more bodies are pulled from the Seine. Perhaps the worst has passed. The vengeance has spent itself. Once the Germans are gone for good, tempers will cool. Once Paris is Paris again, the boulevards crowded with people, the shops full of goods, the restaurants serving steak and sweetbreads, escargots and champagne, the museums showing masterpieces rather than empty walls where they used to hang before they were rolled up and trucked off to châteaux and convents around the country for safe-keeping or stolen by Goering and his henchmen, people will be more interested in enjoying life, the essential Parisian pastime, than in settling scores. Besides, what is she really guilty of? She never provided information or turned anyone in, she reminds herself for the tenth or hundredth time. She never dined on tournedos of beef and bottles of Saint-Émilion with German officials at Le Grand Véfour. She accepted food for her starving child and herself from a German officer, who isn't even a real German officer, only a Jew masquerading as one. She runs through her defenses obsessively, like a madwoman intoning a meaningless chant. Unlike a madwoman, however, she knows the mantra does not make sense. She has slept with the enemy.

July turns to August. The railroad workers go on strike. The police follow. Fewer German uniforms walk the street. When they do, they no longer swagger. They are too busy keeping a sharp eye out for attacks. Barricades begin springing up. Men and women, sometimes singing, sometimes joking, sometimes cursing the boches, pile kiosks, paving stones, benches, the carcasses of dead automobiles and bicycles, even street urinals across roads and at intersections. Children climb the makeshift structures and slide down them. Mothers warn them to be careful, but only halfheartedly. How can anyone be cautious in the face of this euphoria? Charlotte passes two girls—they can't be older than fifteen—in shorts and frilly blouses with rifles slung around their necks and feels the reproach. The city becomes accustomed to gunfire. When it breaks out, people hit the ground or hide behind statues or columns or barricades. When it ceases, they continue about their business. The sangfroid sends a message as powerful as outright resistance.

Though Julian has stopped coming to the shop while it is open, late one afternoon he arrives and begins browsing. He is trying to be unobtrusive, but the ruse is futile. German soldiers no longer browse or shop or do anything but carry out their orders and scheme for ways to get out of this alive. He lingers until the shop is empty, then tells her he will wait in the back room until she closes. She begs him to leave, but he tells her he has one more plan. He is not trying to persuade her to run away with him. This is only to save her and Vivi. She is tired of his far-fetched schemes, but she cannot resist listening.

Finally she locks the door and goes to the back of the shop. Vivi is sitting in his lap while he reads to her. It's not the first time she thinks how much her daughter is going to miss him. She refuses to speculate on what she will feel. She has more insistent worries.

With Vivi still in his lap, turning pages and talking to herself, he outlines his idea. She says it's too dangerous. He says to the contrary, it will be the safest place for her. Just as the army kept him out of a concentration camp, this will keep her out of the clutches of the mass hysteria. The more he talks, the more certain she is that of all the schemes he has hatched, this is the most ludicrous.

"It's impossible," she says when he stops speaking. "I won't do it. I can't do it. It's immoral." She drops her voice on the last word. She knows she has no right to it.

Two days later, another body surfaces in the Seine. The crowd stands around watching the salvage operation with ghoulish curiosity. Charlotte is not among them, but she hears the story later.

"A woman!" one observer shouts as they haul the body, hands and feet bound, a limestone block tied to her neck, onto the quay. Unlike the men, whose clothing had been torn but not stripped from them, the woman has been left in only her underwear. Before the gendarmes cover the body, the crowd reads the words that have been carved into her back. The corpse is bloated and its skin shriveled from the time in the water, but the words are still legible.

Collabo horizontale.

At first Charlotte refuses to believe the rumors about the woman's body, but all around her people are repeating them. Then Monsieur Grassin, her father's old friend, turns up in the shop and tells her it is not a rumor but a mistake.

"A splinter group got carried away. It was bound to happen sooner or later. Too many people going off on their own." Then she hears the phrase that will finally persuade her. "Freelancing revenge."

She shivers.

"That's why I'm here. Strictly between us, I've heard your name mentioned. I know there's no truth to it," he goes on quickly, holding her eyes as he speaks, forcing her to participate in the lie. If they don't share the lie, his conscience will not let him fulfill his promise to her father. He is part of the Resistance. He cannot save a *collabo*. "But I don't want to see any more mistakes made. It would be better if you and the child left Paris."

She starts to list the difficulties as she has for herself, but he cuts her off. He has made arrangements with a comrade. She and Vivi are to be at a café on the Place Pigalle at two the next afternoon. She is to carry a copy of Flaubert's *Salammbô*. The young man will have a volume of Louise Colet's poetry. He smiles. "The secret signs of the intellectuals." They will start for the south immediately.

She repeats that her bicycle no longer has a rear wheel. He tells her the man will have a bicycle for her. With a basket for the child. There is a farm they can reach easily before dark. "It will be dangerous," he adds. "You'd think the boches would give up now that they know they're beaten, but they are too rigid to change course. And too inhuman. Instead they become only more vicious. Like trapped animals. Nonetheless, it will be less dangerous for you and the child than remaining here."

He tells her all this quickly. He is obviously eager to get away. She follows him to the door and asks about her father. He says he has not had word for some time.

"But he would want you to leave. He did."

She thanks him and doesn't add that her father fled

the Germans. She's running from her own countrymen. She thinks of the concierge. And countrywomen.

The next morning she packs a satchel with a few articles of clothing for her and Vivi and the last of the food Julian has brought. She has not seen him since he came to the shop three days earlier with his most recent harebrained scheme, but even if she had, she would not have told him she was leaving. She cannot tell a German officer, even one who is not a real German officer, even one she has come to trust, that she's being spirited out of the city by members of the Resistance. Besides, she wants no good-byes.

The afternoon is warm with an overcast sky. Rain is in the air, but it has not yet begun to fall. She takes that as a good omen. That's what she has come to, reading her fortune in the weather. As she approaches the café, she sees two bicycles chained to a post. One has a large basket strapped behind the seat. Holding Vivi with one hand and clutching her copy of *Salammbô* ostentatiously in the other, she weaves through the outdoor tables and steps inside. Her eyes take a moment to adjust to the dim interior. Two men sit at one table, a man and a woman at another. No one is sitting alone. No one has a book. Then she spots it. A book lies on one of the empty tables. She takes a step closer to read the print on the spine. *Fleurs du midi* by

Louise Colet. Perhaps he has gone to the WC. Only she knows he has not. In a situation like this, a man does not go to the WC. She glances around the café. The waiter is watching her. He starts for the table with the book. "At least," he murmurs as he picks up the volume and begins mopping the table, "it wasn't the filthy gendarmes. These days the boches have to do their own dirty work." The rag goes around and around on the zinc surface. The spill disappears before she can tell whether it is wine or blood.

Still holding Vivi by one hand with her copy of Flaubert in the other, she makes her way out of the café and hesitates beside the bicycles. Nothing is stopping her from leaving the city on her own. Except the chain that secures both bicycles to the post.

That evening she is about to lock up the shop when Julian slips in. He tells her about the woman's body that was pulled from the Seine.

"It was a mistake," she says.

"That is cold comfort to the woman." He glances across the shop at Vivi. "Or to her children, if she had any." He reiterates his latest plan.

"All right," she says.

❦

It takes only a single word on her papers. Julian fills in *juif* in the appropriate space. He also brings a yellow star.

"Are you sure there won't be any more transports?" she asks again as she sews the star onto her dress.

"The rail lines have been bombed. Besides, they don't care about Jews anymore. They're too busy saving their own skins." He gives her a terrible smile. He has lost the one he used to bring out for special occasions. "Trying to save our own skins," he corrects himself.

❦

Despite the August heat, she puts a coat over her dress. A few days earlier, two Wehrmacht guards were assassinated in broad daylight. The only thing more dangerous than a German soldier alone on the streets these days would be a German officer harrying a woman with a star who is carrying a child. A well-meaning bystander might try to rescue her.

He manages to get his hands on a car, not a jeep but a closed automobile. They set out early through a strange kind of rain. Ashes float down, soft as snow, but darker and fouler smelling. When the Germans marched in, the French government burned its papers. Now the Allies are arriving, and the Germans are setting fire to all traces of their thousand-year Reich.

They don't speak. He is busy navigating the streets, on the lookout for barricades, trying to avoid crowds of angry or celebratory Parisians, worrying about German checkpoints. Now that she's on her way, she's sure the scheme will end in disaster.

They manage to get across the Seine but grind to a crawl near Sacré-Coeur. No automobiles clog the roads, but the crowds spilling out into the streets slow them. Finally they reach Aubervilliers, where German guards stop them. Charlotte glances down to make sure her coat is buttoned over the star and hugs Vivi to her. Julian and one of the guards talk in low voices. She doesn't hear what they say, but she can tell by the guard's salacious laugh as he waves them on that he takes her for what she is.

"I'm sorry," Julian says. "It was the only way to get through."

She doesn't answer.

As he is about to turn onto the rue Édouard Renard, he spots the barricade. Paving stones, benches, lampposts, a kiosk, tires that must have been stolen from a German truck, a bed, several mattresses, and other objects rise six feet into the air and block the width of the street. A mob spots the automobile and begins running toward it. He throws the gears into reverse and shoots back down the street they have just come up. It takes them another forty minutes to find a way through.

They smell Drancy before they see it, the stench of filth and excrement and disease. In an attempt to mitigate against the last, he has managed to get his hands on a vial of typhus vaccine at the hospital. At least she and Vivi will not have to worry about dying of natural causes.

The vast rectangle of connected barracks, each rising five or six stories high, open at one end to reveal a muddy central yard, looms into sight. From a distance, the complex doesn't look much worse than dilapidated apartment buildings for the working poor, dirty, in disrepair, but not deadly. As they get closer, she sees the barbed wire around the perimeter; closer still, the mounted machine guns. They face in, rather than out. Searchlights squat like huge ungainly animals, not illuminated now, but surely blinding when turned on at night. Crowds of men, women, and children shuffle through the muck of the open courtyard or merely stand, staring numbly at nothing. This is her safe haven.

He pulls the car to the side of the road, kills the engine, and turns to her. She feels him looking at her but goes on staring straight ahead. He reaches for her hand. She pulls it away. He moves his hand toward Vivi. She tries to squirm out of her mother's lap to get to him, but Charlotte holds her tight.

"You're right," he says. "Someone might be watching."

He climbs out of the car and comes around to the passenger side. An observer would think he was pulling her out, but his touch is more gentle than that.

The sentry at the gate watches them approach. The

dog, tethered by a short leash, pricks up its ears but doesn't growl. Perhaps it, too, senses the war is lost. When they reach the guardhouse, Julian holds out her altered papers. The guard doesn't bother to glance at them. She has opened her coat. He sees the star.

He scowls, first at her, then at Julian. He might be annoyed at having to stuff one more prisoner, two if you count Vivi, into that crowded swamp of pestilence, though it's no longer bursting at the seams as it was at the height of the roundups. Or he might be disgusted by Julian's zealousness at this late date.

Charlotte steps through the gate. She hears it clang shut behind her. She doesn't turn around. The last thing she wants is to remember him.

❦

Four days later the camp is liberated. By then she has no papers, only a number in a ledger, but not, thank heavens, on her arm. That happened only in the east, she will learn later.

The situation in the camp is as chaotic as it is on the streets. Jewish resistance fighters, French officials, Allied representatives, men and women from relief organizations brave the filth and contagion and misery to try to sort out matters and people. Prisoners churn through physical examinations, fill out questionnaires, not always truthfully, and squirm through interviews. Charlotte sits in a make-shift office with Vivi on her lap while a well-meaning but overworked American woman fires questions at her. She never says she is Jewish. She never says she is not. The woman makes her own assumptions.

Taken with the young widow who speaks flawless English and with the child, the first she has seen in the camp who is not one of the army of small scabby skeletons who break her heart but repulse her senses, she asks Charlotte if she knows anyone in the States who might be willing to sponsor her.

The name comes to her out of nowhere. She hasn't thought of him in years. Why would she? She met him only once when her father brought him home for dinner. She was at the Sorbonne then, and he was a successful American editor, older, but still young enough to flirt with her, politely, innocently, flatteringly. He'd turned her head, for a few hours.

She tells the woman of a man in New York. His name is Horace Field. The woman asks if she knows where to reach him. She says she doesn't. Then that comes back to her, too. He is an editor at a publishing house called Simon Gibbon Books.

The woman smiles. She is a voracious reader. "These days it's called Gibbon & Field."

Thirteen

Once again she didn't say she was a Jew, but she didn't say she wasn't. Like the social worker in Paris, the rabbi in Bogotá assumed.

She'd agonized over the letter, or rather over whether to answer the letter, for weeks. A reply was asking for trouble. The less connection she and Vivi had to their past, the safer they were. She'd never heard of people hunting *collabos* around the globe as they did Nazis, but exposure was always possible, and some French didn't mind eating their revenge cold. Still, didn't she owe him something? She kept remembering a photograph she'd seen in a French newspaper shortly after the Liberation. A stream of German prisoners was being marched out of the Hotel Meurice with their hands in the air. Men and women and children danced around them, grinning, jeering, spitting. She was sure she recognized Julian toward the back of the group, though she remembered enough women sitting in darkened cinemas during the Occupation, spotting husbands and sons in newsreels, to doubt her eyes. Nonetheless, according to the letter from the rabbi in Bogotá, Julian's fears about his fate in a Germany returned to what he had believed would be sanity had turned out to be warranted. German gentiles had no interest in helping a Jew. Hadn't Jews been the cause of the war from which they'd suffered so much? Jews had no desire to help a traitor, a Jew who'd murdered Jews, a fake Nazi who was worse than the real thing because he should have known better. Nonetheless, he had managed to make his way to Colombia, no thanks to the various agencies set up to help Jewish refugees. She remembered her own interview with the American woman, and her guilt ratcheted up another notch. It had taken him years, but he had finally found a country that would take him in. Now he wanted to work in a hospital, to try to atone for his sins was the way the rabbi put it, but the Jewish community in Bogotá was suspicious. South America was full of Nazis touting their anti-Nazi past. Some of them were even masquerading as Jews. Again she felt the words as an accusation. What Jew would risk going to a former Wehrmacht officer for medical treatment? The name Mengele was whispered ominously. That was why the rabbi was writing to Madame Foret. What could she tell him about Dr. Bauer's behavior in Paris? Had he persecuted Jews? Had he been responsible for Jewish deaths? I have no authority, he'd said as they'd dragged the professor out of the shop. Or had he tried to save Jewish lives? She saw the orange sitting on the counter beside the cash register, glowing as if lit from within. She saw herself huddled on the shelf in the cramped closet, her hand over Vivi's mouth.

Then suddenly, after weeks of debate, she made up her mind. She wasn't sure what persuaded her. She hadn't awakened sweat-soaked and heart-constricted from another nightmare. She hadn't even given the letter much thought that day. Her mind had been on Vivi. After months of agonizing that all of her friends had got it and she never would—another aftereffect of her early deprivations, Charlotte thought—her daughter had finally got her period. She was the last of the group, but at least she was once more part of it.

Charlotte got out of bed, went to her desk, and brought back stationery and a pen. After all the weeks of torment, the letter was surprisingly easy to write. She told the rabbi that she and her daughter owed their survival to Dr. Julian Bauer.

As she folded the sheet of stationery and put it in the

envelope, she thought again about the rabbi's assumption that she was Jewish. That was when the line came to her. She didn't know where she'd read it. Maybe she hadn't. Maybe Vivi had brought it home, another result of her religious awakening. He who saves one life saves the world. As far as she knew, no condition stipulated the life had to be of any particular denomination.

Only after she'd mailed the letter the next morning did she begin to wonder if what she'd written was true. Had he really saved their lives? Plenty of people had survived the Occupation without compromises. Maybe not as many as claimed purity once it was over, but enough. Maybe she and Vivi would have been just fine without him. Thinner, sicker, but alive. And what about the night of the raid? Had the gendarmes and the Wehrmacht soldiers been on such a rampage that they would have taken in anyone they came across? Her papers had been genuine. The forgery had come only when Julian had written *juif* on the form. But accuracy wasn't the point. She had written out of gratitude. No, that was only partly true. She had written out of love. Now that it no longer mattered, she could admit it.

☙

The day after she posted the letter to Colombia, she was rifling through her own mail on the small table in the foyer when the door to Hannah and Horace's part of the house opened and a man in a topcoat came out. Horace, in his wheelchair, lingered on the other side of the doorway. The man nodded to her as he put on his hat, then turned back to Horace. She scooped up the pile of mail and magazines and started up the stairs.

"Just think about it, old buddy," the man said.

"Nothing to think about," Horace answered.

"You know," she heard the man say as she turned the first-floor landing to climb to the second, "this isn't just about your opinion. It's bigger, much bigger."

She had to smile at that. She'd never met a would-be author who didn't believe his book would change the world. Poor Horace. The man had called him "old buddy," a term of camaraderie left from the war. And the man had come not to the office but to Horace's home. Rejecting books from strangers wasn't the sadistic pleasure writers believed, but turning down the work of an old friend was real pain.

She let herself into the apartment. Vivi was sitting at the small dining table in her usual studying position, her elbow on the table, her chin on her hand, one leg folded beneath her.

"What's cooking?" Charlotte asked. She'd picked up the phrase from Vivi. What's cooking, she and her friends asked one another. Chicken, you wanna neck? they answered. Bacon, you wanna strip? But Vivi surprised her.

She straightened from her book and held a thin sheaf of two or three papers out to Charlotte.

"A-plus," she said, in case her mother couldn't read the red mark on the top of the front page.

"Congratulations."

"Miss Connelly says I'm a born writer."

"Oh, no."

Vivi frowned. "What do you mean?"

"I'm joking, sweetheart. I spend my life working with writers. They're either horribly abused, which is not something I want for you, or horribly abusive, which is not something I want you to become. What's the essay on?"

There was a time when Vivi wouldn't have turned in a paper without running it past Charlotte, but those days were rapidly dwindling if not gone forever. Charlotte was of two minds about that. Vivi is standing on her own two intellectual feet. Hurrah for her. Vivi doesn't need me anymore. Finis for me. It was everyday proof of the old adage that a parent-child relationship is the only love affair that has to end in a breakup to turn out well.

"*The House of Mirth*. I was the only one in the class who picked up on the anti-Semitism."

Oh, no, Charlotte thought, not again.

"I don't mean they didn't know Rosedale was Jewish," Vivi went on. "Wharton calls him a Jew or says he has Jewish traits a couple of times."

"I know."

"I know *you* know, Mom, but you could tell everybody else in the class was afraid to mention it. You should have seen them when Miss Connelly read my essay. Eleanor Hathaway looked as if she wanted the floor to open up and swallow her. Her and her grandmother both."

Charlotte started to say that the book was written half a century ago, that you had to see Wharton in the context of her time, that she wished Vivi would stop looking for trouble, but caught herself. Maybe looking for trouble wasn't so dangerous if trouble was likely to find you anyway.

"You are one courageous kid, Vivienne Gabrielle Foret."

She grinned. "I take after my mother."

"Who says?"

"Me. And Aunt Hannah."

"Hannah said I'm courageous?"

"She said you must have been brave to get both of us through those years in Paris, then come here and make a whole new life. She said you must have been one tough cookie to pull that off."

Charlotte smiled. "That sounds more like it."

"She said something else."

"I'm waiting."

"She said she wishes you'd get married again."

"I bet she does."

"What do you mean?"

"Nothing. Only that married women always want to marry off unmarried women."

"She was only being nice."

"I didn't say she wasn't."

"No, but your tone did."

"You're right. I'm sorry. She was being nice."

℣

Every week the publicity department of G&F circulated to the editorial, advertising, and sales departments a folder of clippings of reviews of the house's books and interviews with their authors that had appeared in newspapers and magazines across the country. Occasionally an editor underlined a sentence or two raving about one of his or her books. Once an editor—no one knew who, but they all had their suspicions—underlined several lines that trashed someone else's book. Editors themselves were never mentioned in the reviews, but on rare occasions they won an accolade from a grateful, or toadying, writer in an interview. No one had ever called attention to any of those references until now. Charlotte sat rereading the underlined passage in an interview with the author of *The Red Trapeze*. The book wouldn't be out for months, but Henry Garrick, the one-man publicity machine, was impatient for fame.

The interviewer said she'd heard that a dozen publishing houses had turned down the book because of its frank depictions of sex and war. "Thirteen to be exact," the author corrected her. "Horace Field was the only publisher with the guts to take it on. A guy who killed hundreds of Japs singlehandedly isn't afraid of a couple of milksops in judges' robes."

She wondered who'd underlined the comment. Her guess was Bill Quarrels. She turned out to be right, though she didn't find that out until later that day. He stepped into her cubicle, folded his big body into one of the chairs on the other side of her desk, and stretched out his legs to barricade her in place.

"Did you see that interview with Garrick?"

"A waste of hard-to-get real estate. The publicity doesn't do any good if the books aren't in the stores to buy."

"Forget sales, *ma petite* French adding machine."

"I like books to earn out, if that's what you mean. As for the rest, I am five feet seven inches tall, an American citizen, and definitely not yours."

"A guy can dream. I'm talking about the part I underlined. About killing hundreds of Japs singlehandedly."

Only a man who had never witnessed bloodshed could be so in thrall to it. Then she remembered the roundups and amended the thought. Only those who had never witnessed it or were drunk on it.

"Who knew," he went on, "that poor guy in the wheelchair got there by being a hero."

Horace wasn't a poor guy any more than she fit Bill's earlier description, but she wasn't going to argue the point.

"That's not the way he tells it." As soon as the words were out she knew she should have kept her mouth shut about that, too.

He leaned forward eagerly. "He told you about it?"

"Only to deny it."

"I knew the story was too good to be true." He sprawled back in the chair. "All the same, you have to admit, like Garrick says in the interview, he had the balls to publish the book."

"Actually, he said guts."

His grin was more leer than smile. "Yeah, that's what they wrote, but you know what Garrick really said."

⚘

This time the man came to Horace's office rather than the house. And this time Horace introduced her.

It was close to six, but unlike on the night Horace had

256

taken her for a ride, the office wasn't empty. Faith Silver was on her way to the ladies' room, to put on a face, she told Charlotte as she passed her cubicle. She was meeting an agent for a drink. The assistant to the advertising manager was hunched over his typewriter, squinting through the smoke from his cigarette as he banged out catalogue copy for the next list. The cigarette, Charlotte suspected, made him feel like the reporter he hoped someday to be. Horace was in his office with the man she'd seen coming out of his part of the house a week earlier. She stopped in the doorway when she saw him.

"I'm sorry, I'll come back later."

"No, come in," Horace said. "We're finished."

"Not me," the man said as he stood. "I'm nowhere near finished. Not on this subject."

Horace introduced them.

"Would you believe," the man whose name was Art Kaplan said, "there was a time when me and this guy"—he jerked a thumb in Horace's direction—"were thick as thieves."

"Foxholes have that effect on people," Horace said.

"Only we lost touch after the war," the man went on. "Then I saw that piece about him in *Newsweek*. I wasn't sure it was the same Horace Field. I figured it probably was. The woods are full of Fields"—he paused to let the joke sink in—"but how many are named Horace? Still, I couldn't be sure until I read the other piece, the interview with that author. Then I was positive."

"He knew I was the Horace Field who'd be likely to publish a pornographic novel," Horace said to Charlotte, then turned to the man. "Which incidentally this is not."

"I knew you were the guy who killed hundreds of Japs singlehandedly."

"He's seen too many war movies," Horace said. "No one kills hundreds of Japs singlehandedly, Art. You know that."

"He can deny it all he wants," the man countered, "but the Jewish War Vets of America know the truth. That's why I'm here," he explained to Charlotte, then turned back to Horace. "This isn't just your medal, old buddy. It belongs to them. It belongs to all of us." He faced Charlotte again. "More than half a million Jews served in the war. Guess how many got the Congressional Medal."

"I have no idea."

"She's not interested, Art."

"Two," the man answered. "Two men out of more than half a million. If that's not anti-Semitism, what is?"

"Remember what I told you about hypersensitivity," Horace said to Charlotte. "This is exhibit A."

"Hypersensitivity, my foot. A general went on the record. 'A Jew getting the Congressional Medal of Honor,' he said. 'Don't make me laugh.'"

"Actually, he said a Jew or a Negro." They both turned to look at her. "Don't ask me where I read that."

"Anyway," the man went on, "it's time to start adding to the list. But we can't do it without this guy." He jerked his thumb in Horace's direction again.

"They figure," Horace said to Charlotte, "if Chips from the K-9 Corps can get a Distinguished Service Cross for taking out a German machine gun nest, why not put Field up for the Congressional Medal?" He turned to Kaplan. "But be careful, Art. When Chips met Eisenhower, he nipped Ike's hand. If you got me up there, you never know whom I might take a bite of."

"Do you believe this guy?" Kaplan asked Charlotte.

"Charlotte believes me." Horace made a show of looking at his watch. "She also wants to get out of here. As do I. Come on, Art, I'll show you where the elevator is."

"I know where the elevator is. I came up in it. But you're not getting rid of me that easily, old buddy. I shall return."

"You and MacArthur," he said as Art Kaplan left the office, then turned to Charlotte. "Don't believe everything you hear."

"That's what I tell Vivi," she reassured him, though she was beginning to believe this.

"The Jewish War Veterans of America need a live body for display purposes. Though a dead one would be even more effective. Nothing tears at the heartstrings like getting killed for your country. But barring a dead body, they'll settle for a live specimen. The point is they need a name, a face, a record they can inflate. And if he happens to be in a wheelchair, so much the better."

She didn't say anything to that.

"Besides, I don't believe in awards."

"How about the Pulitzer, or better yet the Nobel?"

"Okay, I don't believe in awards for killing people."

"Is there any choice in war?"

"There are always choices of one kind or another. You know that, Charlie."

❦

This wasn't the first time she'd witnessed one of his late-night excursions into the yard. Funny, he never made them during daylight hours. At least, she'd never observed him then. Perhaps he didn't want to be seen by her or any of the neighbors in the adjacent brownstones. Or perhaps whatever drove him around and around that walled-in scrap of land came out only under the cloak of darkness.

She stood in the window of her bedroom watching him. Down one side of the handkerchief-sized garden, freed now from its winter wrapping, beginning to green with spring, across the bottom, and up the other side. She lost sight of him as he made his way along the path closest to the house; then he came into view again, hurling himself down the side. Even from this distance, she could see that his hands gripped and spun the wheels as if he wanted to strangle them. When he hooked around the far corner, gravel sprayed. Once again, he was a hot-rodder in a wheelchair, but this was no joyride. She knew she shouldn't go on watching him. She wasn't a voyeur. She'd never watch people in the privacy of sex. Why was she spying on him in the intimacy of his suffering? But she couldn't drag herself away. She wished he'd stop. She wished she could race down the four flights and out the door and hurl herself into his path to stop him.

Halfway up one side of the garden for the fifth or sixth or tenth time, he did stop. He grabbed the wheels to halt the motion and sat looking up at the house. He was looking straight at her window.

She stepped back. The light was out in the bedroom, but the glow from the living room probably backlit her silhouette. She should have thought of that. She took another step back, but went on standing there, looking down at him.

He lifted one hand from the wheel and waved. She stepped closer to the window. He made a motion to open it. She did.

"Come on down," he called quietly. "The weather's fine. But bring a coat. April is the cruelest month."

261

She hesitated for a moment, but only a moment, then nodded and closed the window.

He was waiting for her at the back door. "Take a walk with me. I'd offer a ride, but the occasion doesn't call for celebration." He started down one side of the garden, but more slowly now, as if this really were an evening outing rather than an attempt to exorcise demons.

She fell in step beside him. "Why doesn't it call for celebration? Is *The Red Trapeze* turning out to be a problem after all?"

"Not in the way you mean."

They turned the corner. This time the gravel crunched rather than flew under his wheels. It made a similar sound beneath her shoes.

"Then how?"

They turned the other corner and started up the parallel path toward the house.

"Henry Garrick just can't stop giving interviews."

"I know. He'll have spent all the publicity before the book's even out."

"It's a bit more than that."

"The business about your having guts?"

They took another turn around the garden before he answered. "There's a line from a movie that came out right after the war. You were still in Europe. *The Best Years of Our Lives.*"

"'Why can't they leave a guy alone?'"

His head swiveled to her in the darkness. "How did you know?"

"It was still playing when I got here. Someone told me it would be a good introduction to life in America. Hannah, come to think of it."

"I meant how did you know the line I was thinking of? And don't tell me great minds work alike."

"It wasn't hard after that business in your office with the Jewish Vets of America this afternoon."

They reached the house and started away from it again. Neither of them spoke as they made another circuit, then another after that. The crunching of the gravel seemed to grow louder in the silence. He was picking up speed again. She could feel the anger radiating off him. She began to shiver. He must have noticed, because he stopped and wheeled to face her.

"Come inside. You're cold. And I need a drink."

"It's late. I don't want to bother Hannah."

"You won't. She's out. The institute, I imagine. Though it could be a meeting for some other high-minded cause." He wheeled to the door, held it open for her, and followed her inside. "Do you remember the first time we met?" he asked as he led the way down the hall.

"That's a non sequitur."

"Do you?"

"The night my father brought you home for dinner."

"You were an incorrigible little showoff. Spouting your French philosophy. Parading your knowledge of English literature. God, you were young."

"Look who's talking. The swashbuckling boy editor, out to conquer the literary world. And doing your damnedest to dazzle that callow little schoolgirl. If only your French had been better."

"I resent that. You seemed pretty dazzled to me."

He stopped in the doorway to his study, waited for her to go in, then followed her. Unlike the other rooms of the house, this one held no trace of Hannah. Books and manuscripts and magazines littered every surface. Some were piled on the floor. Nonetheless, she sensed Hannah's presence. No, not her presence, her imminence. She couldn't get over the feeling that Hannah was going to walk in at any moment.

He sat staring at her. "Ever wonder what would have happened if that schoolgirl had been just a little older?"

"Can't say that I have."

"The hell you haven't." He wheeled over to a table with a tray that held bottles, glasses, and an ice bucket and kept his back to her as he spoke. "You forget. I'm the man who took you for a joyride around the office."

She crossed the room, slipped out of her coat, and sat in

the big club chair in front of the windows that looked out into the darkened garden. She'd been in the room before, but now something about the arrangement of furniture in the alcove struck her as odd. Then it came to her. There should have been two chairs, one on either side of the small table. There was only one. On the other side of the table was space for his wheelchair. Funny she'd never noticed it before. Perhaps it was the hour, or his anger, or the tension. Funny, too, how little things brought home the awfulness.

He wheeled into the space, handed her a drink, and took a swallow of his own.

"Well, why the hell can't they?"

The return of anger in his voice startled her.

"Why can't they what?"

"Leave a guy alone. As the character in the movie says."

"The answer in the movie, if I remember correctly, is because they're fond of you."

His laugh was a bark. "Right. The Jewish War Vets of America are crazy about me. And Hannah wants only what's best for me."

"The Medal of Honor isn't exactly an insult."

"Travesty is the word you're looking for in this case."

"Maybe you're just too modest."

"Modest! Oh, Charlie, I gave you more credit."

"I don't understand why you're so angry about it."

"You really want to know? You really want to hear my war stories?"

"If you want to tell them."

"Good girl. You know the right answer. Unlike Hannah, who's been trying to pry them out of me for years. She's convinced that if I just talk to her, she can make it all better. The way she does with her patients. But you don't think you can make it all better, do you? Maybe that's because you have stories of your own."

"We were talking about you."

"Ah, yes, my war stories. But here's the problem. Which ones do I tell you? The fairy tale about my so-called heroism? Or the noir version of that little incident? How I ended up in this chair by saving my fellow man? Or the inside dope on the stupidity and evil of it all? But you have firsthand experience of that. Want to know what I was doing when I got shot? Which, incidentally, I don't think was the work of a Jap soldier at all. I think it was divine retribution. Then again, that could be hubris speaking. If there is a God, he wouldn't have had time to worry about me, or the rest of the company, or the whole damn Battle of Buna. Not when he had Iwo Jima up his sleeve. Now, planning that must have been a challenge."

He gulped down the last of his drink, wheeled across the room to the tray, refilled his glass, and wheeled back, but this time, instead of sitting at a forty-five-degree angle to her chair, he came straight at her and stopped only when their knees were almost touching. There was no affection in the gesture. He was too angry for any other emotion to leak through.

"But I digress. I was going to tell you what I was doing when I got shot."

She waited.

"I was bayonetting Japanese soldiers."

She tried not to wince. "Isn't that what you were supposed to do, what you were trained to do?"

"After they're dead?"

"I don't understand."

"I think you do. You're not as stupid as that line about being too modest made you sound. The story my old buddy Art Kaplan told today isn't entirely a lie. I killed a lot of Japanese defending that bunker, though nowhere near the number he touts. According to the officer who recommended me for the medal—that part isn't a lie either—the number was somewhere closer to fifty. That's a ballpark figure. Counting enemy bodies under the circumstances was difficult. We were a little busy. Though I suppose if you're a Japanese wife or mother or child, or the Jap himself, the exact count does make a difference."

"You were a soldier," she insisted. "You were just doing your job."

"Now where have I heard that phrase before? Oh, yes, some legal proceedings in Nuremberg."

"They felt no remorse. You do. That's the difference. That's what's torturing you."

"I see, we've moved from modesty to a normal human being's regret for taking lives. You still don't get it. I couldn't stop. Even after I'd killed them. And don't give me the line about how good Japs were at feigning death, then springing to life and throwing a grenade into a bunch of medics who were treating the wounded, theirs as well as ours. Those Japs were dead. I still couldn't stop. My brain wasn't functioning. Or rather it was working double time. Hopped up. Giddy with destruction. Drunk on devastation. High as a kite on murder."

He stopped and took a swallow of the drink. "I suppose there's a humorous side to it. Or at least ironic. I went off to war thinking I was a decent man. A child of the Enlightenment. Rational. Humane. Moral. My chosen profession proved it. A book publisher, someone who revered ideas, who valued the written word. Hell, I even published books on art and music. Civilized didn't begin to describe me. One thing I knew for sure. I was no barbarian like those sadistic SS bastards who got their kicks torturing people or the Jap devils who drove men on death marches. Well, the war had news for me. I turned out to be no better than they were. Worse in fact. They were doing it for the Führer or the Emperor or some screwed-up idea of country and honor and all that crap. I didn't even have the excuse of other GIs, the ones suffering from the Audie Murphy syndrome, who went berserk when a buddy got killed. I was doing it for fun."

"Surely not fun."

He leaned closer. "You don't think so? That's because you've never been there. Never seen the look of disbelief on a man's face when he feels the bullet go through him. Comical, really. Never cut through a line of men with one burst of a machine gun. They go down in sequence like the goddamn Rockettes. Never watched a body explode like a piñata, only instead of toys spilling out—" His mouth snapped shut. He backed the chair away and pivoted, but not before she saw the expression on his face. The features were as distorted as a Munch painting.

"History's full of writers and artists drunk on violence," she said to his back. He was at the bar again. "Homer's sacking of Troy. Dante's *Inferno*. Churches filled with paintings and sculptures of the damned writhing in hell."

"Now you sound like that French schoolgirl showing off. I bare my blackened soul, and you give me literary and artistic allusions. Those men were depicting violence, not perpetrating it."

"It was war," she said again.

"Which plenty of men managed to come through without becoming monsters."

"You're not a monster now."

"After the fact doesn't count."

"I think it does."

"That's how much you know about it." He put the glass down without refilling it and turned to face her. "Still, it was a nice try. And I'm grateful. But let's just forget it. I never should have started. Even with you. Come on, I'll take you home before I sink deeper into this trough of self-pity."

She picked up her coat and stood. "I think I can make it to the fourth floor on my own steam."

"Somewhere in my misspent youth my father gave me two pieces of advice."

"Your father went one better than Nick Carraway's."

"My father's advice wasn't as moral as Carraway's."

"What was the advice?"

"First, always see a lady to her door."

"And the second?"

"That had to do with pregnancy, and how to prevent it. He had big plans for me. That made two of us."

"From where I stand, it looks as if you've realized them," she said as she started toward the door.

"Ha!" He wheeled after her.

They stood waiting for the elevator in silence. When it

arrived, he yanked open the outer door, pushed open the cage door, and followed her in. Neither of them looked at the other as the cab rose. When it reached the fourth floor, he pushed open the doors again, and she stepped out. She turned to say good night, but he'd followed her off.

"I think this is where you thank me for a lovely evening."

Suddenly she was annoyed. "For God's sake, Horace, you're not the only one with a sore conscience."

He looked surprised, like the man he'd described who has just felt the bullet go through him.

"You're right. I apologize. Again. Who the hell am I to lecture you?"

"A friend."

He sat staring at her for what felt like a long time. "A friend?" he repeated finally.

"Aren't you?"

"Is that what you think, Charlie? Really? That we're friends?"

"More than that, of course. If it weren't for you, you and Hannah, Vivi and I wouldn't be here. We certainly wouldn't have landed on our feet so splendidly."

He was still watching her. "Oh, I get it. We have a legal relationship. Sponsor and sponsored. How about publisher and editor? Employer and employee? And let's not forget landlord and tenant."

"I'm serious."

He raised his eyebrows. "So am I. You're still missing one."

"Short of getting out the thesaurus, I think we've just about exhausted the list."

"Forget the thesaurus. All you need is imagination. No, I take that back. All you need is observation."

"Okay, I give up."

"Come on, Charlie. Don't make me drag it out of you." She looked away from him, then back.

He closed the small distance between them until they were only inches apart. "Lovers, Charlie. That's what we are. Why do you think I told you all that tonight? Why do you think that sometimes around you I begin to feel I'm not such a freak after all? Lovers. Maybe not in one sense of the word, but certainly in another. Maybe even in the truer sense of the word."

They went on staring at each other for a moment. Then he reached up to draw her to him, and she bent to meet him, and the world lurched. She gripped the arms of his chair for balance, but it was too late. She was already tumbling.

꽃

The realization didn't come to her until later that night as she lay in bed trying to dust herself off from the plunge.

He'd asked if she remembered the first time they'd met, and she'd said the question was a non sequitur. It hadn't been. It had been desperately relevant. He'd been reminding her of the lanky young man who'd come loping into the apartment on the rue Vaugirard that wet evening so many years ago, his eyes quick and inquisitive, his hair, when he took off the rain-soaked gray fedora, still full and golden, his movements easy and graceful. He'd been reminding her of the man he'd once been.

❦

Bill Quarrels didn't so much walk into her office as stride. He was vain about his height. He'd once told her, after a few drinks at a book party, how pleasurable it was to be the tallest person in the room. "I can see everyone, and everyone can see me."

He dropped a mock-up of an ad on her desk, settled into the chair on the other side of it, and stretched out his long legs to make a barricade between her and the door.

She moved the mock-up out of range of her coffee mug. "What's this?"

"What does it look like?"

"Why are you showing it to me?"

"I need a girl's take on it."

"Why, is it a romance?"

"It's a thriller, but it has a strong female character. Two, actually."

She looked at the ad. "I suspect caricature is the word you're looking for. One's a whore and one's a Madonna."

"Is there another category?"

"It looks fine to me." She handed him back the mock-up.

He took it but didn't move.

"What was going on in Horace's office this morning?"

"Don't worry, Bill. We weren't plotting against you. As far as I know your job is safe."

She'd been joking, but when she saw the relief on his face, she almost felt sorry for him. He wasn't much of an editor, though he did have a nose for a certain kind of book.

"I never thought you were."

"Good."

"I just wonder . . ." He let his voice drift off.

She made a show of going back to the catalogue copy she'd been editing when he walked in.

"I just wonder," he started again, but this time when she didn't ask what he wondered, he went on anyway. "I just wonder what you're doing with him. A guy in a wheelchair. Not even a real man. You can do better than that. If fact, if you're looking for volunteers—"

There was no intent behind the action. It was pure reflex. Before she knew it, she was standing beside her desk with the coffee mug in her hand. He didn't move his legs to let her past. She'd known he wouldn't. The mug didn't fly out of her hand. It merely tipped as she tried to step over him. The coffee went straight into his lap.

He jumped up. "Jesus, Charlotte!"

"Sorry."

He took a handkerchief from his pocket and began mopping his crotch. "It's just lucky it wasn't hot."

She agreed that it was lucky and didn't add that she would have done the same thing if it had been. That was how she knew, if she hadn't before, that she was in free fall.

❦

Bill's shout had gone out across the common area where the secretaries sat and into the closer offices. A moment later he came out saying to no one in particular and the entire multitude that Charlotte Foret was a dangerous woman.

The secretaries went on typing, smiling secretly at their keyboards, but when Charlotte left her cubicle for the women's room, one of them followed.

"Thank you," she said. "On behalf of all of us."

Charlotte held her gaze in the mirror over the sink. "It was an accident."

"I was wondering how long it would take you," Faith said when she came into Charlotte's office a little later.

"You, too?"

"Oh, bless your generous nearsighted soul. No one has made a pass at me since the party we threw when Dorothy was nominated for an Academy Award for the screenplay of *A Star Is Born*. But from him"—she tilted her head toward Bill's cubicle—"it isn't a compliment, only a kneejerk."

As the day wore on, the story spread through other departments. Only Horace had nothing to say. By five o'clock she was beginning to hope he hadn't heard, unlikely as that seemed. She was just putting a manuscript in her briefcase when he came into her office.

"Shame the coffee wasn't hot," he said.

She smiled but didn't answer.

"I've been waiting for you to do that."

She still didn't answer.

"Mind if I ask what finally drove you to it? God knows he's given you plenty of cause in the past."

She went on staring into her briefcase. She knew if she met his eyes, she'd never be able to carry off the lie. He'd know her reaction had had something to do with him.

"Just another crack," she said.

"Too salacious for my innocent ears?"

"Exactly." Now she managed to look at him.

"At the risk of flattering myself, tell it to Sweeney."

Fourteen

Later, Charlotte would wonder if the idea hadn't been
Hannah's revenge. You want to dabble in alienation of affections? I'll see you and raise you a couple of notches. But
that couldn't be. Hannah might be vindictive. Charlotte
hadn't forgotten the story her lame-duck editor friend
had told. But to be fair, Hannah couldn't have known
the unexpected consequence of her good intentions.

When Charlotte got home that evening, she wasn't
annoyed to find the note with the pile of mail on the table
in the entrance hall. She was grateful that Vivi wasn't
entirely a latchkey child, as the magazines had christened
the breed, coming home to an empty apartment every
afternoon. She even congratulated herself on having a

daughter considerate enough to leave a note. She refused to think Hannah was responsible for that.

I'm in here, the note said. An arrow pointed at the door to Hannah and Horace's part of the house. *Love, Vivi* was scrawled at the bottom.

She thought of going upstairs and calling from the apartment to tell Vivi to come home, but that seemed ungracious. She rang the Fields' bell. Vivi opened the door. Her daughter was clearly at home there.

"Love your mustache," Charlotte said.

Vivi wiped the crumbs off her upper lip and kissed her mother on both cheeks. "We made brownies."

"So I see." Charlotte brushed a last crumb off her daughter's chin.

"They're going home with you," Hannah said as she came down the stairs from the kitchen and crossed the area that served as the waiting room for her office. "I don't need the temptation. And brownies are Vivi's favorite."

"Since when?" Charlotte asked without thinking. The last she'd heard, her daughter was partial to macarons and biscotti, but then she hadn't made either in a while. By the time she got home from work, she had all she could do to get dinner on the table. Besides, what teenage palate isn't more attuned to gooey brownies than austere biscotti?

"Since Aunt Hannah taught me to make them. Want a bite?" She held the half-eaten brownie out to her mother.

"At this hour?"

"My fault," Hannah said. "But if I know Vivi, it won't ruin her dinner."

"Of course it won't," Charlotte said. If it does, she thought, I'm coming back and personally ramming the entire batch down your smug little gullet.

Hannah went upstairs to the kitchen, returned with a plate of brownies covered with waxed paper, and handed it to Vivi. "Don't forget your coat and books."

"I'll take them." Charlotte scooped up Vivi's things from one of the chairs and started for the stairs.

"Take the elevator," Hannah said.

"The stairs are fine."

"Let's take the elevator, Mom. I don't want to drop the brownies."

They took the elevator.

"I didn't know brownies were your favorite," Charlotte said as the cage climbed past the first floor. How petty could she get?

"They're not exactly my favorite. I like chocolate chips and your biscotti and macarons, too. But I didn't want to hurt her feelings when she said they were."

Charlotte unlocked the door and held it open so Vivi could carry in the plate. "You're a nice kid," she said. "Mendacious but nice."

"Mendacious?"

"Less than truthful. Also, in this case, kind. What were you doing down there besides making brownies?"

"Nothing much."

Something about the offhand way Vivi pronounced the words made Charlotte think whatever her daughter and Hannah had got up to was something very much indeed, but she wasn't going to ask a second time.

"Why don't you attack your homework. I'll call you when it's time to set the table."

Vivi didn't wait for her mother to call her. She came into the kitchen while Charlotte was sautéing the chicken and perched on the tall stool in the corner. Charlotte recognized the position. Her daughter was working up to something. She wondered what Hannah had dangled before her now. A new phonograph that played LP records? A few pearls to add to the necklace Charlotte had started for her? Pierced ears? No, Hannah would never offer something she knew Charlotte would disapprove of. She was too scrupulous for that.

"Remember the article Aunt Hannah gave me a while ago? The one by the woman in Paris who helps people who were separated during the war find one another?"

"I remember."

"Aunt Hannah offered to help me write to her."

Charlotte pretended to concentrate on turning the

chicken pieces. "Why would you want to do that?" she asked carefully.

"To find people, of course."

"There isn't anyone left to find."

"Aunt Hannah says that's what a lot of people who came out of the war think. Then they go to this woman or some other agency and find out they have some relative, even a close relative, they thought was dead."

"Vivi, sweetheart, I'm sorry, but your father did die in the war."

"I know that. I'm not talking about him."

"His parents died in the bombing of Avignon. The details about my father are murkier—he was a good socialist, and the Nazis didn't like that—but friends in Grenoble wrote to me after his funeral."

"I know that, too, but what about others?"

"Your father and I were both only children."

"You make it sound as if you and my father were the last two people on earth. There must be relatives. For all we know, all over France great-aunts and -uncles and second cousins and cousins once removed are dying to meet me."

"That's unlikely."

"But you don't know for sure. We could at least try to find out."

Charlotte turned the flame off under the skillet and faced her daughter. "I understand it isn't easy being stuck with just me and an honorific aunt and uncle downstairs, but do you really think you're going to feel an instant connection to a total stranger just because you share a few ancestors? I'd trust Hannah's affection, and Horace's, too, more than blood."

"Maybe, but I don't see how it could hurt to find out. What's so terrible about wanting a family? Pru McCabe spends a month every summer in Maine with her grandparents, the ones on her father's side, and a whole bunch of cousins and aunts and uncles. They have something she calls a compound, but she stays in the room her father grew up in, and she sails the boat he learned to sail on. She even has his old fishing rod."

"You want to learn to fish?"

"Mom!" She pounded the counter with her fist. "I'm serious."

"I know you are." She took a step toward her daughter to put her arm around her, but Vivi slid off the stool and took a step back.

"I don't understand why you won't do this. I'm not talking about grandparents in Maine or a sailboat or a fishing rod. All I'm asking for is information. Like the names of relatives and where they lived and stuff like that.

There could be people all over Europe, all over the world looking for us. But you don't want to find them."

She thought of the letter from Bogotá. "I just don't see the point."

"If I see the point, isn't that enough?"

"I can't explain."

"Try." The word came out as a sob. "For once just try."

Charlotte reached for Vivi again, but Vivi took another step back.

"You know what you are? You're a self-hating Jew."

"This has nothing to do with religion."

"Then what?"

"Maybe when you're older—"

"When I'm older!" Now she was screaming. "What is this, the sex talk we have every couple of years? It'll be too late when I'm older. I want to know now." She was no longer trying to hold back the tears. She hiccoughed. "Why won't you let me find out? Why are you so mean? Why does everything have to be a big dark secret?" She was moving toward her room. "I hate your secrets. And I hate you. I wish—" The door slammed before Charlotte could hear what her daughter wished.

She crossed the living room and went down the short hall to Vivi's room. "Vivi," she said softly to the closed door.

There was no answer.

"Vivienne."

Still no answer.

She went back to the kitchen to make sure she'd turned off all the burners, then went into the living room, sat, and looked at her watch. She'd give her an hour, half an hour, she decided, then she'd make her open the door. The only question was what she was going to say once she did.

The idea came to her fifteen minutes into her vigil. She'd help Vivi write to Simone, dredging up names, addresses, all the damaging information from her past. Vivi would be satisfied. She didn't have to know whether the letter was ever mailed.

The door down the hall opened. She'd known Vivi couldn't stay angry. But she went on sitting on the sofa. She wanted to give her time, to let her come back in her own way.

Vivi appeared in the archway to the living room and crossed to the front door. She didn't even glance at her mother as she went through.

"Where are you going?" Charlotte asked.

Vivi didn't answer. But Charlotte knew.

The phone rang a few minutes later. It was Hannah. "Vivi's here," she said.

"Thank you. I'm relieved to know where she is."

"She'd like to spend the night."

Charlotte hesitated. She wanted her daughter back. But that was about her, not Vivi.

"I think it's a good idea," Hannah went on. "That's my professional opinion, not my personal one, though the personal side loves having her here. You know that. But I think she needs time to calm down."

"Did she tell you what's wrong?"

"Only that her mother is the meanest mother in the history of womankind."

There was a silence.

"That was supposed to be a joke, Charlotte."

"She didn't say that?"

"She said something to that effect, but we both know she doesn't mean it. She worships you."

Having another woman tell you your daughter worships you was somehow disconcerting. No, having Hannah tell her that was galling.

"I'll bring down clean underwear and a blouse and her books for tomorrow. And her pajamas for tonight."

"Don't worry about pajamas. I have a drawer full of nightgowns."

"I'll bring her pajamas anyway. As long as I'm coming down."

"It's okay, Charlotte. They're flannel Mother Hubbards, not the stuff of Rita Hayworth pinups."

What kind of a mother was she that at a time like this she took note of the fact that Horace's wife slept in flannel?

❧

She was in the kitchen putting away the half-cooked chicken when the bell rang. It took her only seconds to get to the front door.

"I know I'm not the one you wanted to find here," Horace said when she opened it.

"Is Vivi all right?"

"She's fine. I came up to see if you are."

"I'm fine."

"Sure, and I can dance the Charleston. Do you want company?"

She shrugged.

"That's a warm invitation."

"I'm sorry. Come in. Would you like a drink? Or coffee? Or an uneaten dinner?"

"Thanks, but I didn't come up to be fed, watered, or entertained."

She sat on the sofa, across from his wheelchair. The tilted mirror above the mantel reflected the scene. She looked like death, her face pale, haggard, washed of makeup, her hair a Medusa's nest from running her fingers through it for the last hour. Being closer to the mirror, he was visible only from the shoulders up. Even the wheels of the chair didn't show. The reflection was a cruel joke.

"What's Vivi doing?"

"She and Hannah talked for a while. Then Hannah settled her in the guest room."

"Hannah would have made a good mother. She is making a good mother."

"She likes managing people, if that's what you mean. But you're right, she would. You want to know the funny thing about that? She was the one who didn't want to have a child before the war. I wasn't exactly campaigning for one, but she was adamant. She said it wouldn't be fair to the child if I didn't come back. Now that I have, she does want a child. Just not with me."

She didn't say anything to that.

"You want to talk about what happened with Vivi?" he went on.

She shook her head.

"You want me to get out of here?"

She shook her head again.

He sat watching her. "Listen, to paraphrase you on other subjects, you could put what I know about teenage girls on the head of a pin and still have room for a couple of million angels, but isn't this what girls her age do? Scream, cry, rebel against their mothers? And according to Hannah, canonize their fathers in the bargain."

"Vivi doesn't have a father to canonize."

"She has a fantasy father. That makes him even easier to prop up on that pedestal."

"Thanks, but it's a little more complicated than your garden-variety rebellion. She's supposed to be furious at me, but she isn't supposed to have a reason to be furious at me."

"I don't suppose you want to explain that statement." She shook her head again.

"Okay, I'm not going to pry. But I will say one thing. I doubt very much you could have done something as terrible as you seem to think."

"Maybe, but according to you, you were off the mark about your own capacity for evil. Why should your take on me be any more accurate?"

He had no answer for that.

Somewhere around six the next morning, she heard the sound of grinding gears as the elevator rose through the house. She'd been waiting for it for hours. Then she realized the noise wasn't the elevator. It was coming from a sanitation truck on the street.

Nonetheless, she got out of bed, showered, dressed, and put on makeup. The irony of primping for her daughter was not lost on her, but she remembered her reflection in the mirror the night before and had the feeling it would be easier to love, or at least forgive, a presentable mother than an unsightly harridan.

In the kitchen, she made coffee for herself and poured juice and cereal for Vivi, then sat on the tall stool, drinking coffee and waiting.

After her third mug, she looked at her watch. It was almost eight. She carried her coffee into the living room and stood at the window. A few minutes later, Vivi came out the front door. At the gate, she turned back to the house. Charlotte waited for her to look up. She knew her mother would be watching. She didn't look up. She waved toward the door. Charlotte read her lips. *Thank you.* Vivi closed the gate behind her and started down the street. Charlotte's chest grew tighter as the distance between them lengthened. She made her decision. It had nothing to do with willfully failing to mail letters.

ॐ

The scene on the sidewalk outside the school took her back. Mothers and nannies stood, chatting with one another, keeping an eye on the door for their charges. Horace had never objected when, let down by a babysitter, Charlotte had left the office early to pick up Vivi, then worked at home for the rest of the day. She stood watching the younger girls now, some holding hands, others breaking away to run to a mother or nanny, some noisy and demanding attention, others quiet and diffident. She'd give a lot to be back there. It was a cliché, but like all clichés, it contained a nugget of truth. Smaller children, smaller problems.

She should have told Vivi then. But you couldn't ask a six- or seven-year-old to keep a secret. You might as well put a mark of shame on her forehead: I'm different. I have something to hide. And she couldn't have made the announcement to the world. It would have amounted to admitting that she and Vivi were in the country under false pretenses, possibly even illegally. They might be sent back. The agency had been trying to save Jews who'd suffered at the hands of the Nazis, not gentiles who'd managed to survive with German help. She didn't think deportation was likely, but she couldn't be sure. At the least, Horace and Hannah would have felt duped. Instead of saving a victim they'd taken in an impostor.

She caught sight of Vivi coming out the door with Alice and Camilla. It took Vivi longer to spot her mother. When she did, she turned away. Charlotte crossed the sidewalk to her. She knew she had her trapped. Vivi might complain about her mother to her friends—unfair rules, arbitrary restrictions, unreasonable curfews—but she wouldn't make a scene in front of them and the whole school.

The other two girls greeted Charlotte. These were children who had learned to shake hands and say they were pleased to meet you shortly after they emerged from diapers. Vivi didn't say anything. Charlotte offered a lame explanation about being in the neighborhood for a meeting and asked the girls anodyne questions, and the girls replied in kind, then moved off. Vivi stood with her hands in the pockets of her polo coat, staring at the pavement.

"It's a beautiful day," Charlotte said. "More like the end of April than the beginning. I thought we could take a walk."

Vivi went on staring at the sidewalk.

"Or would you rather go for a soda or ice cream?"

"I'm not hungry."

"That's a first."

Vivi didn't answer.

"Fine, we'll walk." Charlotte put her arm through her daughter's and started west toward Central Park. Vivi let herself be led.

They entered the park at Engineers' Gate, and Charlotte turned them south. Lemony sunshine poured through the budding trees, dappling the pavement beneath their feet, and forsythia rioted beside the walk. Charlotte dropped her daughter's arm, but when they reached the path to the Great Lawn, she took it again to steer her in that direction. A baseball game of boys around Vivi's age was just starting at the near end of the lawn, but Vivi didn't even glance at them.

They circled the lawn once in silence. Charlotte knew better than to ask about school or anything else. Halfway through the second circuit, she suggested they sit on one of the benches.

"This is boring. Can't we just go home?"

"It's a beautiful spring day. And I want to talk to you."

Vivi flung herself onto the nearest bench with her legs stretched out in front of her, her hands still jammed in her pockets, her eyes focused on the middle distance. "I suppose I'm going to be punished for screaming and talking back to you and slamming out of the house."

"This isn't about punishment. It's about apology."

"Okay. I'm sorry. You're not the meanest mother in the world."

"My apology, not yours."

Vivi turned to look at her.

"For being so stubborn last night, and before that. For being so difficult when you wanted to go to services at a synagogue and light a menorah and all that."

"My religious awakening, you called it."

"I'm sorry. I shouldn't have been sarcastic about it."

"You were mean." Vivi went back to staring out across the lawn. "You're not the meanest mother in the world, but that wasn't fair."

"I know. And I'm sorry. But there's a reason I was adamant."

"Because religion is responsible for most of the evils throughout history," she said, mimicking her mother's voice. "The Crusades. The Inquisition. You name it, and my mother is against it."

"Do you know anyone who's in favor of the Crusades or the Inquisition? I'm sorry that was sarcastic again. In this case I had a more specific objection."

"Such as?"

"I didn't want you getting carried away about being Jewish, because you're not."

"Here we go again. We're not practicing Jews."

"We're not Jews at all."

Vivi swiveled to her again. "What?"

"I said we're not Jewish. We're Catholic. Or rather I was born and raised a Catholic. Baptism, holy communion, confirmation. All of it. I didn't go to confession to keep my friend Bette company. I went to confess. Until I was sixteen. My mother was upset when I stopped, but my father was an atheist, and he said I was old enough to make up my own mind."

"I don't understand. How did we end up pretending to be Jewish?"

"That was just an assumption the agency made when they found us in the camp."

"An assumption?"

"Things were pretty chaotic."

"I don't understand. If we're not Jewish, why didn't you just tell them?"

"It's complicated."

"In other words, more secrets."

"All right, I didn't tell them because it was a way to get out of France and to America."

"Why did you want to get out of France?"

Charlotte hesitated. In her entire editorial career, words had never been so important to her. "It was more than chaotic after the Liberation. It was dangerous. People had been through all sorts of hell. They wanted scapegoats. People to blame."

"For what?"

"For everything they'd suffered."

"I still don't understand. Why would they want to blame us? Did we do something wrong?"

Charlotte hesitated again.

"Did we?"

"Not we. But some people thought I did."

"You didn't turn in other Jews—I mean Jews—or anything like that?"

"Of course not."

"Then what did you do that people wanted to punish you for?"

"I took food we weren't entitled to."

"You mean you stole?"

"Not exactly."

"Then what?"

"I accepted food I shouldn't have."

"That doesn't sound so terrible. You said people were starving."

She took Vivi's hand out of her pocket and held it in both of hers. "I took it from a German officer."

Vivi sat up straighter. "I guess that's different." She thought about that for a moment. "Why did he give us food?"

Her daughter was no fool. She went straight to the heart of the matter.

"He used to come to the bookshop. He saw how malnourished you were."

"Then it's really my fault. If you hadn't been worried about me, you wouldn't have taken the food, right?"

"How could it be your fault? You were a baby. Once he came to the shop when I was out, and the woman who was taking care of you had been arrested, so you were left alone. He found you sick and undernourished and howling. He was a doctor. He gave you an aspirin to bring down your fever. That might not sound like much, but there were shortages of everything, and I couldn't get my hands on one. It was a terrifying time. Children were dying of pneumonia and measles and all sorts of untreated ailments. After that he started bringing milk and other food. For both of us," she went on quickly. She wanted Vivi to stop hating her, but she didn't want her to start hating herself.

Vivi leaned back against the bench again. Charlotte could see her trying to make sense of the story. "That still doesn't explain how we ended up in the camp."

"He put us there."

"So he wasn't so nice after all."

"He said it would be the safest place for us. Hiding in plain sight, he called it. He'd been doing it for years."

"What do you mean?"

"He was a Jew."

"I thought you said he was a German officer."

"He was, but he was also a Jew. According to him, the safest place for a Jew in Nazi Germany was in the military. As long as no one found out."

"This is crazy."

"That was my initial reaction. But it's all true."

"Okay, so here's this Jewish German officer, and he saved me, but why me, why us? He should have helped people who really were Jewish."

"I told you. He used to come into the bookshop. He was lonely. We were there. And he grew fond of you. It's as simple as that."

Vivi thought for a while. "It doesn't sound simple at all. It sounds crazy," she repeated.

"A lot of crazy things happen during war."

Vivi didn't say anything to that. She was still trying to make sense of the story.

Charlotte let go of her daughter's hand and put her own in her pockets. The sun was sliding toward the art deco towers of Central Park West, lengthening the shadows of the trees around the lawn. It didn't feel so much like spring anymore. She stood. "That's why I was so mean. I didn't see the point of unearthing all that history. I was afraid to get in touch with people. Some of them, like our old concierge and other friends"—she didn't see the need to mention Simone, the one name Vivi might recognize—"were pretty angry at the time. They might still have wanted to settle old scores."

Vivi went on sitting on the bench, staring up at her mother. Charlotte could tell she was still trying to make sense of the story. It was too complicated and too far-fetched. That was because she'd left out an essential part.

"I have one more question," Vivi said.

Here came the missing piece. But Charlotte wasn't going to fill it in. At least not yet.

"My father," Vivi said. "Was he Jewish?"

Charlotte felt almost giddy. She'd dodged the bullet. Then she had to smile at the question. "Sorry to disappoint you, sweetheart, but he was born and raised a Catholic, too. And hated the Church with a passion. As far as I know, you don't have a drop of Jewish blood, whatever Jewish blood is, in you."

Vivi was silent most of the way home. They were almost at the house when she spoke again. "What do I tell people?"

"You don't have to tell people anything, unless you want to. I certainly wouldn't make an announcement. My guess is if you do confide in a friend or two, the news will spread like wildfire."

"What about the camp?"

"I told you, that wasn't a lie. But I wouldn't mention the Jewish German officer. No one would believe it. About his being Jewish or putting us in the camp for safety. Just say we were rounded up by accident or for political reasons if anyone asks, but they won't. People don't ask details about things like that."

"I bet people won't believe me," Vivi said as they were climbing the stairs. "They'll think I'm just trying to pass. That's what Aunt Hannah calls it. She says it's immoral."

"You can't do anything about what people think. All you can do is tell the truth."

They reached the landing, and Vivi stood watching her mother unlock the door to the apartment.

"That's funny coming from you."

"I deserved that," Charlotte admitted.

"I'm sorry. Now I'm the mean one." She followed her mother into the apartment. "You did get us through the war and over here. Like Aunt Hannah said—"

"As Aunt Hannah said."

"As she said, you were pretty brave."

"Or one tough cookie."

Vivi was in bed when Charlotte went in to say good night.

"In case I haven't mentioned it, it's nice to have you back." She bent over to kiss her daughter, then straightened and started out of the room. When she reached the door and was about to turn out the light, Vivi spoke.

"The Jewish German officer. The one who gave us the food."

Charlotte turned back to her. "I know the one you mean."

"Is he still alive?"

"According to a rabbi in Colombia, he was a couple of months ago."

"You went looking for him?"

"The rabbi came looking for me. He wanted a character reference, if you can call it that."

Vivi thought for a moment. "Is he my father?"

"What!"

"Is he my father?"

She hadn't dodged the bullet after all. She walked back to the bed and sat on the side. "I know I lied to you, but I would never lie about something like that."

"I wouldn't blame you or anything. I know about those things. Ava Armstrong's father has a mistress."

"What does that have to do with anything?"

"It means I'm not a baby. And I wouldn't blame you," she said again. "Really. But I want to know who my father is. I have a right to know."

"You do know." Charlotte pointed to the photograph on the dresser. "That's your father. Laurent Louis Foret."

"You swear?"

"Not only do I swear. I'll do the math for you. You were born June 13, 1940. Check your birth certificate, if you don't believe me. That's one document I managed to get my hands on, though it took half a dozen letters from here to Paris. The Germans didn't march in until June 14, 1940. Do you believe me now?"

"I guess."

"You guess?"

"I believe you. It's just kind of weird, all of a sudden being someone else."

"You're not someone else. You're still you. You just aren't the religion you thought you were." She stood. "Look on the bright side. You can always convert."

Vivi made a face at her.

Charlotte was about to turn out the light when Vivi spoke again.

"Mr. Rosenblum is going to be disappointed."

"I think he'll get over it." She flipped off the light switch and started down the hall to her own room, then stopped, turned back, and stood in the doorway to Vivi's room.

"Will you do me a favor?" she asked.

"What?"

"Don't tell Hannah yet. I'd like to tell her, to tell both of them, myself."

Fifteen

The clock on her night table said a little after ten. It was an unconscionable hour to pay a visit, but the longer she procrastinated, the harder this was going to be. She picked up the telephone and dialed the Fields' number.

Horace answered. She said she knew it wasn't exactly a time to drop in, but there was something she wanted to talk to him about. "To you and Hannah both," she corrected herself. "Would it be too inconvenient if I came down now?"

"I've been looking for an excuse to put aside this manuscript for the past hour. I'm in the study. Ground floor, as if you didn't know."

He was waiting for her at the open door. "I got you here under false pretenses," he said as he led the way across the waiting room for Hannah's office to his study. "Hannah's out."

"Perhaps I should come back."

He glanced at her with raised eyebrows.

"I'm not sure I can go through this twice."

"You don't have to go through with whatever it is at all. You don't owe me any explanations. Hannah or me. Maybe you owe them to Vivi. According to Hannah you do. But not to us."

"I think I do."

"Then you might as well have a drink." He went to the bar to pour the drinks, and she took the chair in front of the bay of windows overlooking the garden.

"This is getting to be a nice habit," he said as he handed her one of the drinks and positioned his chair at a right angle to hers.

"You won't think so when you hear what I came to say."

"Let me guess. You want an increase in salary, a decrease in rent, an office with a real door, or all three."

"A bit more weighty than any of that."

"Apparently. Does this by any chance have to do with that business with Vivi last night? I admit Hannah has a tendency to rush in where, well, you know those angels and their fears, but she really did mean well."

"I know that, and I appreciate it."

"Then what?"

She took a swallow of her drink. The ice rattled in the glass as she put it down on the table. "I'm here under false pretenses."

"Aren't we all?"

"No, I mean I really am. The other night Vivi called me a self-hating Jew."

"Why do I hear the echo of Hannah's voice in that statement?"

"It doesn't matter where it came from. It's not true."

He shrugged.

"I'm not a self hating Jew. I'm a guilty gentile."

He sat looking at her for a moment. "What are you telling me? That you've been passing the wrong way, so to speak?"

She nodded. He thought about that for a moment. "I have to admit it's original. And it does explain the lack of antennae." He sat watching her for another moment. "I won't ask why you'd do something like that. It isn't as if you hadn't been through enough, or so I imagine, and had to go looking for more trouble. But if you don't mind my saying so, who cares?"

"Vivi does. I do."

"You want to be Jewish?"

"I want not to have lied to everyone. You, you and Hannah"—she corrected herself again—"sponsored me because you thought I was Jewish."

"Actually, I was surprised that you were. I never thought your father was. But that was what the agency said."

"The agency assumed. I never told them differently."

"So that's it? The big confession? Charlotte Foret has been passing as a Jew?"

"It's a bit more than that." She told him about Julian and the food. She didn't tell him the rest. She didn't have to. He'd know. "So you see," she said when she finished, "I collaborated with the enemy. I was a collaborator." Again she didn't think she had to spell out the *horizontale* part.

"Collaborator. An interesting word. But what does it mean? A while ago, I read in a manuscript I turned down that during the four years of the Occupation, your compatriots, good French citizens one and all, wrote almost a million letters to the German authorities and their French minions denouncing their friends, foes, and even relatives as Jews, socialists, communists, and various other enemies of the Reich. How many did you contribute to that number?"

"You don't have to denounce someone to be a collaborator."

"Oh, I see. You provided other kinds of information. Plans for sabotage, times and places of Resistance meetings, whereabouts of downed Allied pilots in hiding."

"You know I didn't do any of that."

"I'm trying to figure out what you did do."

"I told you. Don't make me go through it again."

"I'm just trying to understand where we draw the line. I can see that taking an orange for a child who hasn't had vitamin C since she was born was a heinous crime, but is saying thank you to a German soldier who holds the door for you a betrayal of your country or a slip of the tongue due to ingrained good manners? Is an inadvertent smile giving comfort to the enemy or an uncontrollable tick of the funny bone?"

"It was a bit more than good manners or reflexive reactions."

"I understand."

"Do you? They were rounding up people and sending them off to die."

"We've already been through that. As far as I can tell, you weren't complicit in those crimes. Listen, Charlie, I never lived under an occupation, but I can guess a little what it was like. Let someone who never showed a shred of decency to the enemy during all that time cast the first stone."

"Some people didn't."

"Bully for them."

"There was a man in my apartment house. A chain smoker. Before the war, I never saw him without a cigarette in his mouth. You could smell him coming two floors away. Under the Occupation, he looked as if he had palsy. He was that shaky from the lack of tobacco. One day I saw a German soldier on the street offer him a cigarette. That was the awful part of it. Some of them could be nice. The man kept going without even acknowledging the offer."

"That certainly advanced the war effort."

"At least he could face himself in the mirror."

"A solipsistic pleasure. Did you ever think you and I ought to spend less time gazing at ourselves and more time looking at each other?"

"That's your solution?"

"Can you think of a better one?" He wheeled closer to her. "Stand up."

"Are you throwing me out?"

"You know damn well I'm not throwing you out. I'm offering consolation. It won't be as jubilant as that night in the office, but a little human warmth never hurt."

"This isn't the time for it."

"This is exactly the time for it."

"Don't you understand what I'm telling you? I wasn't just smiling or saying thank you. I was sleeping with the enemy."

"Stand up, Charlie."

She went on sitting in the chair.

"If you don't need the solace, I do."

"Why do you need solace?"

"I just discovered the woman I love has feet of clay."

He reached over, took her hands, and tried to draw her to him, but she still didn't move. They went on sitting that way. A car cruised down the street. The radiator clanked. Outside the window, a dog barked, a man's voice apologized, and a woman said that was all right, she liked dogs.

"Come on, Charlie, don't make me beg."

She stood, turned, and settled into his lap.

He put his arms around her. "Like coming home, right?"

That was what she had been thinking. She reached an arm around his neck, but she couldn't drop the subject.

"You know what the French term for what I was is?"

"I know."

"*Collabo horizontale,*" she went on as if he hadn't spoken.

"You know what the English words are? Lonely. Vulnerable. And one more. Loving. Though I bet you couldn't admit to that last one."

She turned her head to look at him. "How did you know?"

"Because I know you."

"I don't deserve you."

"There are two ways to take that. I'm too good or I'm too repellent."

"Repellent?"

"Come on, Charlie. We've confessed our moral crimes to each other. Let's not get coy now. I do know I'm not exactly heartthrob material. But for the record, unlike Clifford Chatterley, I am not hors de combat. Not that you asked, but I just wanted to enter that into the record."

"Oh, Horace."

"Oh, Horace?"

She stroked his cheek. "It's not your physical condition. It's your marital state."

"Hannah wouldn't care. There's no love between us anymore."

"You may know me, but you don't know your wife. She'd care." Maybe not for the right reasons, she thought but didn't say. Hannah might not want something, but that didn't mean she could bear anyone else having it.

"She'd be mildly annoyed. And mostly relieved."

"I doubt it."

"She could stop feeling guilty."

"What do you mean?"

"Young Federman, the budding analyst with the headful of romantic curls. She thinks I don't know. I know. I just don't care. Hell, I'm happy for her. It's the perfect relationship. She's older, supposedly wiser, and entirely in control. Does that make you feel any better?"

"Not really," she said, and started to stand, but he went

on holding her, and she gave up and settled back in his arms. As she did, a phrase from her childhood came back to her. Two wrongs don't make a right, nannies and nuns and teachers had warned. Hannah's behavior was beside the point. Only her own concerned her, and she was the one who was cutting moral corners again. They weren't committing adultery. That particular transgression was clear-cut. Infidelity was more amorphous. That had to do with what they felt as much as what they did. Locked together in that chair, they were committing infidelity, and then some.

Sixteen

As soon as Charlotte got home from work the next evening, she called Hannah and asked if she could come
down for a few minutes. Horace had said she didn't owe
either of them any explanations, but she knew she did.
She also knew Hannah would judge her more harshly
than Horace or even Vivi. Still, she dreaded that conversation less than she had the other two. She'd been terrified
of Vivi's condemnation. She'd feared Horace's disappointment. But she didn't really care what Hannah thought of
her. Or rather she knew what Hannah thought of her.
Hannah found her lacking as a mother, unconfiding as
a friend, and insufficiently grateful. And that was before
they figured Horace into the equation.

Hannah led her through the small waiting room and into her office. Charlotte didn't think that was an accident. The house was joint territory with Horace, but the office was Hannah's realm. The blinds were closed. A lamp on the desk and another behind a leather club chair pierced the gloom but didn't illuminate it. A day bed, also leather, stood against one wall. A desk and two chairs took up the rest of the area. Shelves lined the walls. Here and there, small pre-Columbian statues stood among the books. The space was clearly a lair for Hannah. It would be a nightmare for a patient with claustrophobia.

Charlotte hesitated in the doorway. She didn't want to sit across a desk from Hannah for this conversation, but she didn't like the idea of the day bed either.

Hannah took the big leather chair with the lamp behind it. Charlotte looked around again, then moved to the day bed and perched on the edge. Now the light was in her eyes. Hannah noticed and adjusted the shade. Charlotte told herself this wasn't going to be so bad after all. Compassion was, if not Hannah's natural predisposition, then her chosen profession.

The confession Charlotte made to Hannah was a variation on the sanitized account she'd given Vivi and the self-flagellating story she'd told Horace. Hannah's reaction was different from theirs, too.

"So I'm here under false pretenses," Charlotte said when she finished, "and I owe you an apology for that."

"I'll stand in line after Vivi and six million others."

Charlotte tried not to flinch under the blow. "I suppose I deserve that."

"Suppose?"

"I deserve that."

"I'm sorry, Charlotte, but if you heard the stories of suffering I do hour after hour, day after day, if you wrestled with the long-term effects of all that horror and torment and inhumanity, you'd be all out of sympathy or even understanding, too. Or rather you'd be saving it for the victims who deserve it."

"I didn't expect sympathy or understanding. I merely thought I ought to be honest."

"I appreciate the honesty. I just can't offer exoneration in return."

"I suppose you'd like me to move."

"I would if you were alone, but Vivi doesn't need any more disruption in her life."

Charlotte stood. "Thank you."

"I'm not doing it for you. I'm doing it for Vivi," she repeated in case Charlotte hadn't understood.

"Nonetheless, I'm grateful."

Hannah stood, too. "Still, I can't imagine how you did it."

Charlotte went on staring at her. No, she thought, you can't. Because despite the hours and days you spend listening, you weren't there.

🍂

Charlotte turned out to be right about the news spreading. Vivi told her two best friends. By the end of the week, the entire school knew.

"The funny thing about it," Vivi said as they stood waiting for a traffic light to change—they were walking down Fifth Avenue to the Metropolitan Museum—"is how relieved everyone is."

"I'm not surprised."

"I'm disgusted."

Now Charlotte was surprised. Vivi was frequently disgusted by lima beans or cough medicine or the wrong haircut, but she had never used the term in response to her peers' behavior, not even when Alice had cheated on the Latin test.

"It's as if all of a sudden they don't have to feel sorry for me or tiptoe around me or anything like that. All except Aunt Hannah. Now she's the one who feels sorry for me."

"Because you're not Jewish?"

"Because of my identity crisis. She says it's hard

enough figuring out who you are at my age, but having the rug pulled out from under you while you're trying to do it doesn't help. She says she doesn't blame you, but you should have thought of me."

"She does blame me, and she's right to."

The light changed, and they started walking again.

"No, she isn't. I'm glad I was Jewish for a while. I mean, I was angry at you at first. For all the secrets. And then it was funny finding out I wasn't who I thought I was."

"I keep telling you, you're still the same person."

"You know what I mean. But I think I learned a lesson, no matter what Aunt Hannah says."

"By thinking you were Jewish?"

"By being Jewish for a while and then not being Jewish. I think the whole world ought to go through that. Same about being Negro. Though I suppose that would be harder. But I bet if they did, there wouldn't be any more prejudice in the world. No Nazis, no Ku Klux Klan, and no Eleanor's grandmother."

"Just one big happy family."

"Don't make fun of me."

They were at the foot of the wide steps leading up to the museum, and Charlotte stopped and put her arm around her daughter's shoulders.

"That's the last thing I was doing. Or maybe I was teasing because I didn't want to preen with pride. No, pride is the wrong word. That implies I had something to do with it. Awe is *le mot juste*. I'm in awe of your compassion and decency and intelligence."

"You mean I have a moral compass like my dad?"

"The very same."

They climbed the steps. When they reached the top, Vivi spoke again. "You can be proud. You did have something to do with it."

"Thanks. I hope so. But I can't hold a candle to you and your father."

Now Vivi reached an arm around her mother's shoulders. That was how tall she was getting. "Maybe, but you're all I've got.

"Incidentally," she went on as they crossed the soaring entrance hall, "I told Mr. Rosenblum I wasn't Jewish. I know you said I didn't have to go around making public announcements, but I thought I ought to tell him. I mean, after the business with the menorah and everything."

"What did he say?"

"That nobody's perfect."

Charlotte smiled and shook her head. "I always thought he was a dour old man. But you bring out the comedian in him."

"You just have to know how to talk to people, Mom."
"I'll keep that in mind."

※

A week later, Charlotte went to the hardware store to buy light bulbs. She'd considered going over to Lexington Avenue for them. Vivi brought out the comedian in Mr. Rosenblum, but she didn't think he'd find her a source of humor. He hadn't before, and he certainly wouldn't now. But the store on Madison was more convenient. And she'd have to face him eventually. Nonetheless, she found herself skulking in the aisles and waiting until he went off to help another customer before going to the cash register. But it was no good. He caught up with her on her way out. It was the first really warm day of spring, and he'd shed his sweater, but his shirtsleeves were buttoned tightly around his wrists.

"So, some news Miss Vivienne brought."

"I'm sorry, Mr. Rosenblum."

"What's to be sorry about? You were taking up room in a camp that maybe somebody else wanted?"

"It was a mistake. We shouldn't have been there."

"Who should?"

"I mean it was a mistake, and I used it to save us."

His worn face creased in that terrible too-white smile.

"For six million, being Jewish was a curse. What's so terrible if for Mrs. Foret and her daughter it's a blessing?"

"Thank you, Mr. Rosenblum."

"What're you thanking me for? Those light bulbs you found on your own. But I tell you one thing, that's one nice daughter you're raising."

"Thank you," she said again.

"You noticed I didn't say one nice daughter you got. I said one nice daughter you're raising."

"If I stand here another minute, I'm going to start to cry."

"So nu, don't stand here. Go home. You got supper to make. I got work to do."

She didn't know she was going to do it. Later she'd be embarrassed by it. She leaned over and kissed him on the cheek.

When she pulled away, he lifted his hand and touched his face where she'd put her lips. "Like daughter, like mother," he said.

Seventeen

This time the letter came to the apartment rather than the office. This time she didn't toss it in the wastebasket. But she didn't open it immediately. She waited until Vivi was asleep. She'd told her daughter the story, but she didn't want to add any new chapters to it. At least not yet.

She sat on the sofa in the living room, staring at the envelope for longer than she should have. She had nothing to fear. They were safe here in America. Vivi knew the truth. So why was she afraid to open it?

She turned over the envelope to read the back flap. He was still in Bogotá. So he was safe, too. There was nothing more she could do for him, nothing more he could ask of her.

She pried open the flap of the envelope, took out the

single sheet of stationery, and unfolded it. His handwriting was small, regular, and neat. She thought of the prescriptions she'd got from doctors here and had to smile. That was a good sign. She could smile about him now.

Dearest Charlotte,

I have written this letter many times in my mind, but now the time has come to commit it to paper. My writing it cannot affect you at this point, but it is important to me. Please forgive any infelicities. My English is even weaker than my French, but you are American now so I am writing with a dictionary at hand. Please also forgive me for writing to you a third time. Perhaps you did not get the first letter from Germany or the second from Bogotá. Or perhaps you chose not to answer them, but I cannot believe that. You replied to Rabbi de Silva. I am grateful. Those first letters asked a favor of you. I needed someone to vouch for me, and I am grateful to you for doing so to Rabbi de Silva. This one is to unburden myself.

After the war, others were not as forgiving of a Jew masquerading as a Wehrmacht officer as you were. A rabbi in Berlin whom

I went to for help emigrating called me a killer. An uncle whom I wrote to in Palestine answered that it would have been better if I had died in a concentration camp. Who can blame them? How could I expect them to forgive me if I could not forgive myself?

I carry an image in my mind from those days in Paris. I carry many images. Some are happy, or at least not raw with pain. The first time I walked into the shop and saw you sitting with a book, bathed in light, like a girl in a Dutch genre painting. The sun was behind me, but in your eyes. You were about to say *bon soir*. Then I took a step closer, and you saw my uniform. The disgust with which you swallowed the welcome went through me like a bullet. There are other images as well. You standing at the door of the shop in the predawn darkness, your hair in disarray, your face soft with love. Yes, love, though you denied it always. And Vivi, of course Vivi. I see her looking up at me with those big trusting eyes. I remember her crawling into my lap and nestling there as I read. These are the images I carry like talismans against the shame. But there is one image that is equally sharp, and that is not a talisman but an indictment. I see the gendarmes dragging the professor out of the shop while I stand by and tell you I can do nothing. The other images are of you and Vivi, but that is my self-portrait. Warts and all, the saying goes. Warts are all in that portrait.

But here is the other side of the ugly picture, and it is why I am writing to you. In my worst moments, and there have been many, I think of you and Vivi, not only of the images of love, but of the knowledge that perhaps in some way I saved both of you from the worst. It is not, as the axiom goes, saving the world, but it is better than standing by while an innocent man is dragged off to prison. You are my only bulwark against the knowledge I did that.

Thank you for what you gave me during that terrible time and for the solace the memory of you has given me since. Without it, I would not have survived this long.

All my love,
Julian

She sat for a long time with the letter in her lap. She had images, too. For years she'd fought them, but now they came flooding back. Her conscience ached again, not for collaborating with the enemy, not for giving in to Julian, but for withholding from him, and from herself. She had refused to admit the truth because of the lies she had to tell the world.

She stood, finally, carried the letter to her bedroom, and put it in her night-table drawer. She wanted it close at hand, though she had no idea why.

❦

The thought followed her around for the next several days. He hadn't asked for an answer to his letter. If anything, the tone was elegiac. I am thanking you. The chapter is closed. But the more she thought about that time, the more vivid he became in her memory. She saw him standing in the shop, holding a book in one hand while the fingers of his other tied an imaginary surgical knot. She heard him singing to Vivi in that sad voice that was always just a little flat. She felt his hands on her body and her own on his, the two of them crazy with hunger and loneliness and desperation. Or was she merely summoning those memories as a defense against Horace? She was an immoral woman, careening from collaboration to

infidelity and back again. In any event, she had no intention of answering the letter. But then why did she keep
thinking about it?

A week later, another letter arrived from Bogotá. This
one was from Rabbi de Silva again. He regretted to in-
form her of the death of Dr. Julian Bauer.

She stood in the living room staring at the words. Of
course. How had she been so stupid? The elegiac tone.
The statement that he had written the letter often in his
head, but now the time had come to commit it to paper.
The last line about her providing the solace for him to
survive this long. She'd read a love letter. He'd written a
suicide note.

Nonetheless, she had to be sure. She wrote back to
Rabbi de Silva. Had Dr. Bauer been ill? Had there been
an accident? Surely he could give her more information.

He could not, the next letter said. Now she was sure.

For some reason she became obsessed with how he had
done it. The rabbi's letters had been on the stationery of
a synagogue. There was a telephone number as well as an
address. One morning after Vivi left the house, Charlotte
went to the phone on the table in the living room and
dialed the international operator. It took some time to get
through, but finally she heard the phone ringing on the
other end. She wasn't sure how long that went on before
it occurred to her that today was Saturday. Apparently

Vivi had taught her more than she'd realized. No one in a synagogue would answer the phone on the Sabbath.

She called again when Vivi went out on Sunday but had no more success. On Monday, she left the office early. Bogotá was an hour behind New York City. Vivi had a rehearsal for the spring play—they were putting on *Our Town*—and wouldn't be home until after five. She had plenty of time. She dialed the international operator again.

When she finally reached the rabbi's office, she had trouble getting through to him. The rabbi, his secretary explained, was a busy man. In her rusty Spanish, Charlotte said she realized that but asked the woman to tell him that a friend of Dr. Julian Bauer's was calling. The secretary told her to hold on for a moment. Charlotte knew from the change in the secretary's voice that her instinct had been correct. A woman who worked for a rabbi would be accustomed to dealing with death. A woman with religious scruples, not to mention an old-fashioned sense of social shame, would have more trouble dealing with suicide.

The rabbi came on the line. His English was better than her Spanish.

She asked again if Dr. Bauer had been ill.

He had not.

She asked if there had been an accident.

There had not.

"Then what was the cause of death?"

"All I can tell you, Mrs. Foret, is that Dr. Bauer died peacefully. He was not a violent man, his tour of duty in the German army notwithstanding."

"You mean he didn't shoot himself?"

"Dr. Bauer died peacefully," the rabbi repeated.

"Did he take pills? Did he get in a bathtub and cut his wrists?" She was shouting now. "How did he do it?"

"Dr. Bauer found the peace he was looking for," the rabbi said, then the phone went dead.

The images haunted her. She saw him sitting on the side of a bed in a lonely room, counting out the pills, lining them up on the night table. She saw him go into a bathroom and return with a glass of water. Did he swallow handfuls or take them one by one? One by one, she thought. He was—correction, had been—a methodical man. She saw him taking off his shoes, stretching out his long thin body on the narrow bed, waiting for the peace the rabbi insisted he'd found.

Or had he chosen a more natural method? He could have gone to another town, Cartagena or some other place on the Caribbean or Pacific coast. She saw him checking in to a hotel. He'd carry a suitcase in order not to arouse suspicions. At sunset or sunrise, depending which way the coast faced—she had a feeling he would want to walk into the sun—he would go down to the beach. He'd be wearing a robe over his swimsuit. He was a proper as well as a deliberate man. She saw him taking off the robe, folding it, laying it carefully on the sand beside his shoes. His body would be older now and probably thinner than the one she'd known so intimately. He would turn and begin to walk into the long rays of the rising or setting sun, just as he'd come walking out of them the first time she'd seen him.

She began to cry, finally. The reaction was a relief but not an abandonment. At a little before five o'clock, she went into the bathroom, washed her face, and bathed her eyes. She did not want Vivi asking what was wrong. She had spent her cache of explanations.

❦

One more envelope arrived from Bogotá. This one was oversized. She opened it carefully and warily. Inside was a large parchment document. She took it out and sat staring at it. The words *Medical Faculty of the University of Heidelberg* ran across the top. *Julian Hans Bauer* was written at the bottom. She ran her fingers over the elaborately scrolled name. It was ludicrous but somehow logical that she had never known his middle name.

There was a piece of stationery in the envelope as well. It was from the same synagogue.

329

Dear Mrs. Foret,

Dr. Bauer had few effects. He left his books
to our synagogue. He asked that I forward
his medical degree to you. He wanted you
to remember him as a man who wished to
first do no harm.

> Yours truly,
> Rabbi Sandor de Silva

This time she didn't cry. The pain was numbing.

She'd thought the images would fade as the days passed,
but at odd moments—reading the paper on the bus, editing
a manuscript in the office, sitting across the table from Vivi
at dinner—she saw him lying on that narrow bed waiting
for death or walking into the ocean to meet it. And just as
she wondered how he had done it, though it hardly mattered, she tried to decipher what she felt. Grief certainly.
Guilt as well? Anger at her own hardheartedness? It didn't
seem fair that he had saved her and Vivi from the worst
of the Occupation but hadn't been able to salvage himself.
Reason assured her nothing she could have done would have
made a difference. Her conscience told her another story.

She wouldn't be bothering anyone. Horace had driven to
Connecticut to spend the weekend working on a manuscript with one of his writers. Hannah was at a conference
in Boston, with young Federman, Charlotte was willing
to bet. And when she'd moved into the apartment, both
of them had told her to feel free to use the garden at any
time. She rarely had, but on this Friday night, walking
from empty room to empty room—Vivi was off at another slumber party—finding the ghost of Julian lurking
in every shadow, she felt the need to escape. She pulled on
a sweater, though the May night was mild, poured herself
a glass of wine, and, because she didn't want to spill it,
took the elevator down to the ground floor.

The scent of lilacs assaulted her as soon as she stepped
into the yard, except she wasn't in the yard but back in
the Luxembourg Gardens. Let me help you, he'd said,
and she'd slapped away his hand. Where had she got the
nerve to strike a Wehrmacht officer? Even then she must
have known whom she was dealing with. That was why
she'd got on her bike and pedaled away as if all hell were
after her.

She made her way down the path and sat in one of
the wrought-iron chairs arranged around a small table.
The aroma of lilacs was even stronger here, part fragrant
memory, part olfactory punishment. On either side of
the yard, lighted windows made blank crossword puzzles

of the neighboring brownstones. Farther afield, the illuminated windows of the taller apartment houses on Fifth and Park Avenues flamed in the darkness. The sound of passing cars hummed quietly in the distance. Occasionally a horn shattered the quiet.

She didn't know how long she'd been sitting there when a light went on in the study and a beam spilled through the bay windows and down the path to her feet. She was only a shadow in the darkness, but if someone were looking out the window, the shadow would probably be visible.

The door to the garden opened, and Horace came out. He looked around as if to get his bearings, then started down the path to the wrought-iron table and chairs.

"I thought you were away for the weekend. Cutting and slashing Bullock's new biography."

"I was supposed to be, but the atmosphere was not conducive to editorial work. This afternoon when Bullock went out for his daily constitutional, Mrs. Bullock took the opportunity to go through his desk. She said she was looking for a stamp. What she found was bills and receipts for restaurants where she'd never eaten, hotel rooms where she'd never slept, and a Tiffany bauble she'd never got a chance to wear because it was dangling from some other woman's neck, which, she was shouting as I arrived, she had every intention of wringing. I said

I'd come back another time. Want company, or is this a solitary commune with nature?"

"I'm not particularly pleasant to be with."

"My favorite kind of companion."

They sat in silence for a while. A light went off in the house next door. A cat appeared on the wall between the yards, prowled along it, then disappeared into the night.

"Want to talk about it?" he asked finally.

"No."

"I didn't think so. Okay, we'll just sit here and smell the lilacs."

She felt the tears start again and turned her face away, but she was too late.

"Vivi again?"

"Vivi's fine. It appears I'm even forgiven."

"Then we should be celebrating. Another joyride around the premises. But you don't appear to be much in the mood for that. In fact, you look as if you just lost your best friend."

She didn't say anything to that for a while. "Not best, but a friend," she admitted finally.

"I'm sorry."

"He committed suicide."

"By *he* I assume you mean the German doctor you knew in Paris."

"My God, Horace. You're a publisher. Your stock-in-trade is words. When did you start speaking in euphemisms? The German doctor I *knew*? And he wasn't a doctor. Or rather he was a doctor. But he was also an officer in the German army."

"That's it, Charlie. Keep up the self-flagellation. All right, you did more than know him, unless we're speaking in the biblical sense. And he wasn't just a doctor. He was an officer in Hitler's army. For all I know, he was a Nazi. An SS. A Gestapo."

"He wasn't any of those things," she shouted, then stopped. "Why are you deliberately provoking me?"

"Because I'm tired of your either running away or strutting around in your hair shirt, which amount to the same thing. For years you couldn't admit that anything had happened. Now all of a sudden you're responsible for the whole damn Occupation."

"I collaborated with it."

"We've been through all that. Tell me one thing. Would you have admitted you loved him if he weren't a German officer?"

"Of course."

"Really? You wouldn't have felt it was a betrayal of your dead husband? Or of Vivi? You wouldn't have thought you didn't have a right to love someone or to be loved because you were alive, your poor young husband was dead, and all around you people were suffering while you were managing to survive?"

"Now you sound like Hannah."

"No one can be wrong all the time."

"That was unkind."

"Come on, Charlie, we both know how you feel about Hannah. How we both feel about Hannah. But I'll tell you what is unkind. Throwing away life with both hands. It's worse than unkind. It's stupid and reckless and wasteful. You're sitting out here wallowing in sorrow for that poor man, who I admit deserves it, and pity for yourself, who doesn't, because you're damn lucky. You're sitting out here on a soft May night with a man who loves you. That's a gift, Charlie. Take it!"

She thought about that for a moment. "I don't know how to."

"I have some idea."

"I've already told you. I may dislike Hannah, but I don't want to start disliking myself."

"Let me tell you about Hannah and me. It has nothing to do with young Federman. He's an effect, not a cause. It doesn't even have to do with the war. It has to do with the fact that we misled each other. Or maybe we misled ourselves. The match was so appropriate, the surface so shiny, that neither of us bothered to lift the hood of this perfect pairing and look beneath it until it was too late. And now all that's left is the surface, tarnished with wear and tear and mutual antipathy. So tell me, whom would we be hurting?"

She didn't answer.

"All right, I'll put it another way. Whom did you hurt with your German officer?"

She still didn't answer.

"He didn't take his life because of you. From what you've told me, from what I can imagine, he took it because he was a Jew serving a regime determined to destroy Jews. I'm not blaming him. I'm in no position to make moral judgments. But did it ever occur to you that he might have been in worse shape without you?"

She turned to him in surprise. "That's what he said in his letter."

"I rest my case. Don't throw it away, Charlie. If not for your sake, then for mine."

His face was coming closer now, his eyes violet in the darkness. Again she met him halfway.

Neither of them spoke going up in the elevator. She was too frightened. She couldn't even look at him. Her eyes focused straight ahead, watching the floors as they passed. She'd told him his condition didn't offend her. That was true when she was sitting across from him or even in his lap. But this would be . . . she didn't know what this would be. That was the problem. Suddenly she remembered something. The conversation she'd over-heard the night Vivi had lighted the menorah. He and Hannah had been arguing, and their voices had carried into the foyer.

"You may not be stupid," Horace had shouted, "but you're lousy at hiding disgust."

"I was trying to help," Hannah had replied.

Was she supposed to help? Or not help? And what did that mean? Was she supposed to avert her eyes? She'd loved looking at Laurent. Julian, too, though she'd never been able to admit it, even to herself. Was she supposed to pretend there was nothing out of the ordinary?

She was still staring straight ahead at the passing floors when she felt him take her hand.

"It's going to be all right, Charlie. I promise."

The elevator cab arrived at the fourth floor. He pushed open the doors. She stepped off. He followed her.

"There is one more problem," she said as he closed the door to her apartment behind them. "I realize this isn't exactly romantic—"

"Don't worry about romance. I've got enough for two. And if you're worried about precautions, remember my father's advice. I come prepared. You see the effect you have on me. I'm a kid again."

He followed her across the living room and down the hall to her bedroom, then closed the door behind them.

She was standing beside the bed. "I'm not sure what to do," she admitted.

He wheeled over to her. "Just leave everything to me."

He reached up and began unbuttoning her blouse. She started to help him, but he pushed her hands aside. "I don't need help. I've been preparing for this for a long time." He slid the blouse off her shoulders. She shivered.

"Cold?"

"That's not from the cold."

His hands moved around to her back. He unhooked her bra. She closed her eyes. Then suddenly his hands were gone. She opened her eyes. He was staring at her.

"I'm memorizing you," he said, "in case you disappear."

She leaned over, took his hands, and put them on her breasts. "I'm not going anywhere," she murmured against his mouth.

Together they undid his tie and got him out of his jacket and shirt. She wasn't helping. She was impatient.

"Now comes the acrobatic part." He swung himself out of the chair and onto the bed. He was still watching her. "Thank you," he said.

"For what?"

"For not averting your eyes. For not struggling to hide your distaste."

She climbed on top of him, bent until their faces were almost touching, and moved her body against his. "Does this feel like distaste?"

Somehow they maneuvered out of the rest of their clothes, a joint effort of mutual unbuttoning and un-zipping and tugging. When they were both naked, she climbed on top of him again. Then she was falling and he was rising, and they both forgot the awkwardness and the tragedy and the heartbreak of his condition, and then his condition itself, moving slowly at first, then faster, then more slowly until she thought she would howl with the pleasure, and finally, lost to herself, lost to him, her back arching in a frenzy she couldn't control, his body bucking beneath her, she did howl. The shudder went through her like an earthquake. The aftershocks shook him a moment later.

He spent the night, though neither of them slept much. It wasn't the narrow bed. It was the waking each other up, once to make love again, several times after that merely to touch in the darkness as if to make sure the other was there, then just before dawn to make love a third time.

The sun was coming up as she walked him to the elevator.

"I should be consumed with guilt," she said. He stopped to look at her. "But I'm not."

"I'm going to send out a press release. 'For the first time in recent memory, Charlotte Foret is not consumed with guilt.'"

"But I have a feeling I will be."

He shook his head. "What am I going to do about you? More to the point, what are we going to do about us?"

"Nothing."

"Don't say that."

She leaned down to kiss him good-bye. "Aren't you supposed to be the one who isn't afraid of the truth?"

Eighteen

∽◦∾

At first she refused to go. "I can't leave Vivi."

"Take Vivi with you. School will be out. It'll be the best thing for her."

"I can't afford it."

"The house is paying your expenses. I think we can swing a little extra for Vivi."

"What will she do while I'm working?"

"Do I have to give you a guidebook? Notre Dame. The Eiffel Tower. The Louvre."

"But she'll be on her own. She's only fifteen."

"She's a New York City kid. She knows how to navigate a metropolis. And what fifteen-year-old wouldn't kill for a few hours a day on her own in Paris? But if you're really worried, I know people there. So does Hannah. I bet you do, too."

She sat looking at him across her desk. "Isn't that the problem?"

"Times have changed. It's been ten years since the end of the war. All is forgiven, thanks to the political acumen of your namesake Charlie de Gaulle."

"It would be nice to think so, but I'm not so sure."

"Go, Charlie. Vivi will see Paris, G&F will end up with some good foreign books for next year, and you'll lay some demons to rest."

"I doubt that."

"Try."

॰

They sailed on the SS *Independence*. They could have flown—everyone was saying that in a few years no one would spend six days crossing the Atlantic when they could do it in less than one—but she needed the time at sea. It would take longer than a few hours to get ready to face her old persona.

Some of Vivi's friends came down to the ship to see her off. They crowded the cramped stateroom, erupting in giggles and excitement and, from those who had already been to Europe, worldly advice.

Charlotte and Horace left them to it and went up on

deck. The July sun was strong, but the salt breeze took the sizzle out of it. In the distance, the skyscrapers of the city pulsated in the heat. She found her dark glasses in her handbag and slipped them on. He took a pair from the breast pocket of his jacket.

"I still think I'm making a mistake," she said. "With all due respect to de Gaulle's political acumen, people aren't as forgiving as you make them out."

"There's only one person who can't forgive," he said, still looking off at the skyline.

"Look who's talking."

He turned to her, but his eyes were hidden behind the dark glasses. "As I keep saying, we're two of a kind. That's why we deserve each other." He looked back at the skyline. "You are coming back, aren't you?"

"Where else would I go?"

He shrugged. "You're not as American as you pretend. You can still roll a wicked *r* when it comes in handy. Paris might turn out to be home after all."

"I'm coming back."

"Then what?"

"Then nothing. A few weeks in France aren't going to change anything here."

"I keep telling you, Hannah would be glad to get rid of me. She can marry Federman, or her next trainee."

"I still doubt that, but to tell the truth, it's not Hannah

anymore. It turns out I'm too selfish for that kind of sacrifice."

"Vivi?"

"She's forgiven me a lot, but I don't think she'd forgive me this. She adores Hannah. And kids are judgmental about things like marriage."

He turned to her and took off his dark glasses. His eyes were ice blue in the hot afternoon. "She isn't going to be a kid forever. Not even for much longer."

"She still wouldn't forgive me."

"I'm not so sure. She worries about you."

"I know, and I wish she didn't."

"Maybe she wouldn't if she thought you were happier." He smiled, the wicked grin she remembered from the photograph taken before the war. "Sorry, Charlie, but you walked straight into that."

The first warning to go ashore sounded. He stopped smiling. "Mind if I say something you're not going to like?"

"Yes, but that won't stop you."

"It wasn't Hannah. And it isn't Vivi. They're excuses. It's you. Did you ever think that it might have been better if you'd stayed in Paris? Maybe you would have had your head shaved and suffered the rest of the ugliness." He read the horror in her face. "I'm not making light of how awful it would have been. But at least you could have hated them for it. Now the only person you have to hate is yourself. You got off scot-free, and you can't forgive yourself for that."

She stood looking at him. "That's quite a bon voyage speech."

"I figure you're a big girl."

"Or as Hannah says, a tough cookie."

"Exactly. You can take it."

The second warning to go ashore sounded. He started toward the gangway, then stopped again. A few departing visitors piled up in a logjam behind them. A man shot them a dirty look, then noticed the wheelchair and murmured an apology. Horace wheeled over to the port deck, away from the starboard side where passengers were already positioning themselves to wave good-bye. She followed.

"I just changed my mind," he said.

"You don't think I should go? Or you don't want me to come back?"

"I don't want you to bury the demons in Paris. I think you should go looking for them. And your German officer. Goddamn it, I can't keep calling him that. What was his name?"

"Julian." She remembered the medical degree he'd left her. "Julian Hans Bauer."

"Go looking for Julian Hans Bauer. And yourself. Remember the moments of joy, though I bet those damn near killed you. Remember what you gave him. More to the point, think about what you withheld. You want to flagellate yourself about something, try that."

"Are you finished?"

"For the moment."

He started toward the gangway again. She fell into step beside him.

"Then come home," he went on. "I'll still be here."

They arrived at the gangway, and the seaman standing beside it reached out to position the chair to go down it.

"I can manage," Horace snapped, then looked at her and shook his head. "As I keep saying, two of a kind." He turned to the seaman. "But thanks all the same."

He started down the gangway. "Whatever you do," he called back, "don't fall for some smooth-talking Gauloise-smoking French lothario."

"Not much chance of that," she said, though she didn't know if he heard her.

She stood watching as he disappeared in the crush of people leaving the ship. A moment later she caught sight of him at the bottom of the gangway, then lost him again.

She made her way along the deck toward the bow of the ship and took a position at the rail. When she looked down at the pier, he was across from her. He wasn't smiling or waving; he was just sitting there watching her.

Suddenly Vivi was at her side with several rolls of colored streamers. She began hurling them to her friends on the pier. All around them, passengers were tossing paper ribbons, and people on shore were trying to catch them, and the summer afternoon vibrated with a rainbow of tangled lines. Charlotte took a roll from Vivi, raised it above her head, and flung. It streaked across the water and down to the pier, where Horace reached out a long powerful arm and caught it.

The horn sounded again, and the tugs began nudging the ship out of the slip. She and Horace went on holding either end as the distance between the deck and the pier widened. Gradually, one after another, the ribbons around them were snapping. She felt the streamer that stretched between them break. She went on holding one end. Across from her on the pier, he was holding the other.

A Note on Sources and Acknowledgments

Though memoirs by and books about the women who fought in the Resistance or spied for the Allies during World War II abound, their sisters who were not blessed, or cursed, with their unholy courage have attracted less attention. It is those legions of more ordinary women who aroused my curiosity and inspired this novel. Three books proved invaluable in researching it. *When Paris Went Dark: The City of Light Under German Occupation, 1940–1944* by Ronald C. Rosbottom is an exhaustively researched and wonderfully lively account of day-to-day existence under the Occupation, including a perceptive consideration of the nuances of collaboration. Shortly after starting the research for this novel, I came across, thanks to the open stacks of the New York Society Library, a volume called

Hitler's Jewish Soldiers and its companion, *Lives of Hitler's Jewish Soldiers*, both by Bryan Mark Rigg. At first I thought the titles must be a play on words or a provocation, especially since most of the historians I spoke to had never heard of the thousands of Jews and part-Jews who served in the Third Reich's military. The stories of those men expanded and deepened what I had originally conceived as a novel about identity and survivor guilt.

In addition to those books and countless histories of the Occupation, many diaries kept by girls and young women painted more vivid and personal pictures of what it was like for Jews and gentiles alike to live under the German thumb. To mention only a few of the best: *Diary in Duo* by Benoîte and Flora Groult; *The Journal of Hélène Berr*; *Rue Ordener, Rue Labat* by Sarah Kofman; *Maman, What Are We Called Now?* by Jacqueline Mesnil-Amar; and one by a woman who did serve in the Resistance and paid mightily for it, *Résistance: A Woman's Journal of Struggle and Defiance in Occupied France* by Agnès Humbert.

In addition to these books and memoirs, many people provided professional and personal support. I am grateful to the staff of the New York Society Library for their expert help and unfailing good humor, and for the Frederick Lewis Allen Room of the New York Public Library, which provides a safe haven for research and writing. I am also indebted to Judy Link, JoAnn Kay, André Bernard, Ed

Gallagher, and, for encouragement above and beyond the call of duty, Laurie Blackburn. Richard Snow and Fred Allen once again kept the literary and historical egg off my face. Liza Bennett contributed more to this book than she knows. My thanks also to Emma Sweeney, ace agent and good friend, and to Margaret Sutherland Brown and Hannah Brattesani at the Emma Sweeney Agency, to the entire team at St. Martin's Press, and especially to Elisabeth Dyssegaard, who is not only a superb editor but a gracious and generous woman.

A BOOKSHOP IN PARIS
by Ellen Feldman

- An Interview with Ellen Feldman
- Books Set in Bookshops
- Reading Group Questions

 An Interview with Ellen Feldman

Many of your previous books dealt with real characters, such as Anne Frank. Where did the fictional Charlotte and her moral dilemma come from?

Charlotte came from her moral dilemma. Most books about the women of World War II feature those who displayed enviable, or hard to fathom, courage—women who spied for the Allies or worked in the Resistance or risked their lives covering the action. I stand in awe of those figures. But as I read those accounts, I kept wondering, what did women who were not blessed, or cursed, with such guts do, what would I do if faced with choices between what is conventionally thought of as right and wrong, moral and immoral? It is, I suppose, the eternal question of the bystander. Charlotte is, if not my answer to it, then my exploration of it.

Yes, but how did Charlotte, the particular character in the novel, come into being?

I find all my characters, even the historical figures—because of course they're not the real historical figures, only my understanding and representation of them—come into being the same way. When I begin a book, I have in mind a vague character defined mainly by name and circumstances, the individual's history, and where I want her or him to go, though the latter rarely is where that character ends up going. Only as I get deeper into the story does the character begin to take on a reality of her or his own. Frequently the people on the page refuse to do things I'd intended to have them do. They make it clear, as the writing goes on, that a particular action or emotion is not in keeping with who they have become.

You list some of the sources you relied upon in researching A Bookshop in Paris. *Do you have a particular method for delving into the past?*

I begin by reading general histories of the period, then go on to personal memoirs, magazines and newspapers, and archival material if there is any. I love getting lost in libraries, and I love the thrill of coming across a little-known or even previously unknown letter or diary entry or scrap of paper that brings the character or period to life. In a more general sense, even the ads in old newspapers and magazines can untether you from the present and pull you back to another time. Once, while reading an old magazine, I came across an ad for a sweater I thought would make a perfect Christmas gift for my husband. Only when I started to jot down the information did I realize that the magazine was from 1945, the store no longer existed, and the sweater I was so eager to buy had probably been eaten by moths decades ago.

Are some eras more difficult to research than others?

For some aspects of *A Bookshop in Paris* I had to do almost no research. Several years ago I worked in a New York City publishing house. While by that time the business had changed considerably from the 1950s, human nature hadn't.

Does the research ever change your original conception of a book?

Absolutely. In *A Bookshop in Paris*, I had started out thinking about what Charlotte would do in certain situations and how she would live with the repercussions of her actions for the rest of her life. In other words, I was interested in survivor guilt, though I didn't use the term to myself at the time because I think starting a novel with a high-falutin philosophical or psychological concept is the kiss of death for a good story. The library where I do most of my work has open stacks. One day as I was looking for another book about France under the Occupation

I came across two volumes called *Hitler's Jewish Soldiers* and *Lives of Hitler's Jewish Soldiers* by Bryan Mark Rigg. I was so astonished I sat on the floor of the history stacks and began reading. What I found there not only altered but deepened and expanded the story I had set out to tell. Suddenly, I had the beginnings of a character I'd never dreamed of, more survivor guilt than I'd bargained for, and the additional issue of identity and how we perceive it.

At what point in the research do you begin writing? Where do you work? When do you work?

After a certain amount of time, and it differs with each book, I can't keep the characters and the ideas in any longer. They're shouting to get out of my head and onto the page. That's the point—and I've heard many writers use this image—at which I leave the research room, close the door behind me, and walk into the writing room. Closing the door is essential because in fiction characters and story always trump history, and you don't want the former to get lost in the latter. But there is a caveat. I sometimes have to go back to the research because, before I start the writing, I often have no idea what I'm looking for when I'm reading. Sometimes a stray fact that seemed irrelevant when I came across it inspires a scene or makes a character take a different course. So while the two processes are separate, they are also intertwined.

I do the actual writing in the writers rooms of two libraries: The New York Society Library, which is a subscription library on the Upper East Side of Manhattan and New York City's oldest library, and the New York Public Library. Both have silent oases for writers that I am fortunate to have access to. The walk to the library each morning gives me time to think about what I'm going to write that day, as does an early run around the Reservoir in Central Park; the walk home in the evening allows time to decompress, or, all too often, the eureka realization that the scene I spent the day writing simply doesn't work and has to be either completely rethought or tossed out.

Are you currently at work on another book?

I am always at work on another book. The idea for the current work in progress sprang from two sentences about a character I came across in my research for *A Bookshop in Paris*, but that's all I can say about her now.

📖 *Books Set in Bookshops*

When I started writing *A Bookshop in Paris*, I had no idea that Charlotte was going to run a bookshop in Paris during the Occupation. I did know that once she arrived in New York, she would go to work somewhere in the fashion industry, either in a designer's studio or shop or on a magazine. I'm not sure why I chose that career for her. Probably because in my childhood I'd heard of and later read about women who'd fled Europe for the States and ended up in that field, if they worked outside the home at all. But though the Charlotte who began to take shape as I wrote cared about fashion—she is, after all, a Frenchwoman—her real passion was for books. The better I got to know her, the clearer it became that when she arrived in New York City, she would get a job in publishing, as I had when I was young in the city. From there it followed, or preceded, that she would work in a bookshop while in Paris. Perhaps I was inspired by the stories of the various bookshops and publishing houses that survived under the Occupation. Perhaps I was influenced by other books I'd read about bookshops. The following is a brief list of some of my favorites.

The Bookshop by Penelope Fitzgerald is not only my favorite book about a bookshop, it is one of my favorite books of all time. In 1959, in the seaside town of Hardborough in East Anglia, there is no fish-and-chips shop, no launderette, no cinema except on alternate Saturday nights, and certainly no bookshop—until Florence Green, an unremarkable local widow, decides to use her small inheritance to open one. Purchasing a small property known as the Old House that turns out to have a leaking roof, a flooding cellar, and a possible ghost, Florence nonetheless manages to make a success of the undertaking, thereby enraging less prosperous shopkeepers in the town and arousing the envy and ire of another local woman, who considers herself the arbiter of all things cultural in Hardborough. A piercing look at small-town social ambitions, vicious rivalries, and woman's cruelty to woman, this slim but powerful novel breaks my heart every time I read it, and as with so many books I love, I have reread it at various stages of my life, always hoping against hope it will end differently.

Perhaps I'm cheating when I include *The Uncommon Reader* by Alan Bennett in books about bookshops. This perfect gem of a novella begins not in a bookshop but in the City of Westminster traveling library, which every Wednesday parks just outside the palace grounds. In my mind, however, libraries, in which I've been hiding out since childhood, are solid buildings where silence and decorum reign. This small van crammed with a motley collection of odd volumes is more informal and louche. One Wednesday the Queen enters the van to apologize for the din her barking dogs have set up and feels it is her royal duty to take out a book, though books have always been "something she left to other people." Soon one book leads to another, as books have a habit of doing, and the Queen undergoes a transformation that builds to a delicious denouement in this enchanting novella that resonates far beyond its sly, hilarious story to explore the power, delights, and dangers of reading.

The Bookseller of Kabul begins when the author, Åsne Seierstad, wanders into the shop of a man who loves books with such passion that each time a new regime demolishes his store he rebuilds it. But the man who reveres books reveals himself to be a tyrant who destroys souls. When Seierstad moves in with the bookseller and his family, sleeping on their floor, sharing their communal meals, venturing out in the hated and suffocating burka, and enduring their hardships in this broken, war-torn country, she discovers a fiercely hierarchical society that degrades and crushes not only women but the less powerful of both sexes. As head of the extended family, the booklover rules with a hard heart and an iron hand. *The Bookseller of Kabul* is an unflinching account, impossible to look away from, of the power of books to open minds and of the cruelty and destructiveness of minds determined to remain closed.

The Big Sleep has only two scenes set in bookshops, but both are so shrewdly drawn and drolly realized that it's hard not to include the novel when thinking about fictional bookshops. Since this is Raymond Chandler territory, both stores are meticulously observed. One has wall-to-wall blue carpeting, blue leather easy chairs, and finely tooled leather volumes, most behind glass, that are clearly intended for decoration rather than reading. The other is a small, unprepossessing store crammed with books from floor to ceiling. The two women who mind the disparate bookshops are even more of a contrast. The first, an ash blonde who knows nothing about books, wears "a tight black dress" and walks "with a certain something [Marlowe] hadn't often seen in bookstores," while the second is a small dark woman with a finely drawn face, a knowledge of first editions, and a gift for observation that Marlowe, the narrator, says would make her a good cop. "I hope not," she answers.

George Orwell's "Bookshop Memories" is not a book but an essay about the experience of working in a bookshop, which, according to Orwell, is pictured as a "paradise where charming old gentlemen browse eternally among calf-bound folios" only by those who have never worked in one. Orwell finds the customers boorish, more "first edition snobs" among them than true lovers of literature, the kind of people "who would be a nuisance anywhere but have special opportunities in a bookshop," because that's the only place you can hang about for hours on end without spending a penny. Nor do the booksellers who run these dusty pits of pretension and despair escape his scorn. He cites one bookshop's ad for Boswell's *Decline and Fall* and another's for *The Mill on the Floss* by T. S. Eliot. But he does find one redeeming feature of the book trade. Bookshops, he predicts, can never be squeezed out of existence by large conglomerates. Orwell wrote the essay in 1936.

Influenced, perhaps inspired, by Orwell's essay, *Diary of a Bookseller* by Shaun Bythell, who on a whim and a bank loan ended up owning The Bookshop in Wigtown, Scotland's largest second-hand bookshop, also manages to puncture every romantic fantasy about the joys of retiring to a bucolic village and living with and off books. Bythell spares no one. His is a granular, gimlet-eyed view of trying to run an old-world business in a new age with Amazon breathing down his neck and cutting into his meager profits. The frustrations are endless—but there are moments of joy, as well. The thrill of stumbling upon a book signed by Sir Walter Scott and another by Florence Nightingale. The pleasure of meeting customers who truly love books and not merely the idea of being a booklover. The passion of discovering an author or book he'd never heard of. This is a witty, waspish account of the horrors of running a bookshop by a man who clearly loves doing it.

 *Reading Group Questions*

1. Charlotte is continually trying to reassure herself that she didn't really collaborate. She wasn't dining on tournedos of beef and bottles of Saint-Émilion with Nazis. She never turned anyone in. Are there degrees of collaboration, and if so, how do you determine where to draw the line?

2. Was Charlotte right to raise Vivi believing a lie? If not, how and when could she have told her the truth?

3. Mr. Rosenblum, who has survived a concentration camp, absolves Charlotte of guilt. Hannah, who spends her life listening to tales of horror and trying to minister to those who have suffered it, refuses to forgive Charlotte. What do you think their different reactions are based on? Does someone who has not suffered have as great a right to judge as someone who has?

4. Julian believes he sacrificed honor, honesty, and his family to survive. If he had refused to serve in Hitler's army would it have done any good?

5. Why do you think Charlotte answered Julian's letters after the war and tried to help him?

6. The book begins with a quote from a young girl who lived in Paris during the Occupation about being able to hate in the abstract but not in individual instances. This phenomenon is generally recognized as an antidote to prejudice. If you live next door to a member of a minority, it is harder to hate that minority. How does this phenomenon apply to the hatred of oppressors and tyrants?

7. Charlotte spends a good deal of time worrying and talking about moral compasses—her own, her daughter's, her late husband's, her lover Julian's. Hannah spends her time doing good. Can people who commit immoral acts be moral people? How does this relate to Hannah and Charlotte?

8. If your child was caught in a moral bind between turning in her best friend for cheating and ignoring the infraction, what would you advise her?

9. In the last scene in the book, Horace tells Charlotte she would have been better off if she'd stayed in Paris and suffered the consequences of her choices rather than getting off scot-free and spending the rest of her life punishing herself. Do you agree with this sentiment? Why or why not?

About the author

Ellen Feldman is the acclaimed author of *Scottsboro*, which was shortlisted for the prestigious Orange Prize, *The Boy Who Loved Anne Frank*, which was translated into nine languages, *Next to Love*, *Terrible Virtue*, *The Unwitting* and *Lucy*. A former Guggenheim Fellow in fiction, she has a BA and MA in modern history from Bryn Mawr College and after graduate studies at Columbia University, she worked for a New York publishing house, like Charlotte in *A Bookshop in Paris*. She has lectured around the US, Germany and the UK. She lives in New York and Amagansett with her husband and rescue terrier Charlie.